PARKWAY 12

ALSO BY DENNIS CARR

Coastal Confessions
Corporate Rules
The Eight Vital Signs (Nonfiction)

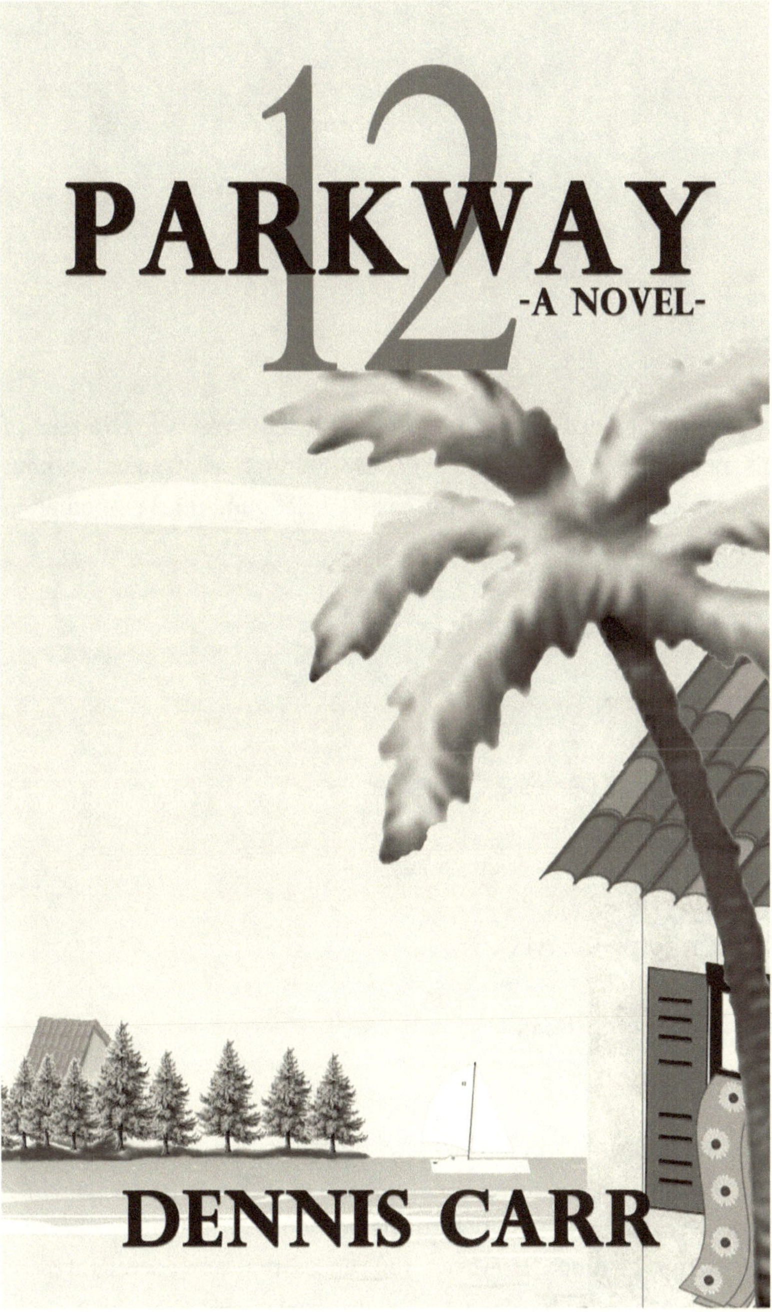
12
PARKWAY
-A NOVEL-
DENNIS CARR

Published by MedEcon Analytics, LLC

FIRST EDITION

Cover design by Dennis & Cheryl Carr

Author photograph by Scott Quady

Editor at Large: Cheryl Carr

ISBN 978-0-9881-8643-9

This is a work of fiction. Characters, corporations, institutions and organizations in this novel are the product of the author's imagination, or if real, are used fictitiously without any intent to describe their actual conduct. However, references that are documented in footnotes are accurate.

If anyone supposes that he knows anything, he has not yet known as he ought to know . . .

—THE APOSTLE PAUL

CLASSIFIED AD

Exclusive new listing in Parkway Community. Architecturally designed manufactured home nestled on a quiet street overlooking palm-lined private lake. Home features 3BR, 2BA, 2 car garage, separate breakfast nook, and incredible amenities. Nice neighbors, spectacular views, community dock, swimming, boating, fishing, and hunting. Special owner financing available. A nice place to live.

New Listing—Won't Last!

Parkway Community
-A Brief History-

In the Seventies, back in the days when Parkway Community was little more than rolling hills, pine trees, and swampland, a Southern gentleman nicknamed Ol' Man River won a poker game that would change my life forever. A bold statement to be sure, given that I wasn't around when it all started. In fact, it would be another seven years before I entered the world. Most of what I gleaned about Parkway's history came at a later date, in a transitional period when I was blind to how life can sometimes play tricks on you.

By all accounts Ol' Man River was a successful, yet good-hearted man. In his prime they said he could be seen daily around town in his signature jeans, houndstooth jacket, and fancy cowboy hat with its braided leather band. Local legend has it that he was wearing that very outfit the night he won the land in a poker game at the Ritz-Carlton in Atlanta.

Four men and a lady faced off that night, but only Ol' Man River and one other remained at the table as the final hand played out in the wee hours. Ol' Man River bet the ranch on little more than a wing and a prayer, getting the better of an opponent who was unaccustomed to coming up on the short end of the stick. But his luck had run out, and the rival was forced to reveal a secret of his own—he had no cash to his name, only a pair of lizard-skin boots, a worthless land deed, and an empty bottle of Gentleman Jack. Since the boots didn't fit, Ol' Man River departed with the deed.

Not long afterwards a recession hit, and like many others, Ol' Man River's business fell on hard times. During the downturn he paid a visit to the property he had won, only to discover it was three hundred acres of swampland in the North Georgia foothills. But that much he had already figured, and through his adversity decided to change his way of thinking, knowing full-well there was nothing to lose by dreaming big. When inspiration struck, he jumped in with both feet and developed the wasteland into what was to become Parkway Community. He transformed the site into a getaway for upper middle class suburbanites—a community of second homes within easy driving distance of the city. Aiming to make prices affordable, he restricted floor plans to five architecturally designed doublewides. When all was said and done, it was a labor of love that produced only a handful of lots, all situated around a horseshoe-shaped street and nestled next to a scenic lake beneath the tall Georgia pines. The home sites featured spectacular views and a full array of amenities: covered dock, sandy white beach, boating, fishing, hunting, tennis, heated pool, and an A-frame lodge. At the Highway 141 entrance he chiseled a sign from a tree trunk that read:

PARKWAY COMMUNITY
-A Lakeside Retreat-

The development was an instant success and functioned more like an extended family than a neighborhood, but that was before the demographic shifts set in between the Nineties and the dot-com bubble. The upwardly mobile homeowners began to slip away during this era, taking their leisure activities further north to the shores of Lake Lanier. Parkway slowly transitioned into a collection of full-time residents, and fortunately each new wave promptly warmed to the unique vintage setting. It was about this time Ol' Man River decided to relinquish day-to-day control of the property, allowing community members to vote in a board of directors, along with a healthy dose of protective covenants. It was his way of ensuring a legacy.

As the new millennium rolled in, the Atlanta suburbs marched northward, adding cachet to what was quickly becoming prime real estate. Parkway Community found itself squeezed in by subdivisions, golf courses, and shopping centers, but somehow managed to maintain its original charm. As the economic pendulum swung, the northern corridor turned into a seller's paradise. Parkway prospered, and every time a doublewide hit the market it would be snapped up by an anxious buyer.

The turnover continued for the next thirty years, which was about the time I entered the picture—and mind you—it wasn't by choice. I was one of those unfortunate souls who got wiped out by the 2008 downturn, better known for its tsunami of toxic mortgages. Life had been pretty good up until the crash, but from that point forward Wall Street charted a new course, forever setting me adrift in its unforgiving wake. Few of the experts predicted the economy would languish as it did, so who could have dreamed my life would implode so quickly in the aftermath? Destiny has a funny way of making mice out of men, and well, I'm here to tell you it happens. In my case, it struck in one fell swoop . . . I lost my job, our home, the country club membership, and a boat.

A really big boat.

Fortunately, there was one person I could always count on through thick and thin. But to my surprise, even that changed. It all happened after a remark she made that has stuck with me to this very day. "It might be an answer to prayer," she said. A cliché to be certain, but those were her exact words. And even though I was doing my best *not* to be sensitive about the whole mess, I slipped up and spouted off at her anyway. Chalk it up to bad timing, because that was the day Ol' Man River's poker winnings entered my life. Lot number twelve at Parkway Community hit the market—quite mysteriously, actually. And if the truth be told, I bought it. Hook, line, and sinker. But we'll get to that.

As it so happens, residents referred to the parcel as the Dorsey Place. And despite the fact that living in a trailer park wasn't my cup of tea, at the time I was focused on the bigger picture. If I appreciated anything, it was the certainty that the Wall Street meltdown hadn't buried me. I was upright and breathing, but otherwise things were headed south—*fast.*

By my way of thinking Parkway was more or less a detour, yet it did represent the beginning of a new chapter in my life. So it may come as no surprise that the last *good* thing I remember before the so-called interview that started it all was flipping on a football game, curling up on the sofa, and thanking my lucky stars for the one person . . . that predictable little ray of sunshine standing between me and the abyss . . . *Tracie.*

I fell asleep that afternoon clinging to one solitary assurance: *Tracie was the spark that would sustain me through it all.* She was the one I could count on . . . that special someone who believed in me.

And that was the day my true destiny unfolded.

Chapter 1

Midtown Atlanta
Sunday, October 6th
7:30 P.M.

I'll never forget the day I first sold out. It was a line from one of those celebrity CEOs who was doing time in federal prison for stealing millions from his company. At the present, I was trying hard to forget I had ever read about it, but I knew for a fact I had to block that little jewel from my thinking. *Pronto.* It had been—*what*—less than twenty-four hours, and here I was second-guessing myself. Gazing up through my car's moonroof, I studied a mosaic of constellations that peeked down from the sky. At the moment they looked more like a host of random stars wandering across a vast, empty universe. Something stirred within me, probably a guilt pang reminding me why I was here.

It was just after dusk when I pulled around back of an empty two-story parking deck and stepped out of my car. The place looked like a landfill, a perfect match for the depressing thoughts swimming inside my head. I had no idea it would come to this, but then again denial had been twisted into my DNA long ago. Barely in my thirties, my options were fading faster than the sinking sunset behind me. Life had become hard. In fact, it was impossible. And it was the force behind my total desperation, as good a reason as any to bow out. Right here and now.

The parking lot was cold and dark, gloomier than the weatherman had forecasted, even though the King Plough Arts Center was tucked away in a trendy corner of Midtown Atlanta. The setting reminded me that stiff drinks are best suited for moments like these. *Has it really come to this?* I thought. The place was deserted and next to a construction site cordoned off by a chain link fence. The only sign of life was a bum with a brown paper bag, who lay curled up in front of a rusty gate. In my mind, I imagined a pack of Dobermans snarling out of the shadows to put me out of my misery.

When the dogs didn't materialize, the stillness somehow calmed me—a peace that seemed out of place. I tugged at my cufflinks and propped my elbows on top of the car, re-examining the sky. The stars were growing brighter. A meteor streaked across the horizon and disappeared behind the distant skyline. As crazy as it sounds, I wasted a perfectly good wish on wishing I had sent my suit to the one-hour dry cleaner.

I took out my wallet and cracked it open. There was a silky-smooth lining in the main compartment, nothing else. I raised it to my nose and sniffed the rich leather before thumbing through a half-dozen credit card cubbies, all but one empty. Double-checking each of them, I hoped to strike a vein of rainy-day cash. As expected, I found only a single gold American Express card. *My lifeline.*

I put away the wallet at the sound of a car pulling into the lot. The headlights blinded me as the vehicle accelerated and bore down in my direction. I recognized the shape—it was a beast of a Mercedes. *Maybe this is it,* I thought. The oversized sedan screeched to a stop within inches of my rear bumper, which was attached to a car I loved with all my heart. She was a limited edition BMW, affectionately nicknamed *Goldfinger.*

Understandably, pride got the better of me, so I stepped between the two automobiles and squinted into the light. I wasn't sure how much longer this calm would course through my veins. It wasn't like me.

The door swung open, and a driver who reminded me of a stallion in pinstripes stepped out. Clad in a pair of dark sunglasses, the mane of jet black hair was slicked back like an Olympic swimmer. Without so much as a snort in my direction the driver rounded the car, offering a glimpse of a sleek physique and an impressive muscular chest. Slinging a leather bag over a shoulder, the stallion reached for the rear door of the Mercedes. A bald man slipped out, straightening his jacket like a bad habit. His frame was as solid as a concrete pillar, and his pate had a sheen that was a bit intimidating, particularly in the bad lighting. As he stood there towering a good two feet over the roof, the suit hung just a little too perfectly. He took his sweet time to survey the lot, with his eyes settling on a classic lime-green Pontiac next to the parking deck.

The ground unexpectedly shook, and I was surprised when I turned to spot a locomotive pulling out from behind the Arts Center. The building was an ancient factory, clearly past its prime, but partially refurbished with a chic glass and steel patina. Boxcars appeared from the shadows and headed down the tracks, picking up speed as they rattled off into the darkness.

When I looked back, the stallion had slipped over to the gate, stopping to poke the bum with a boot. I squeezed between the cars and made my way toward the bald man.

"Gustav?" I called out.

The man didn't flinch, maintaining his fixation on the Pontiac.

I narrowed the gap and extended a hand. "I'm Trevor Wentworth."

Still in his stoic posture, he greeted me with a crushing grip, not uttering a word. My knees nearly buckled before he let go.

"What's the deal with this place?" I said, looking down at my hand. I flexed my fingers . . . realizing the calm had just passed. A train whistle blew in the distance. "I thought you were going to show me a lab?"

"*Trust* is a noble quality," Gustav said.

The accent was Latino with a Southern twist.

"You *do* have offices?"

"Yes, we have recently broken ground."

"I didn't catch your first name on the telephone."

"Dr. Gustav will do just fine."

"*Oh* . . . you're a doctor?" It was a reasonable question, but I could tell by his expression it was best to let it go. "So you found me on social media?" I said, suddenly struck with the notion this was no place for an interview. "Why don't we get out of here and head over to Six Feet Under to talk? It's just—"

"Let's walk," Gustav said, starting toward the fence. "Your résumé indicates you worked for McKinsey."

We stepped over the bum and entered the gate, sidestepping construction debris as we weaved our way toward a suite at the end of the building. For the life of me, it looked abandoned.

"That's right. I handled strategic issues for health care companies," I said. "That's my forte."

"Excellent. We could use those skills."

I looked ahead and spotted the stallion.

"On the telephone you mentioned you were in the drug testing market. I did an Internet search, but didn't get a hit for your company. I take it you're early stage?"

"You understand well," Gustav said, stopping in front of some crumbling steps.

Just past the corner of the building, I could make out the train tracks. The stallion climbed the stairs to a narrow alcove and stared into what amazingly turned out to be an optical scanner. The front door beeped open, unleashing an eerie glow from inside.

"Consolidation is the name of the game these days," I said, pretending everything was business as usual. "Have you thought about competitive positioning?"

"We wish to build market share," Gustav said.

"So—*initially*—you'll want to focus on pricing," I said, teasing him with a little free advice. "How about capital? For funding, you'll need—"

"No outside investment is required."

"It'll take millions . . . but I like the sound of that."

Behind me, I heard cars beginning to trickle into the parking lot. I turned, noticing a lighted marquee halfway down the Arts Center. It reminded me of a theatre sign and advertised an Old 97's concert.

"Do you have a job title in mind?" I said to Gustav.

"A matter to be addressed, *if* we offer you the position."

"I understand . . . Executive roles are typically aligned with experience. But let's not waste time. What kind of compensation are you offering?"

"Not so fast, my good friend. Perhaps you can explain why McKinsey let you go?"

"Downsizing," I replied, short and sweet.

Gustav looked up at the stallion, who was holding the door open. "For negotiating purposes, someone of your caliber might expect to start at your former salary plus an additional twenty percent. Yes . . . that should put you in the ballpark. However, we're getting ahead of ourselves. I have a test for you."

"What do you mean?"

"Please, come with me."

Gustav ushered me up the steps and through the door, just as the stallion flipped a switch that engulfed the cavernous space in blue light. The inside had been gutted. Walls were being framed up front, but the rest of the suite was a warehouse. There was a loading dock out back.

"Our new offices," Gustav said with outstretched hands.

I looked at the door where we had entered, holding my tongue as long as I could. "You realize there's a concert venue a few doors down? It's not exactly medical space."

"We are trying what you might call . . . a new business model."

"You've got that right," I said, raising my eyebrows. I checked out the brickwork. The lighting cast a cool pattern across the nooks and crannies.

"Our primary business will be conducted in the field, but this location will serve as our base of operations."

Gustav snapped his fingers, and the stallion hurried over with the leather bag. I admired the well-manicured fingernails as a lump of plastic with clear tubes was extracted from the bag.

"This is a prototype of our device."

"That's your testing device?" I said, no longer concerned with appearances. "It looks like something you'd use to check chemicals in a swimming pool. I thought you had proprietary technology."

"*Veeery* good," Gustav said, nodding approvingly. He reached into the bag and dug out a single cylinder. "This is the real prototype. It incorporates a five panel test in one tube. We utilize digital sensors to detect traces of drugs in urine. The lights on the cap indicate results by color: orange for cocaine, yellow for marijuana, red for opiates, blue for amphetamines, and green for methamphetamines. Soon we will introduce a blood test that will be as simple to use as a glucose monitor—proprietary technology, as you call it. And it will deliver flawless results."

"*Huh* . . ." I said.

"Over there we will construct a state-of-the-art lab." Gustav pointed. "But first we launch our mobile strategy. Now watch. You have a single tube that handles all five tests." He took a liter bottle from the bag and screwed the cap off, pouring in liquid with a metallic smell. After checking the bag, he looked over and barked something in Spanish.

The stallion pulled a prescription bottle out of a pocket and handed it over, rattling off a response in a higher, yet similar accent.

Gustav checked his watch.

"Are you guys in the country . . . *legally*?" I said.

"What kind of question is that?" Gustav said.

I knew when to back off. "If the blood test pans out, it could be a game-changer."

"Precisely," Gustav said. "Unfortunately, I am late for another appointment." He emptied the device and returned it to the bag. Then he struck a match and dropped it on the floor. The liquid burned in a rainbow of colors until it flickered out.

"To move things along, why don't I take the device and try it on my own?" I said. "If it's as simple as you suggest, then I'd be happy to provide feedback . . . for free."

Gustav's head snapped up, delving into my eyes like he was shrinking me.

"You know . . . *trust*," I said.

There was a moment of hesitation, but the remark drew a smile.

"Very well. The Rx bottle contains simulated oxycodone tablets for your specimen. Place one in the tube, along with the chemical, and insert the probe. Observe the lights on top—the red one will light up." He gestured for the stallion to hand over the bag.

"So the process works without a controlled environment?"

"One reason we're going to blow away the competition," Gustav said.

"Do you have any additional information about the company?"

"You have everything you need."

Gustav directed me outside onto the steps, the stallion following along, hot on our heels. "Let's arrange a follow-up. I want my device back tomorrow."

I spotted a posse of girls in cowboy boots strolling across the parking lot. "How about we talk in the morning?"

Gustav descended the steps, saying nothing until we reached the Mercedes. I had to scramble to keep up with him.

"The address on your résumé is Parkway 12?"

The question threw me. "That's right. It's a . . . small community of lakefront patio homes," I said, hoping to impress him.

"Sounds *very* nice." Gustav pulled out a cigar. "We will continue the discussion tomorrow."

For the first time, I looked deep into his eyes. They were gray with fiery centers, reminding me of a solar flare. He paused to light up. "A word of warning . . . Don't try anything foolish."

"I understand."

"Is there anything else you wish to tell me?" A cloud of smoke hung over Gustav's bald head.

"I'll do the demo tonight."

Gustav slid into the Mercedes and closed the door.

As the stallion started the engine, I chaffed at the thought of the interview ending on a wayward note. I tapped the window, and it lowered halfway. "You *can* trust me," I said. The motor revved, and I stepped back as the car sped away.

Hurrying over to Goldfinger, I tossed the leather bag in the front seat after checking out the scene over at the music venue. The line had disappeared, but the cowgirls were lingering out front, laughing and flirting. I could hear a band warming up inside.

Climbing into the driver's seat rather proud of myself, I hunched over and extracted a Ziploc bag from behind the dash. Pulling out Gustav's device, I poured chemical in the tube. Instead of using his simulated oxy, I added a pinch of white powder from the Ziploc and swirled the contents. The digital readout on top blinked, and then turned orange. "Jackpot," I said, immediately starting to pack everything away. Then I snickered, "A lakefront patio home."

Tussling my hair, I hopped out of Goldfinger and ditched the coat and tie. Then I fished out my wallet and extracted the AmEx, making a beeline for the girls. They seemed to be carrying on about the band's front man, Rhett Miller. When I strutted past the Pontiac, I was so worked up I didn't notice the bum crouched behind the wheel.

Chapter 2

Burke County, Georgia
Monday, October 7th
11:00 A.M.

The Lexus pulled off Highway 80 into a depression-era gas station, at least that's what Tracie thought it was.

"I found it," she said into her smartphone, then ended the call.

There was a faded orange and blue Gulf sign out by the road, but the entrance looked like it had seen better days. The car bounced as it struck a pothole, and she slammed on the brakes, stopping next to a raised concrete island where gas pumps once stood. Metal poles were planted in the center, supporting a rusty awning that extended to the office thirty feet away and shading a patch of asphalt resembling a drive-thru. She noticed water stains on the front of the block building and a pair of bay doors at the far end, both raised. The front end of an early model Grand Prix stuck out of one, basking in the morning sun.

Tracie heard music drifting in the breeze, barely audible above the sound of her engine. The retractable top on her car was down, and a few leaves fluttered into the passenger seat. She looked closer at the office. The oversized plate glass windows were milky, as if they had been coated with a thin layer of soap film. There was a boom box outside on top of an old Coke machine, thumping out a Kenny Chesney classic—*She's Got It All.* Inside, she spotted a man in a ball cap sprawled out in a lounge chair. Pulling the car forward, she felt it lift out of the pothole, then turned off the ignition before getting out.

Tracie closed her eyes, swaying to the rhythm just long enough to take the edge off her worries. When she opened them, she noticed a cotton field across the highway running as far as the eye could see. The rows ran straight as an arrow and arched toward the horizon. When she turned for a look behind the station, there was a pecan orchard that wrapped around both sides to the highway. She reached into the car and grabbed her phone. Checking voicemail, there were a dozen messages—twice as many as an hour ago. She stuffed the phone in her purse without listening to them and headed for the office.

By the time she reached the awning, Tracie figured the man inside was asleep. There was an open book draped across his chest, and the bill of the cap sat low over his eyes. He wore a pair of cowboy boots that were propped up on a stack of burlap bags. The office door was open and a sign on the glass panel read: *Neely Pecan Orchards.* She stepped in the doorway clearing her throat, but the man didn't budge.

Tracie knocked on the jamb and was greeted with an index finger that raised ever so slowly in a "just-a-minute" gesture. From where she was standing, he was a hunk . . . maybe in his mid-twenties . . . wearing Lucky Brand jeans. She could spot them a mile away. A Burke Truck & Tractor logo was stitched on his cap. The finger remained in place until he snapped the book shut, stretching as he stumbled to his feet.

"Yes, ma'am," he said, letting out a yawn and tossing the book in the chair.

"Are you Neely?"

"Yeah . . ." he said, looking a bit surprised. "How'd you know?"

Tracie pointed at the sign on the door.

"Silly me," Neely said.

"I don't remember this place being here."

"Is there a problem?"

"Do you have a restroom?" Tracie said, ignoring the enquiry.

Neely took his time, checking out the designer sunglasses in her hair, fitted top, jeans, and Steve Maddens. When he was done he leaned his head ever so slightly, sneaking a peek at the Lexus.

"Are you—*uh*—interested in buying some pecans?"

"Maybe some other time," Tracie said, fully aware she had just been sized up. She turned to follow his gaze.

"Waynesboro is just a few miles down the road. They've got food, gas, and restrooms. You may want to hold it until you get to town."

"*Meaning* . . . you don't have one . . . or I have to buy pecans to use the facility?"

"I was just pointing out how close you are to—"

"I know where I am."

"Okay, okay. That's cool. Don't shoot the messenger." He raised his hands. "I'm not selling you anything, babe."

Tracie cut her eyes over at the chair. The book that had put him to sleep was upside-down, but she was able to pick off the title: *Forensic Accounting*. "What exactly are you doing here if you're not selling pecans?" She glanced around the office. Burlap bags were stacked everywhere.

"Let's just say pecans aren't exactly my bailiwick." Neely took off his cap and messed up his hair.

"And the verdict on the restroom is . . ." Tracie smiled, raising her hands in the air.

"Aren't you a bit young to be driving a Lexus?"

"*Brother* . . . what is it with men and cars—"

"No, ma'am," he cut in. "It just sort of—"

"Maybe you can point me—"

"My momma drives one just like it, only hers is black. Of course, she prefers to call it obsidian."

Tracie hitched a hand on her hip and started talking to herself, visibly annoyed. "I don't know—maybe I'll just relieve myself over there behind that pile of bags."

He looked down at the floor with a schoolboy grin, and then rocked his head like he thought she was funny. "The ladies' room has been broken for years, but you're welcome to try the boys'—if you're up for an adventure."

"I was a Girl Scout, so I think I can manage."

"Then you'll want to go around back." He gestured in the general direction. "The door doesn't close all the way, but nobody's gonna be looking. If you see any lizards, just blast them with the spray can next to the toilet. They crawl in this time of year to keep warm."

Tracie looked out at a patch of waist-high weeds through a side window. There was an overturned trash can and paper strewn everywhere.

"Excuse me . . . Why did you say you are here?" Tracie sat down on a burlap bag and crossed her legs.

"My daddy owns the place, orchards and all," Neely said. "I'm just helping out temporarily."

"You're not planning to take over the family farm?"

"Not right away," he said. "I'm headed up to Chicago to dabble in commodities and work on my MBA."

"And then you're coming back?"

"I suspect I'll get homesick for the South sooner or later."

"If you want my advice, enjoy life before it bites you in the . . . Well, you know."

"Are you from around here?"

"Once upon a time. I grew up on the other side of town," Tracie said.

"That explains why you don't look familiar. I know every babe on this end of the county."

Tracie gave Neely a full sweep, head to toe. "Good to know. Anyway, I've probably got a few years on you."

"Can't be more than ten," he agreed, giving her another once-over. "But to tell you the truth, I actually prefer older women."

"Look—I'm just biding a little time, so don't go ape on me. When I get to town, they're not exactly going to roll out the Welcome Wagon."

"You're pretty feisty, even for a blonde. What kind of trouble are you facing in town? . . . And what's with that accent?"

"I lived in New York for a few years."

A semi pulled off the road in front of the station, throttling the conversation. Behind it a mobile home extended from one entrance to the next, completely wrapped in plastic. The air brakes let out a hiss as the truck came to a stop. A man sporting a camo bandana and long hair leaned out the window, looking their way.

Tracie turned to Neely, red-faced.

He glanced over at her, then back at the road. "Somebody you know?"

"It's not what you think."

Neely walked over to the door. "You don't even want to know what I'm thinking." He studied the rig for a spell. "That's a doublewide . . . at least, it's half of one. Are you on the lam?"

"Is that anything to be asking a stranger?"

"Hey, I was taking a nap and minding my own business when you blew in here . . . acting a little crazy, if I say so myself. Now this sideshow pulls up." Neely pointed at the rig. "What's the story?"

"None of your business."

"What possessed you to pull into a run-down place like this?"

"I told you."

"Well, talk some more, sister . . . or I'm gonna have to ask you to leave."

"No!"

"Why not?" Neely said.

"Because then I'd have to kill you."

Chapter 3

Suwanee, Georgia
Monday, October 7th
6:00 P.M.

I grabbed my wrist and screamed like a banshee. When I looked up, my fishing rod was dangling mid-air beneath the fronds of a palm tree. The cork grip had been ripped clean out of my hands, leaving a nasty burning sensation.

"Got your line fouled up," I heard someone call out from a distance. I turned to a man in a well-worn camel hair jacket, jeans, fancy leather belt, and cowboy hat, ambling toward me sporting two days of beard stubble.

When I cut my eyes back at the rod, it was bouncing up and down in the breeze, head-high. I reached out with both hands, jerking it first to the left, then to the right. Amidst the swooshing sounds, my palms caught fire again. I let loose with a "son-of-a—"

"That ain't the way to do it," the man interrupted, shaking his head. I noticed the letters *CBJ* on the oversized belt buckle. He tipped the brim of his Stetson and squatted down, snapping a weed off the ground. Taking his time, he slipped it in his mouth and studied the top of the tree.

I yanked one more time for good measure, rattling palm fronds overhead. But they refused to give up the fight. Beaten,

I leaned over and picked up a bottle of Bird Dog whiskey and stared out across the lake.

"Your fishing lure's stuck up in the top," the man said, squinting. "I can't say I've ever seen a bright red one quite like that. I suppose it's something new and improved."

"Whatever," I said, determined not to engage with him.

"Where'd you get it?"

"Get what?"

"That fancy crankbait up in the tree."

"Over at—"

"Boy bass or girl bass?" He fired off without waiting for a response.

I shifted my weight, leering into the sun. The ripples on the lake sparkled like diamonds. I turned loose of the rod and let it hang there. "What did you say?"

"Oh, I was just thinking about how that lure of yours was probably designed for boy bass. You know, the same way a young man yearns for something flashy, like a sports car."

I let the comment pass, certain it was a jab at Goldfinger parked within eyesight up at the house.

"Testosterone, they call it. It's what makes us boys chase after all kinds of nonsense." The man's words were articulate, like maybe he had read them in a medical journal.

"I thought that was, like, a hormone that causes men to develop?"

"That's a fact," he said, leveling a finger at me. "But we're talking about fishing." He stood and offered his hand. "Clayton Beasley."

I steadied the fishing rod before accepting Clayton's hand. "Trevor Wentworth," I said. His grip was like steel.

Clayton reached for the pole and rolled it in his hands, eyeing the markings. "Zebco 303—it's still got the price tag on it." He raised it over his head and reeled in line until it was taut.

Cutting his eyes at me, he gave a swift tug. Fronds snapped overhead and the lure plopped on the ground next to my loafer. "Do you fish often?"

Still working on a brush-off, I turned my attention to a yellow sailboat sunning on a patch of sandy white beach. Just past it, a dock with a shiny tin roof seemed to float on the water. "Only when I drink," I said, feeling a swarm of wild locusts stirring in my gut. In a moment of weakness, I tossed him another tidbit. "I'm actually working my way through a setback."

"Ain't we all," Clayton said without skipping a beat. He handed over the rod. "Me and the missus were once in the same—"

"I don't think so," I cut in.

"I owned—"

"Not to be rude, but this is different," I said, trying hard not to stare at his ratty sport coat. The handmade belt was actually pretty neat.

"Fair enough. Then let's hear it," Clayton said.

I clicked a button on the reel. "You wouldn't understand."

"Try me," Clayton said.

I took a sip of whiskey.

"You might not believe this, but I know that look in your eyes. In fact, I had it once myself. I'm a better man today because I had someone to talk to."

"Okay, *Clayton*," I blurted out. "I lost my job."

"Whoop-de-do. It happens every day, especially in this economy. And I know firsthand—it's embarrassing. In my case it was a whole damn business."

"This was an important job—McKinsey & Company."

"The spice people?" Clayton said.

"The what?"

"The folks that sell spice. You know—pepper, garlic, sea salt. What did you do for them?"

"You're not even close."

"Hold on a minute . . . I think I got it."

"McKinsey is the most—"

"McCormick!" Clayton snapped his fingers.

"Are you listening to me?"

"What's your favorite spice?"

"My favorite—"

"Cinnamon . . . You look like a man who craves the stuff."

I squeezed the grip on the fishing rod so tight my fingers turned white. Then I sliced the air, forcing Clayton to step back. "McKinsey doesn't sell cinnamon or pepper—no spices," I said. "What I was trying to explain is they're the most trusted advisory firm in the world."

"So you're with one of those outfits that don't produce anything?"

"That's . . . not exactly how I would describe it. But yes. Only, not any more. We advised important clients."

"Like who?"

"Technology companies, but mostly pharmaceuticals and biotechs."

"Done any work for the spice people?"

"I'd—*uh*—have to check."

Clayton smiled. "Don't get so bent out of shape. I know about McKinsey. Where'd you work before you started peddling advice?"

"Why is that important?"

"The way I see it, if you're some kind of industry expert—"

"Biotech is my expertise."

"So tell me about your biotech experience."

"It doesn't work that way. I'm focused on strategic issues."

"Okay, tell me about that."

Annoyed, I reared back and kicked a rock. It skipped across the beach and splashed in the lake. "I deal with high level matters."

"You mean—like profits?"

"That's one area."

"So what do you tell these biotechs?" Clayton said.

"That depends on the circumstances."

"Give me a for-instance."

I rolled my eyes, stopping short of a total snub. "Listen, I can't talk about this right now."

"I understand. Man's got a right to plead the fifth when he's in a bad sort of way. Mind if I change the subject?"

"Be my guest," I said, looking down at my loafer. The rock had left a gash.

Clayton made a slow turn toward Lakeside Circle, the horseshoe-shaped street just above us. His eyes stopped on the nearest residence. "Where's the other half of your house?"

What was left of my self-esteem vaporized on the spot. I refused to look up. As long as I faced the lake, I didn't have to be reminded that I lived in a trailer park. The image of my dismembered home was seared into my brain, so I didn't need anyone rubbing my nose in it. I wanted to climb under the rock I had just kicked in the water.

"I know for a fact the Dorsey Place was a doublewide when I shoved off for work this morning," Clayton said.

Halfheartedly, I peeked up at the street, taking in an assortment of homes scattered among the pines and grassy areas in Parkway Community. In the distance, headlights dotted the highway through the trees. Twenty yards up the grassy bank from where we were standing, the doublewide in question—*my home*—had a perfect view of the water. The cream-colored siding was trimmed in rust tones set off by a faux terracotta roof. Goldfinger sat out front next to a palm tree. A garage, formerly attached to the front corner, sat lopsided in the backyard. From where we stood, the back of the house looked as if it had been sawed off. Right down the middle.

"It's . . . a long story," I said.

"Clayton!" a woman called out.

Her voice beckoned from the dock. I glanced over and spotted string lights draped around the eaves of the tin roof, giving it a Caribbean flare. They were just beginning to glow as the sun dipped behind the trees. Underneath, I noticed an arrangement of Adirondack chairs as the sound of country music floated up to us.

"Coming, Honey Bunch!" Clayton hollered back, looking over at me. "I apologize if I've poked my nose where it don't belong. I'm just trying to be neighborly."

"That's cool," I said, feeling an uneasy tug at my heart. I looked him in the eyes as he came closer.

Clayton gestured at the lake, where the colors on the surface now reminded me of a postcard I had once seen. "Them boy bass don't seem to be biting this evening," he said. "Why don't you come join me and the missus for dinner?"

Chapter 4

Midtown Atlanta
Monday, October 7th
6:00 P.M.

Gustav paced the floor at the Arts Center warehouse with a laser pointer in hand. When he had made a full sweep, he took aim and traced out a large area that ended at his feet.

"This is where we will locate the secure storage," he said, turning. "A thousand square feet should be sufficient."

The stallion paced off the dimensions, marking the floor with a piece of chalk.

"Tell me about the concealed entrance," Gustav said.

The stallion responded in a throaty, almost sexy voice. "Based on the measurements, the adjoining lab will extend into the warehouse and provide the only access into the storage area. For effect, we will stage work benches, equipment, sinks, and refrigerators in the center of the room, with oversized cabinets positioned against the back wall."

"A fully compliant laboratory, I might add," Gustav said.

"The cabinets are custom high-density metal and capable of withstanding an explosion. The one designed to be our entryway will be fitted with hinges that allow it to swing open."

"So the entire unit becomes a door?"

"Yes. One that weighs eight hundred pounds with magnetic locks," the stallion said. "The rest of the equipment, I leave to you."

"I am negotiating the purchase of an entire lab setup, which should be finalized shortly. How are we progressing with the construction plans?"

"The remaining materials arrive tonight, and then our technicians will come in to do their magic."

"When do they wrap up?"

"Before sunup."

"Once we have a full test of the security system, we will bring in the inventory," Gustav said.

"We should be operating within twenty-four hours."

Gustav gave the stallion a long, approving look. "Now, about the other matter you wanted to discuss."

The stallion's green eyes drifted.

"What is this?" Gustav beckoned with a finger, and the stallion obeyed, easing over. Gustav wrapped his arms around the stallion's waist, squeezing possessively. "I am an unhappy man when you're like this. We will paint the town tonight . . . wine . . . veal parmesan . . . maybe a little dancing. So tell me what's bothering you."

The stallion blushed, surrendering a pearly-white smile before turning serious again. "I messed up. That bottle of pills I gave Mr. Wentworth . . . it seems they were real."

Gustav loosened his grip, taking a step back. "You gave him oxycodone?"

"It's not traceable."

"Perhaps not to the original source."

"I know, I know . . ." The stallion tensed up.

"What am I to do with you, my darling?" Gustav said, extracting a cigar from his jacket. He ceremoniously snipped off the end, searching deep inside himself for leniency he reserved for but one.

"Why did you trust him with the device?" the stallion said.

"It is not so much a matter of trust . . . as necessity."

"We must take additional precautions."

"Unfortunately, we have our lingering problem . . . And now this," Gustav said, turning his back. "I intend to keep Trevor Wentworth on a short leash until we get to the bottom of the Parkway issue. As it turns out, he has my device and refuses to take my calls."

"And my stupidity has only complicated matters. Perhaps, I should pay him a visit."

"For what purpose?"

The stallion smiled, slinking up next to Gustav. "Must I tell you everything?"

"We will give him twenty-four hours. After that . . . it's the carrot-and-stick routine for Mr. Trevor Wentworth."

Chapter 5

Waynesboro, Georgia
Monday, October 7th
6:00 P.M.

Tracie had a feeling she might have overstayed her welcome at the pecan stand. Not that Neely had asked her to leave, she just didn't appreciate people butting in where they didn't belong. Especially, when it came with an attitude. But she was rather proud of the way she had managed to charm a bit of kindness out of him, doing her best under the circumstances. Making an effort to lighten up as she stood in the concession stand line at the Burke County Fair, she summoned a host of all-but-forgotten childhood memories. Over her shoulder, a Ferris wheel with flashing lights lit up the sky, as shrills filtered down from on high. Flanked on each side were colorful displays of sideshows and carnival booths. In the distance, she heard an organ grinding, painting musical images of prancing merry-go-round horses and starry-eyed children. She caught a whiff of French fries, just as a clown strolled by with a bouquet of floating balloons.

The man in front of her finished up at the counter, and Tracie stepped to the window, ordering corndogs and Diet Cokes. After paying, she spun around a little too fast, slamming headfirst into an unfortunate soul who had shown up at the wrong time. The cups launched out of the cardboard carrier like scud missiles, exploding into a shower of Coke and ice as they found their mark. The man's hands went out as he jumped back in total shock.

Tracie nearly dropped the corndogs as she froze in place, analyzing the mayhem she had just created. *Not this*, she thought. As she slowly raised her head, she spotted a Coke stain the size of a basketball in the center of the man's chest. She braced herself for an old fashioned chewing out as her eyes lifted. Then she dropped the corndogs.

"Well, I'll be damned," Neely said.

"What—are—you—doing?"

"I came over to give you a hand."

"I'm so—"

"I'm sure you are," he interrupted.

"Let me . . ." Tracie didn't know what to say, so she cut her eyes to the counter. "I'll get some napkins."

When she returned, Neely was sitting on a picnic table in a black t-shirt, smiling. "Is this your way of trying to get rid of me?"

"I wish you would yell—or something."

"Actually, I'm feeling pretty refreshed at the moment." Neely held up the soggy shirt.

"This is awful," Tracie said, taking a sleeve. "I'm *really-really* sorry about this."

"I know you are, but I kind of like things this way."

"Just call me an idiot."

"No, I'll stick with Tracie."

"What can I do to make this right? I'll pay for the dry cleaning."

"I'm still hungry. What do you say I buy us—"

"No you don't. If anyone's buying anything, it's going to be me," Tracie said, cutting him short. "Stay here. I'll be right back."

When she returned, Tracie set the food on a makeshift tablecloth Neely had made out of a newspaper, handing over a stack of napkins. "*Those* are in case the idiot reappears," she said. "I'll just get some ketchup and—"

"None for me," Neely interrupted. "I take mine naked."

Tracie stopped. "Me, too."

Neely stood up. "Have a seat. And if it wouldn't be too much to ask, wipe that guilty look off your face." He sat down. "You bought me a corndog, so let's just call it even. Okay?"

"Actually—I bought you two," Tracie said, taking a seat across from him. "But I also owe you for allowing me to hang out at the orchard all day."

"You're starting to keep score, like my mom."

"For the record, let's get one thing straight. I don't exactly care for the mom analogies. I'm not that old, just in case you haven't noticed."

"Sensitive are we?" Neely said, snickering. "Weren't you the one telling me to call you a name just now?"

"That was different."

"I thought I made it clear this morning. I like older women."

"Then go find yourself one. We're practically in the same demographic."

"And you're pretty . . . *I mean* . . . you were pretty quiet all day. Why are you traveling alone anyway? And that's quite a rock on your finger. What's the story there?"

"Enough with the questions," Tracie said, mooning him with her eyes. "I'm not alone. My mom and dad are over in the 4-H pavilion helping set up. I snuck over and peeked in on them earlier."

"And?"

"That's all there is to it."

"Is that so? Well you're a big fat liar." Neely picked up a corndog, ripped off the wrapper, and took a bite. "You're not coming home. You're hiding out. And in case you haven't noticed, I'm not buying it."

"That makes two of us," Tracie said. "And don't talk with your mouth full." She grabbed a corndog and started drumming it on the table. "Listen, what do you say I pay for the shirt, and we part company on good terms?"

"This morning you said something about killing me."

"It's a figure of speech."

"I'll say."

"How does twenty bucks sound?"

"Are you crazy?" Neely tossed the shirt over and pointed at the label.

Tracie took a look, shaking her head. "Never heard of it."

"Twenty dollars wouldn't buy a collar stay. It's an artisan design from up in Nashville."

"It's western wear. What are you trying to do, scam me?" She started with the drumming again.

"Okay, back up just a minute," Neely said. "I'm sorry I compared you to my mom, because I can see it puts you in a bad way. I won't do it again. Besides you're much prettier than her. But don't tell her I said so." He reached over and placed a hand on hers.

"No, that's not it," Tracie said, studying his hand.

"If that's true, then I'd wager it has something to do with that rock you're wearing."

Tracie's phone rang, and she almost jumped out of her skin. She pulled her hand free and fished inside her purse, mostly to skirt the conversation. Setting the phone on the table she waited for the voicemail chime, and then punched the screen.

Neely leaned across the table for a closer look.

"You've got fifty-four messages from a guy named . . . Trevor?" He grabbed the phone and scrolled down the list.

"Never mind that. Just give me your contact information, and I'll send you a check." Tracie crossed her arms, turning her back to him.

Neely started typing. "First, tell me about the doublewide." He laid down the phone and entered her number into his.

"It's being delivered to a field behind my parents' house as we speak," Tracie said. "I was buying time with you until I was sure they weren't home."

"Where's the other half?"

"Oh, boy. That's where the Rock enters the picture."

"And that would be Trevor?"

Tracie said nothing, just reached around for her drink.

"I've got the picture now," Neely said.

"I don't think so."

"Regardless, I'm sorry."

"It's not your problem."

"No—*I mean*—I may have misled you," Neely said.

Tracie twisted around. The look on her face said it all, even though she had no idea what he meant. Neely let out a snicker and wagged his head.

"I've never told anyone, but I don't particularly care for corndogs. In fact, they're kind of disgusting." Neely wadded up the wrapper and dropped it on the table. "I was supposed to meet a blind date over at the Bonsai Sushi House half an hour ago . . . and you . . . sort of messed up my plans."

"I didn't tell you to come here. How's that my fault?"

"I don't know. But there's one thing you can be sure of. I intend to find out." Neely grabbed the shirt and stood up, stuffing her phone in his pocket. “You’re coming with me, young lady. I know exactly how to get to the bottom of this.”

Chapter 6

Suwanee, Georgia
Monday, October 7th
6:45 P.M.

We had just crossed the gangway onto the Parkway Community dock, when I got a better look at the bombshell Clayton referred to as Honey Bunch. She was standing at the railing with her back to us, her hips swaying like a coconut palm as country music rattled off the tin roof. I suddenly felt dizzy.

There was a thump, rattle, and splash. When I came to my senses, I realized I had just dropped-kicked my fishing rod into the lake. Freezing in my tracks, I returned for another glimpse of Honey Bunch. She turned to see what the commotion was all about, and it was at that moment I stared into the face of the sexiest creature I believe God had ever put on this earth. She opened her eyes wide, displaying an alluring pair of baby-blues. One hand was gripping a spatula and the other a glass of red wine.

"Wow—" I stammered.

"Well, what do we have here?" Honey Bunch said, waving the spatula in the air. Her voice was a pitch higher than the music.

"How about a beer?" Clayton called out, apparently oblivious to the latest developments.

I held up the bottle of Bird Dog, unable to utter a word. Honey Bunch's Lee Riders were tucked inside a pair of leggy cowboy boots. The skintight denim stretched up to her waist, where there was a western belt with a silver buckle. Above it, a pink muscle shirt had *KENNY* silk-screened across the front. Her arms and neck glowed in the evening light, bronzed to perfection. Bobbing above her shoulders was a pair of silver and turquoise earrings, dangling like wind chimes in an ocean breeze. The blonde hair had been pinned up, accentuating a matching coral necklace lassoed around her neck.

Her pink glossy lips were moving, but I was so dumbfounded I hadn't heard a single word.

"I'm sorry," was all I said, shaking the cobwebs out of my head.

"About what?" Clayton said, somehow still out of the loop. He turned down the boom box, and then pecked Honey Bunch on the cheek.

In the corner, a hibachi grill came into focus . . . and a delicious dinner, from the smell of things. It was an awkward moment, so I raised my nose and just stood there sniffing the air.

"Sweet Moses, Clayton! I've told you to warn me when you're bringing strangers to dinner."

"Trevor's no stranger. He's our neighbor."

"I'm Betty Jean," she said with a little curtsy.

"Again, my apologies," I said.

"Land alive, for what?" Betty Jean set her wine on the rail. "Where'd you get those cute little camper shorts?"

As she pointed, I noticed her fingernail polish matched the turquoise jewelry. Looking down at my distressed cargos, I stuffed my hands in the pockets. "Oh, these—"

"My little brother used to wear shorts like those every summer."

"Betty Jean!" Clayton said.

"I'm just messing with you, *Trev.* I see that fancy pony on the pocket."

Trev? I thought. Feigning a smile, I sucked in my gut to tame the wild locusts that seemed to be teaming again. I waited for Betty Jean to look away, and then swallowed hard. Suddenly, my problems seemed a million miles away. I felt something I hadn't felt in a long time. But this couldn't be happening. *She's at least fifty.*

"Take a load off, sport," Clayton said as he dropped into a chair, popping a tab.

"What were you boys doing over by that palm?" Betty Jean said, returning to the grill.

I made my way over to the gangway and stared into the water. Just below the surface, I spotted my rod. Kneeling down, I fished it out.

"Are you a Kenny Chesney fan?" Betty Jean said over a shoulder. It didn't seem to bother her that no one had responded to the previous question. Her boots were tapping out drumbeats. "If you are, I just might keep you."

"Not so fast," Clayton piped in. "This one's what you might call a professional advice-giver. Last time I checked, manly advice don't exactly shine your boots."

"That depends on which end of the horse . . ." Betty Jean broke off mid-sentence, mouthing words to the song.

I took in a deep breath and stood up, clinging tight to the dock rail.

"Sure you don't want a beer?" Clayton said.

"I'm good."

Betty Jean waltzed over with dinner plates, and Clayton helped her into a chair as I reluctantly joined them.

Once we were all seated, Clayton raised a hand in the air. "May the Lord grant us peace and gravy. Amen."

"Amen," Betty Jean said.

I cut my eyes at them . . . not sure what had just happened.

"You caught us on a special night," Clayton said, lifting his plate for a whiff. "Ahi tuna with a ginger-plum glaze over linguini."

"We're out of Pellegrino, but I've got a nice pinot if you're into wine," Betty Jean said.

I reached for the silverware, and in a split-second Betty Jean zeroed in on my hand like an advanced radar system.

"So . . . I see you're married."

It was a bullet to my heart. I dropped the fork, and it bounced off the dock before splashing in the water.

Clayton reached for Betty Jean's hand, shaking his head. They both watched silently as the color drained from my face.

"You . . . *uh* . . . want to talk about it?" Clayton finally said.

"I'm sorry if I said something wrong," Betty Jean said. "It's really none of my business. Let's just enjoy our dinner."

I reached for the Bird Dog, leaving them with their tuna as I returned to the rail. I proceeded to drown my sorrows, and when the bottle was empty, I tossed it in the lake.

"I'll have that beer now," I said to no one in particular.

Chapter 7

Waynesboro, Georgia
Monday, October 7th
7:30 P.M.

Tracie sat across from Neely at the Bonsai Sushi House with her elbows planted on the table. Neely's plate was clean, except for a few scraps of rice. A sake bottle and two small wooden cups, called masus, sat between them. Tracie's was still brimming from the first pour. The restaurant had a casual flair and was quiet except for an occasional banging of pots and pans in the kitchen. The decor was bright red, with paper lanterns hanging from the ceiling. A dragon mural covered the back wall, its jagged tail adorning their corner booth.

"That's better," Neely said, tossing down a pair of chopsticks. He leaned into the table, mimicking Tracie's posture.

"No doubt about it . . . Raw squid sure beats those nasty corndogs any day of the week."

Neely lowered his eyes and snickered, giving his now familiar head-bob. "That's what I love about you."

"That *stuff* you just ate is nauseating. I suppose the sauce is supposed to cover up the taste?"

"No, that would be the alcohol."

"And what's the deal with bringing your own sake? How hard can it be to ferment rice?"

"Pretty easy compared to running off with half a trailer," Neely said, leaning back in his seat.

"That's real cute."

"Now . . . about those voicemails—"

"Which part of *I don't want to talk about it* do you not understand?"

"There's a new one from a local number, so it must be your parents." Neely had Tracie's phone out on the table and was poking around. He tapped the screen.

"I'll deal with them when I get home."

"I checked a few of Trevor's messages, and you may want to listen to the first one," Neely said. "It sounds important."

"I'll decide what's important. Just give me a little space, okay?"

"It's something about a bag," Neely said, ignoring the remark. He drained his masu, then refilled it.

"What are you talking about?"

"Evidently, he has a job interview and needs a bag from the trailer. He thinks you have it."

"That's just like him to misplace something and accuse me of taking it."

"Those corndogs sure did a number on you," Neely said.

"And that's enough about the corndogs."

"Trevor says the bag is in the guest bathroom."

Tracie picked up her masu and sniffed.

"Do you think it's out at your parents' place?" Neely said.

"How would I know? He leaves his crap all over the house," Tracie said, setting down the masu.

"He sounds pretty desperate."

"If you want desperate, I'll tell you a thing or two about desperate."

"All right, just lower your voice," Neely said, checking to make sure no one was staring. "Did you leave him because of his employment situation?"

"What do you think I am—some kind of superficial bimbo? Of course I didn't leave him over a job."

"You're not giving me much to go on."

"Now you're catching on, Einstein."

"I'm doing you a favor." Neely poured another shot of sake and drained it.

"Tell me this . . . Why are you so interested?"

"I can't help myself. It bugs me when things don't make sense. Besides, I like you."

"By the way, did I happen to mention that I don't like it when you call me *older*?"

"Women," Neely said, shaking his head. He refilled his masu. "They sure didn't teach this in school."

"Did I ask you to bring me here?"

"Try the tempura. It'll make you feel better."

"What's the deal with guys and sushi anyway? Trevor swears by the stuff."

"I got hooked on it a few years back when I was in Tokyo on business. Is that a crime?"

"But do you really like it? The texture . . . the *smell*?"

"Let's just say it's an acquired taste," Neely said.

"At least, you're honest."

"And I fessed up about the corndogs, didn't I?"

"Trevor's into omakase."

"Wow . . . Big spender."

"Don't get me started."

"You know, when you're mad it brings out the best in you," Neely said.

"I perfected it when I was on the college debate team."

"I don't believe it. You had to learn to be charming?"

"It's an acquired skill," Tracie quipped.

"Say what you like, but I'm here for you," Neely said with a smile. He reached over and squeezed Tracie's hand, then slid the masu closer. "Free your mind and the rest will follow."

"How original," Tracie said, fingering the masu for the last time before draining it. She shuddered, and then opened her eyes wide. "We're going to need another bottle."

Chapter 8

Suwanee, Georgia
Monday, October 7th
7:30 P.M.

I slammed beer number three on the armrest, sinking low and wiping my mouth with the back of my hand. The tuna sat on the opposite side, untouched. I slid out of the Adirondack, helping myself to the cooler.

"Anybody want a beer?" I said, flipping the lid shut before they could answer. I plopped down and stretched out, then reached over and thumped the tuna. A shard went airborne and landed in Clayton's lap. I popped open the beer.

"That's high gravity brew, sport. You may want to pace yourself," Clayton said.

"I'll heat up your dinner," Betty Jean said, going for my plate.

"Don't bother."

"Why don't you eat something?" Clayton said.

I slapped my palm on the armrest.

"It'll make you feel better," Betty Jean said.

"Like . . . tuna's going to solve my problems," I said.

"It can't hurt," Clayton said.

"Sometimes, it helps to get things out in the open," Betty Jean said. "I don't always know how to express myself."

Clayton stifled a laugh, just as Betty Jean booted him. She got up and turned off the boom box.

"We moved down last year," I said, leaning back and looking up into the tin roof. "I was working for McKinsey in the New York office at the time."

"That's a fine organization," Clayton said.

Betty Jean cut her eyes at Clayton, warning him to button it.

"An executive with my largest client decided to join a startup, called Zuritech, here in Atlanta. I contacted him about his new company and discovered they were developing a drug that was sure to be a blockbuster."

"Blockbuster?" Betty Jean said.

"That's how we pharma-types refer to products that generate at least a billion dollars in *s-sales*," I said, my words starting to slur.

"That's billion with a *B?*" Clayton said.

"Every damn year," I said. "We're talking megabucks."

"Holy Toledo," Clayton said.

"I convinced the partners it was the perfect opportunity to expand our practice down here. We both grew up in the South, so Tracie was beside herself when I told her we were coming home to Georgia." I took a sip of beer.

"And when was that?" Betty Jean said.

"Last summer. We moved into the Golden Bear golf community down the road." I thought that would get a reaction, but there was only the belch of a bullfrog somewhere out on the lake.

"Yeah, we know about *The Springs*," Clayton finally said. "They're the ones that protested the new Walmart."

"Anyway, a few months later Cal Hunter . . . that's the CEO at Zuritech . . . he uncovered fraud and blew the whistle on the company. Now they're under investigation, and I never landed the account."

"Blew the whistle, *huh*?" Clayton said.

"Like a traffic cop at a school *c-crossing*."

"I hate to bring it up because you're going to say I don't understand, but don't you think it's a good thing you didn't get in bed with that outfit?"

"Good point," I said, shaking a finger at Clayton. "But I took a risk by coming here, and I failed. So I lost my job . . . *j-just* like that." I tried to snap my fingers, but they didn't cooperate.

"And you moved into number twelve—ten days ago? What have you been doing for the past year?" Clayton said.

"Looking for work. But this economy is a *mutha*. I've conducted a nationwide search, and so far . . . *zilch*. And the thing is—I had cash flow problems right out of the shoot, especially with the new house."

"Over at *The Springs*?" Clayton said.

"Bingo," I said with a nod. "And then the mortgage market went to hell."

"Did you have one of those toxic mortgages?" Betty Jean said.

"Yes, ma'am. At least, I used to." I squeezed my beer can and it crackled, spewing a geyser out the top.

"I'm so sorry, darling," Betty Jean said. She patted my hand. "I've read about those subprime mortgages, but I never thought I'd actually meet someone who had one."

"It's not exactly something to brag about," Clayton said.

"We lost the house a couple of weeks ago. I managed to sell my boat before the bank repossessed it. That's how I bought the *D-Dorset* Place."

"The Dorsey Place," Betty Jean corrected. "Leland and Sarah were nice people."

"How did you land in Parkway Community?" Clayton said.

"The mortgage company trashed our credit." I shook a fist in the air. "We couldn't even rent an apartment. Those people looked at me like I'd robbed a bank."

"The scoundrels," Clayton said.

"I think my appetite's coming back *n-now*."

Betty Jean hopped up and slipped over to the grill. "I'm going to take care of you, *Trev*."

Trev? I thought, smiling.

"I'll get you a beer," Clayton said, taking my crumpled can. He walked up behind Betty Jean, who was reheating the tuna, and gave her a pat. Then he pulled a beer from the cooler.

"From what I hear those bankers are nothing but a pack of thieves," Betty Jean said. "I wouldn't worry about what they think."

"My account balance is starting to look like one of those endangered *s-species*. And they're upside-down on my mortgage, just like all the others. Maybe I'll bail them out when I get back on my feet."

"Now you're talking," Clayton said. "Of course, at the moment I'm worried about that trailer of yours. It's split right down the middle. Everything you own is exposed to the elements."

Popping open the beer, I tipped the can for a sip. Most of it dribbled in my lap.

"But I can tell you're the kind to rise above this sort of thing. And you'll be a better man for it," Clayton said.

"And he's a wonderful judge of character," Betty Jean chimed in from the grill.

"It's like this," I said. "Tracie wasn't a happy camper, and I can't blame her. She trusted me . . . I let her down . . . and *n-now* she's gone."

"She was here at sunup," Clayton said. "Where'd she go?"

"That's just it. She left me high and dry. I was shagging golf balls at the driving range this morning, and when I came home she had flown the coop."

"Why in the world did she take half the trailer?" Betty Jean said.

"It's a message," I said, stopping to drain the beer.

Clayton sensed my despair and thought twice before going to the cooler for another round.

"What do you mean?" Betty Jean said.

"When I was fishing this afternoon, I figured something out." I reached over and popped the tab while the beer was still in Clayton's hand, nearly dropping it when he turned loose. "Of course, it could be the *brewski* talking." Setting down the can, I hoisted myself out of the chair and stumbled. Clayton and Betty Jean rushed over to prop me up.

"Easy there, sport," Clayton said.

"*Trev*, it may be none of my business—"

"I like it when you call me, *Trev*," I said to Betty Jean.

"What's the message?"

"It's like a message in a *b-bottle*," I said, staring into Betty Jean's blue eyes. "Tracie sent me a message."

"But what is it?"

"Tracie . . ."

"I'm listening, darling," Betty Jean said.

"Tracie, the love of my life . . . she's leaving me once and for all."

Chapter 9

Midtown Atlanta
Tuesday, October 8th
6:00 A.M.

It was getting light outside when Gustav entered the Arts Center through the loading dock. The interior was bathed in blue light as he marched the perimeter, taking in the overnight progress.

A small lobby had been framed at the front entrance. Behind it was a narrow hallway lined with offices that included an executive suite. An opening in the middle of the hall provided access into the warehouse area. The secure storage had been constructed just behind the offices, where he and the stallion had stood last night. Beyond that was the lab. The back wall was covered in gypsum board, and he could make out markings where the concealed entryway was to be located. As he continued his inspection, the stallion appeared.

"This is nice work," Gustav said.

"We have a new completion timeline," the stallion said, turning for a look over a shoulder. "Some of the materials are on backorder. We now estimate that everything will be wrapped up by the weekend."

"I signed the contract for the lab across town. I want you to go over and take pictures of the layout so we can transfer the equipment in next week. Everything must be precisely to specification in the event of an audit."

"Would it not be easier to purchase new equipment?" the stallion said.

"The lab is fully validated with certifications in place. Once everything is installed on site, the seller has agreed to ensure it is in proper working order . . . The perfect front."

"So you want to mirror his current footprint?"

"Verbatim," Gustav said. "Down to the certificates hanging on the wall."

"Consider it done."

"As for our other matter, I have been unable to reach Trevor Wentworth. For some reason, he still refuses to answer his phone."

"I can investigate, like we discussed."

"In due time," Gustav said. "We must not get sloppy, seeing how there is ample suspicion that Parkway is being watched. Get in touch with our people and have them do a thorough background check on our Mr. Wentworth. If his situation has changed, notify me immediately. We must be prepared to exploit his vulnerabilities—that is—if he refuses to work with us."

Chapter 10

Burke County, Georgia
Tuesday, October 8th
6:00 A.M.

Tracie had a bad feeling when she woke up, starting with the fact that she had to pry open her eyelids. She wasn't sure where she was, and the chill in the air didn't help matters, probably the reason her legs felt so stiff. She opened her eyes wide, rubbing away the sleep as she worked a kink out of her neck. The light around her seemed gray and dusty.

Once everything came into focus, she noticed the inside of a car door next to her outstretched legs. Directly across her left shoulder she spotted a small window, and it dawned on her she was in the backseat of a two-door. Looking forward, she stared down at her legs. They were fully extended and propped up on the back of a bucket seat that had been lowered. The seat's headrest was just beyond her bare feet, with the steering wheel and dashboard visible above her toes.

Where am I?

She suddenly felt a throbbing and raised a hand to her forehead. Outside the car, a breeze rattled leaves around on the ground. She closed her eyes and rested her head against the seat, doing her best to recall the previous night. Unfortunately, the images came quickly.

The Bonsai Sushi House.

As Tracie's eyes popped open, she spotted a second pair of legs to her right. Fearing the reality she was about to face, she twisted her head ever so slowly to spot Neely sprawled next to her. Barely an arm's length away, he was fast asleep with his feet stretched across the front passenger seat. His head was buried in the far corner, and there was a corduroy jacket crumpled between them, covering her right hand.

With a gentle touch, she reached over and pulled the coat into her lap. In the process, a wallet fell out, but more alarming was the fact that Neely's hand was resting on top of hers. Down in the floorboard she noticed a pair of boots and an empty sake bottle. Taking another look at Neely, she realized he was still wearing the t-shirt from last night.

Trying to focus, Tracie looked at the wallet on the seat. Next to it was a sleek-looking business cardholder. Fumbling with her left hand, she grabbed for both and knocked the cardholder into one of the boots. Not wasting any time, she opened the wallet and found a driver's license inside, holding it up for better light. The photo bore a good resemblance of Neely. Then her eyes zeroed in on the birthdate.

Tracie snatched her hand free from his.

Neely groaned, took a couple of raspy breaths, and reluctantly opened his eyes. When he spotted Tracie with the wallet, he sprang into action, swiping it out of her hand. She jumped back in the seat.

"Hey, what's the idea?" Neely coughed out. He started flipping through the contents and suddenly stopped. "Where's my cardholder?"

Tracie said nothing, only gestured at the boot.

Neely fished it out. "Did you look at this?"

Tracie sat quietly, wondering what he was up to. For the most part, Neely had been a gentleman, even though last night was still a bit foggy. She lifted the coat with two fingers—like it was toxic—and dropped it in his lap.

"Never mind that. *Perhaps* we should address this matter of age difference," she said.

"That's not what I asked you."

"I looked in the wallet, okay? What's the big deal? You've been playing twenty questions with me. Maybe you're the one who's hiding something."

Neely did a change-up with his classic head-bob, letting out a snicker.

"And stop trying to sway me with that cute little head thing of yours."

"A girl robbed me a few years ago, and I'm a bit guarded about my personal stuff."

"That makes two of us," Tracie said. "So you're saying this kind of thing happens frequently?"

"What kind of thing?"

"For starters . . . what are we doing here?" Tracie peeked out the window. They were parked in one of the bays at the pecan stand.

"You don't remember?"

"I woke up in the backseat of a Grand Prix with a strange man. Do you think these are the brains the Good Lord gave me?"

"That depends," Neely said with a grin.

"And for the record, you're barely a year younger than me."

"You say that like it's a crime."

"You . . . and all that older woman crap."

"You're the one who's acting nuts. If sleeping in a car with a stranger isn't your thing, then maybe you should ask yourself why you're here in the first place."

"*No* . . . it's not my thing," Tracie said, mocking. She bit her bottom lip. "So what's the story? Am I being kidnapped, or am I free to go?"

"For someone who's lived in New York, you sure didn't learn much."

"Did you bring me here under false pretenses?"

"*Jeez* . . . what an imagination."

"You lied to me." Tracie shoved on the door, but it wouldn't budge.

"I brought you here because you had too much to drink, and I couldn't let you drive to your parents' house in that condition."

Tracie squeezed the door handle, thinking for a minute. "What's in the cardholder?"

"First, you tell me what Trevor stashed in that trailer of yours."

"I'll do better than that. I'll sell it to you." Tracie caught a glimpse of her bare feet and rummaged around in the floor-board for her shoes.

"Why exactly is Trevor so hot to get his hands on that bag?"

Tracie slipped on her shoes, all the while staring out the window. Her Lexus was parked in the adjoining bay. "You want to know about Trevor? Let me tell you about him, and I'll make it short and sweet. He's a self-centered, candy-coated, rotten little sack of pecans. Does that answer your question?"

"I was hoping . . ."

Tracie shoved open the door and got out, sick and tired of Neely's nagging. She reached inside for her purse. "I believe you have my phone."

Neely dug it out of his jeans and handed it over.

She checked the time. "What are my parents going to think?"

"I'm glad you brought that up," Neely said. "I used your phone to text your mom last night. Don't thank me now, but she thinks you slept over with a friend."

"How convenient . . . And you can just wipe that smirk off your face."

"Do you really think I'm cute?" Neely said.

Chapter 11

Suwanee, Georgia
Tuesday, October 8th
6:30 A.M.

I was snuggled all comfy in the crisp, clean sheets as a mental fog began to lift. Before I could stir, a loud banging jolted me and I clenched, sending a lightning bolt through my head. The pain intensified into jackhammer blows until the noise faded away and my temples settled into a mild throbbing. Without warning, the banging started up again. I jerked my head, and something sharp pierced my upper lip, causing me to let loose with a yelp. As fast as it had come, the sound vanished.

My eyes popped open, and I realized I was on a bed, flat on my back. A first glimmer of morning light drifted in, illuminating a familiar popcorn pattern on the ceiling. A fast learner, I limited my next movements to rolling my eyes toward the light. Just above the headboard I spotted a pair of flowered curtains. I recognized them as the ones in the front bedroom at Parkway 12—the only bedroom now that Tracie had made off with the other two.

The pounding cut loose again and caught me off guard, only this time it came rapid-fire. With nerves on end, I attempted to ease my head off the pillow and felt a firm tug at my lip. I instantly froze, drawing a hand up to a tender area, which resulted in a swift jab to my finger. Unable to hold still any longer, a squadron of stings descended on my lip and finger like a swarm of yellow jackets. Somehow I managed to suppress a scream long enough to cross my eyes for a look at the attack zone. Just beyond the tip of my nose, a red blob came into focus, sparkling in the morning sunlight.

Breathing in to regain my faculties, it didn't take long to identify the enemy. Staring back at me was four inches of beady-eyed terror, shrouded in hooks. It was my new fishing lure. The first hook was planted snuggly in my upper lip. A second was connected to the lure's belly and dangling ever so delicately over my gaping mouth—I could have poked it with the tip of my tongue. A final one near the tail had snagged the index finger of my right hand only seconds ago. On the lure's nose, I spotted a silver loop attached to a fishing line that was stretched tight across my cheek. In my periphery, I noticed the fishing rod plastered to the side of my face. The Zebco 303. *It's still got the price tag on it*, I heard Clayton say inside my head. My heart quickened a beat or two as I realized that my right arm was looped around the rod. The freshly-hooked finger began to quiver in place, mere inches from my nose.

I took a deep breath and tried to recall the events of the previous night. There was the dock, dinner, and of course—drinking. But I didn't remember coming home or crawling into bed, much less tangling with a fishing pole.

My options seemed to be rather limited, so I went for a simple solution. I crossed my eyes once again and positioned my thumb and pinky on opposite sides of the lure's beady little eyes, and then applied pressure to stabilize it between my lip and finger. Waiting for the hook over my mouth to stop swinging, I reached around with my left hand and took ahold of the fishing rod.

I counted to three and rolled onto my stomach, allowing my feet to slip over the edge of the bed. I wiggled a bit, managing to raise my upper body off the sheets. The tension on the line didn't let up, so I maintained a firm grip as I got to my feet and tip-toed over to the door. It was closed.

With my hands predisposed, I couldn't come up with a way to work the doorknob and hobbled back to the bed. Using my big toe, I probed for the reel's release button, certain it was somewhere down around my ankles. Seconds later, there was a "click", and like an answer to prayer—no pain.

Using my fingers like tweezers, I spooled out enough line to allow the top of the rod to pull away from my face. When there was enough slack, I laid it on the bed and worked out a few more feet. With the lure still hooked to my lip and finger, I made my way to the door a second time, listening as the fishing line whirred behind me.

I carefully opened the door, checking behind me to make sure nothing was going to snag as I took a first step into the hallway. Before I knew what hit me I tripped, stumbled forward, and smacked face-first into a sea of blue tarp. The tarp bowed outward under my weight and snapped back with a fluffing sound that reminded me of a trash bag. Launching me backwards, I lost my footing and slammed to the floor in a full sprawl. I let out a deadly scream.

Reeling from the agony, I laid motionless on my back, praying for a wave of dizziness to pass. Moments later, I managed to get to my feet and spotted the culprit that had tripped me up—a toolbox. I turned for another look at the tarp, which appeared to be a makeshift wall where the two halves of the trailer had once been joined. I wasn't sure how it had gotten there, but it was a stark reminder that Tracie had taken off with half of the house.

Only yesterday, the back bedroom had occupied a spot diagonally across the hall. Next to it had been the guest bath. I tugged on the line to make sure there was ample slack and started to look for help. With the tarp now on my left, the first door I came to on the opposite wall was the laundry room. There was nothing of interest there, so I continued to the next opening, a combo kitchen/breakfast nook wallpapered in a Southwestern pattern. For some reason, it now struck me as a bit flamboyant for my taste. A little further, I eased past a foyer that adjoined the front entrance, and then continued to a doorway at the end of the hall. Inside, I took a right and entered the master bath.

Flipping on the light, I stepped up to the vanity and got a first glimpse of myself in the mirror. There was a trickle of blood where the hook had pierced my lip. From the looks of things, yanking it out probably wasn't a good idea. The hook in my finger had to be dealt with first. Opening a drawer, I scrambled around, looking for something to work with.

Out of the blue, a new round of banging kicked off, and I jumped. Pain pulsed through my wounds, triggering another blood-curdling scream. There was a heavy thump down the hall, and I reached up and gripped the lure in my left hand, snatching my finger loose. As I shrieked holy terror, footfalls hastened in my direction. I felt a jerk on the fishing line and opened my mouth to scream, but nothing came out. As my eyes started to roll up in my head, I could feel myself blacking out, when suddenly Clayton's image appeared in the mirror.

"What the tarnation's going on in here?" Clayton yelled, shaking a hammer in the air.

I grabbed the vanity to keep from buckling, and then managed to raise the bleeding finger.

Clayton made an attempt to stifle his reaction, but couldn't hold it. "Damn if you didn't catch a boy bass, sport." Without warning, he reached out and snatched the lure out of my lip.

I wheezed as my lips pulled back, exposing a row of teeth resembling a rabid dog.

Clayton glanced down at the lure in his hand, tracing the line out the bathroom door. "I knew I shouldn't have left you alone last night."

I cut my eyes to the mirror, a bit shocked by the maniac staring back at me.

"Last time I saw you, you were clinging to that fishing pole like you were in love with it," Clayton went on.

I let out a couple of gasps before I managed to say anything. "You left me alone—*in my condition*—with a deadly weapon? What's wrong with you?"

"It's a fishing pole."

I snapped a bottle of Sea Breeze off the counter.

"Good thing you kept your pants on, 'cause I sure wouldn't want to explain that one down at the emergency room," Clayton said.

"What is all that pounding?" I said, doing my best to tame the monster.

"The back of your trailer was wide open, so I've been sealing her up this morning. Do you know it took nearly sixty feet of tarp?" Clayton paused. "You don't remember a thing, do you?"

I gave him a deadly look. "What do you think?"

Clayton grabbed the bottle. "For starters, I wouldn't put this stuff on those wounds. You're libel to say things you'll regret."

"Why don't you take your tarp, your sorry-ass cowboy self, and just get out," I said, pointing toward the door.

"Clayton!" Betty Jean called out in the distance.

"Sorry, I left the front door open," Clayton said. "Betty Jean has breakfast ready."

I snatched the Sea Breeze from him and slammed it on the vanity.

"Listen, I'm sorry about all of this. I apologize for everything. It's a lousy thing to happen to a nice guy like you. I was only trying to help." Clayton removed his hat. "I just don't want you to go and do something stupid."

"Like what?"

"Do you realize how worked up you are over Tracie and this job situation?"

"Is that your way of saying it's my fault?"

"Did I say that?"

"You were laughing at me."

"Laughter is mighty fine medicine sometimes. Anyway, I apologize."

"Just so you know, I had an interview on Sunday—an important one."

"Then what do you say we sit down to breakfast, and you can tell me all about it?"

I stepped out in the hall, casting my eyes down the length of tarp to where the guest bath once stood.

"What's wrong?" Clayton said.

"Tracie took off with something I have to get my hands on in a hurry."

"Have you tried to get in touch with her?"

I stuffed my hand in a pocket and pulled out my phone. There were several missed calls—none of them Tracie's. They were ones I had been avoiding for good reason. "Tell Betty Jean I'm on my way."

I stepped out on the stoop and waited for Clayton to cross the street, and then headed around the corner of the trailer. The doublewide next door was visible, but there was no sign of life. Clinging close to the house, I looked over my shoulder, and then crawled underneath and pulled a handful of insulation out of a dangling junction box. It had formerly connected the air conditioning ductwork, that is, before Tracie chopped the trailer in half. I stuck my arm inside up to the elbow and extracted a wad of Ziploc bags, all filled with white powder. I made sure there were six before stuffing them back in, along with the insulation. Scooting back out, I retrieved my phone, dialed Tracie for the hundredth time, and headed for breakfast.

Chapter 12

Suwanee, Georgia
Tuesday, October 8th
7:30 A.M.

I did a double-take at a man dressed in Rambo gear down on the beach as I crossed the tip of Lakeview Circle en route to the Beasleys'. The back door was ajar, so I let myself in. Halfway inside, I froze in my tracks, instantly dazed by what I saw. Across the room, I noticed a Viking stainless steel range, and in front of it was Betty Jean swaying in a silk kimono and cowboy boots. The kimono was pink and cinched tight about her waist, accentuating her golden legs that meandered like a river down into the boots. She tapped out a two-step, singing along as Kenny Chesney serenaded from a boom box.

"Not again," I said under my breath.

Clayton looked up from a bistro table, and then called out to Betty Jean. "Turn it down, Honey Bunch. Our guest is here."

Betty Jean dropped a frying pan in the sink, then turned and winked at me. "Morning, *Trev*," she said, not missing a beat. The mention of my name warmed my soul, like a stiff shot of Bird Dog.

"Sorry I'm late," I said.

"Grab yourself a plate and take a load off," Clayton said, standing up. "I've got to finish getting ready for work, but make yourself at home." He headed down the hall.

"I think I'll just have a coffee to go," I said to Betty Jean, trying not to stare.

Betty Jean didn't make the task easy, doing a little twist that left me dizzy. I pulled up to the sink to steady myself.

"Oh my," Betty Jean said, moving closer. She reached out to my lip. "Honey, I'd put a new blade in that razor, if I were you."

I couldn't help but notice the shade of turquoise on her perfectly manicured fingernails. "Rough morning," I said, slipping over to the table.

"What's on your agenda for today?" Betty Jean said, filling a coffee cup. She picked up a plate and set it on the table.

"I'm—*uh*—testing a prototype for a new product."

"You mean, like an invention?"

"Actually, it's for a job interview." I took a bite of toast.

"Well, I'm sure you'll dazzle them," she said. "I've got left-over ginger-plum sauce, if you want some on your toast."

"That's a nice kimono," I said, lapsing into la-la-land for a second. *Idiot.* A bead of sweat broke out on my forehead.

"You seem to be feeling better this morning," Betty Jean said, rolling her big, blue eyes and ignoring the compliment.

I stuffed the rest of the toast in my mouth, totally uninterested in explaining anything about my morning.

"I've got to skedaddle," Clayton called out, barreling down the hallway. He walked over and pinned Betty Jean to the counter, giving her a kiss that lifted one of her boots off the tile. Then he turned to me. "You gonna be all right?"

I set down my coffee. "Do you have a second?"

"As Steven Tyler once said, 'walk this way'." He headed out the door.

"Stop by if you need anything, *Trev*," Betty Jean said.

I could feel my cheeks flushing, so I hurried after Clayton. "Thanks for breakfast," I said over my shoulder.

"Any time."

Outside, I pointed across Lakeview. "From this angle, you hardly notice that half of my trailer is missing," I said to Clayton. The lawn was manicured, and Goldfinger sat under the palm out front. There was a *Beware of Dog* sign nailed to it.

"Not bad, *huh*?" Clayton said.

"The sign is a nice touch."

Clayton turned and started up the street, heading away from the lake. "I picked it up at Home Depot last night."

"Let me know what I owe you," I said, hustling to catch up. We followed along from the tip of the horseshoe where Clayton and Betty Jean's home was situated at lot thirteen, moving toward the highway. I spotted Clayton's tractor trailer rig across a grassy area, parked on a green slab near the second of two entrances. When we reached it, he climbed up in the cab and started the engine. I noticed a *CBJ Logistics* logo on the side. It roared to life, settling into a throaty rhythm. He hopped down to where I was standing.

"Clayton, I've got to find Tracie."

"I'm with you on that, sport." He kicked a tire.

"I tried calling her again this morning. All I get is voicemail."

"I know a guy who trucks mobile homes all over the state. I'll bet you a silver dollar he's the one who hauled your unit out of here."

"Give me his number and I'll—"

"Not so fast. You just let me handle it. This fellow ain't exactly one of those bluebloods you're accustomed to hobnobbing with." Clayton looked me in the eyes, and then climbed up on the rig.

"I'll leave my cell number with Betty Jean in case you need to reach me."

"Ten-four," Clayton said. "Have a good 'un." He slammed the door.

The engine revved, and I watched as he pulled out onto Highway 141. When I looked across the parking pad, I spotted the Parkway office about thirty feet away. It was an odd stucco building that backed up to the woods. Out front a man dressed in a green flight suit sat on a bench that resembled a church pew. Near the front door was a sign carved out of a tree trunk that read: *Parkway Community, A Lakeside Retreat.* A shingle hung beneath it on a pair of rusty chains with the words: *No Singlewides Allowed.*

Chapter 13

Waynesboro, Georgia
Tuesday, October 8th
7:30 A.M.

Tracie stared out the bay window at the lush landscaping that surrounded the swimming pool at her parents' house. There were lounge chairs down one side, and in the far corner a table with a striped umbrella. A breeze ruffled the fringe, reminding her how much she liked autumn.

She slipped into the kitchen for a cup of coffee, and after wrapping her robe tight, grabbed the morning paper and snuck out the back door. Pulling out a chair, she spread the newspaper on the table before positioning herself directly into the sun. Nestling in, she paused to study the ripples on the water.

The morning air was crisp. She inhaled what to her was the most wonderful scent in the world. She didn't know how to describe it . . . because it wasn't so much a smell as it was a feeling. Maybe it was her love of fall, the changing colors, warm sweaters, or the excitement of the upcoming holiday season, but she couldn't help it. Taking a sip of coffee, she slapped a hand on the newspaper to keep it from flying off with the breeze. She put away the paper, leaned back, and closed her eyes. Forgetting about last night, she sighed and let her thoughts run free. They rambled at first, but eventually found a heavenly memory.

She was twelve at the time, but could still recall the fall festival that year. There were silly games, a contest for best costume, hotdogs and marshmallows over a crackling fire. But that was after a few brave souls had taken to the dance floor at the National Guard Armory, wiggling like a barrel of monkeys to tunes on a cassette player. Afterwards, everyone loaded up on a bus and came to her house for a hayride and bonfire. She remembered Tommy Jenkins holding her hand as they bounced down a dirt road on a trailer behind her dad's tractor. He was scared stiff that Tracie's dad would turn around and misjudge his intentions. She also recalled how he had later handed her the most perfectly roasted marshmallow she had ever seen on a stick. The look in his eyes was pure innocence, an insecurity known to just about every preteen on earth. When she accepted the marshmallow, she had batted her eyes and held it up between them, offering him the first bite. As he leaned in for a taste, she took a nibble on her side of the stick. Their lips never actually touched, but it was the closest thing to bliss she had known in all her years. She still got goose bumps thinking about it.

Maybe it was the chilly night or the blazing bonfire, but Tracie remembered how Tommy had blushed when their eyes met. He had gooey marshmallow stuck on his face, and the color in his cheeks was pumpkin-orange, arguably from the dancing flames.

She laughed, thinking how it all happened twenty years ago in a cornfield only a hundred yards away from where she was now seated. She licked her lips, wondering if that kind of sweetness would ever come again.

"That must be some cup of coffee," her mother said, slipping up to the table. Tracie's eyes popped open. "I'm surprised you made it in so early this morning, darling. I heard you in the shower." She swooped in for a kiss on the cheek. "Your message didn't say where you were staying last night."

"I was just thinking about things we used to do in the fall," Tracie said with a slight of hand. She sat up straight.

Her mother pulled up a chair, glancing down at Tracie's bare feet. "Like getting frostbit toes?"

Tracie wiggled her peachy toenails. "I was always good at sneaking out of the house, barefoot."

"As if I didn't know. If I had a dollar for every time I had to pull a splinter out of those mischievous little feet, we'd be having coffee on the French Riviera."

Tracie laughed, and it felt good. Pressing her feet down on the cement decking, she felt a chill start up her toes. She tugged at the robe and perched her feet up on the edge of the chair, draping terrycloth around them before taking a sip of coffee. "Mom, was I ever a difficult child?"

"Compared to your brother, you were sugar and spice. Of course, that's not exactly an objective opinion."

"I know . . . But was I ever unreasonable?"

"Just once when you wanted a Malibu Barbie. I can remember preparing breakfast while you sat glued to Saturday morning cartoons. Like clockwork, there was Malibu Barbie flaunting her stuff on the beach with her hunk, Malibu Ken. I guess the toy people had it figured out a long time ago. Anyway, as if her platinum hairdo and suntan weren't enough, Barbie had a pink Corvette and just about everything a plastic girl could want."

"But you never bought me a Malibu Barbie."

"Exactly, and you turned out just fine."

Tracie stared into her coffee. "Then what happened to Cliff?"

"Your brother? What makes you think there's something wrong with him?"

Tracie covered her mouth. "I wish you could see the look on your face."

"You'll understand *that* when you have children of your own. And speaking of boys, how are you feeling about yours this morning?"

Tracie's eyes darted to the field behind the house. "I'm wondering why I don't miss him."

"After what you've been through, I'm surprised you didn't strangle him. Why in the world would you be missing him so soon?"

"So you think I'm doing the right thing?"

"I didn't say that, darling. You've been hurt—that's all. Some of us eat chocolate, others tend to cry. You, on the other hand, drive away with half a house."

"Mom, I just moved into a trailer park for Pete's sake. How would you feel?"

Her mother studied Tracie's face, noticing a tear in her eye. "That all depends. But this isn't about me. I know you, and this isn't about a trailer park either."

The comment silenced Tracie, but not for long. "That's easy to say when you're living in a house with a pool in the middle of Hundred Acre Woods." She swiped the tear away.

"Now, I know you don't mean that. You're here because you need support, and that's exactly what your dad and I intend to give you."

"But you can see how depressing it is, can't you? I'm thirty-two years old and moving back in with my parents."

"Tracie, you're not moving anywhere. You're here to sort things out, which is perfectly natural when you're facing a milestone in your life."

"But it's embarrassing." Tracie raised her palms in the air, like a set of scales. "My dad is president of a bank, but my husband is unemployed." She tipped the scales, shifting her eyes from one hand to the other. "My dad built a nice home for his family . . . my husband gets a foreclosure notice. You have the bridge club, and I have total humiliation."

"Which explains why you found your way home again. You just need time to think."

"But I don't feel anything. Doesn't that say something about me?"

"You feigned near death when you didn't get Malibu Barbie."

"That's different," Tracie said, looking over just in time to catch an expression on her mother's face. "What?"

"Houses? . . . Jobs? . . . Bridge clubs? Those can be kind of silly at times. Taken out of context, they're a lot like Malibu grown-ups."

"Houses and careers don't sound important to you?" Tracie said, brushing a wisp of hair out of her face.

"Don't get me wrong. Of course they are, but not *that* important."

"Compared to what?"

"Love, darling," her mother said.

"Are you serious? I'm madder than hell and you want to bring up love. What makes you think of that at a time like this?"

"You're numb because you've lost something precious. It's a defense mechanism. Otherwise, you'd be out partying with your friends and trying to forget about Trevor."

"Mom . . . to be honest . . . I came here to get over him."

"Then why did you bring part of a house that you hate?"

"It's called marital assets. Half of everything is mine."

"But you just said it was an embarrassment."

"But it's mine."

"And what about your heart, dear?"

"I thought I just explained that."

"You said you couldn't feel it. And that says something important, but I don't think you're ready to hear it."

"Tell me. I'm a big girl now."

"You said half of everything is yours. Well, it seems you may have left something behind." Her mom paused.

"Are you going to tell me what it is?"

"It's your heart. I don't think you brought even half of it with you."

Tracie shot out of the chair and marched toward the house. When she reached the steps, she spun around and folded her arms. In the distance, she caught a reflection in the cornfield, forcing her to squint. Her mother peeked over a shoulder at the trailer and raised an eyebrow.

"For your information, I'm driving to Tybee Island tomorrow to visit someone who happens to be a little closer to my age—a friend who understands me," Tracie said. "She thinks a little fun in the sun will do me good."

"She told you that?"

"It doesn't matter. I'm going to the beach, regardless of what anyone thinks. And I'm going to forget about Barbie, trailer parks, and most of all—Trevor Wentworth. And if I wanted you to know where I was last night, I would have told you."

Chapter 14

Suwanee, Georgia
Tuesday, October 8th
8:00 A.M.

I crossed the parking pad and headed for the office. As I approached, there was little doubt about the man in the flight suit. It was Fate Tanner, better known as the property manager. When I was within shouting distance, I could tell he was oblivious to me, staring off into the distance. Following his line of sight, I could see nothing of interest that might be distracting him.

"Is something wrong?" I said, stepping closer.

Fate sat on the church pew, adjusting a pair of horn-rimmed glasses and silent as a stone. He sported a shock of gray-white hair that was straight out of *The Call of the Wild*. I half-expected to hear wolves howling any second. When he remained in the trance for another couple of minutes, I took a second look in the general direction. Nothing.

Fate unexpectedly stirred, coming to life. "Love the sound of that diesel. Sometimes I can track her halfway up to Route 400. Not today, no *sirree*. Rush hour's put the kibosh on that. Drowned her out, just like that." He snapped his fingers.

Confused, I waited until I had his full attention. "You're listening to an engine?"

"Not just any engine. It's Clayton's Kenworth. Six hundred horsepower of raw muscle. When that baby roars, she's like a mountain lion on the prowl. But I lost her about a mile up the road."

"You must have good ears," I said, feigning interest.

"Have you ever been inside that truck?"

"Just a peek."

"The interior is prettier than your momma's bedroom. Clayton treats that rig like a spoiled child. Have a seat," Fate said, motioning to the bench.

"You're Fate, right?"

"That's right. Fate Tanner. Born in nineteen hundred and thirty-three."

"And you collect the rent?"

"Rent's due the first of the month, late on the fifteenth. Interest accrues daily thereafter. Let's see . . . you're in number twelve."

"The old Dorsey Place."

"Leland and Sarah, now they were what you call good people."

"You stopped by when we moved in."

"It's one of my duties. I was appointed by the homeowner's association for a term of two years to collect rent, make sure the grounds are maintained, and refer all complaints to the board of directors."

"By the way, I'm Trevor Wentworth."

"I know all twenty-seven residents in this community—every last one of them."

"That's impressive."

"Can I get you a drink, *Trev*?" Fate said, not really asking. He hefted himself off the bench and disappeared inside. A minute later, he plopped down with two ice-cold cans. "I hope you like Dr Pepper."

"Nothing for me," I said.

"Normally, you'd have to put a quarter in the cash box. But no worries, we're conducting business here." Fate winked and handed me the soda anyway. "Most folks around these parts are absolute Coca-Cola fanatics."

"So Fate, do they know you drink on the job?" I said with a smile.

Fate popped the top on his can, taking a long sip. He fell into a trance, making me think another rig might be coming. Straight-faced, he turned to me. "Comedian, *huh*? I like a good laugh every now and then. It keeps a man young."

"Can I ask you a question?"

"If it's a complaint, I'll have to take it to the board."

"It's not a complaint—"

"Have you ever heard the story about that parking pad?" Fate nodded at the green concrete.

"No, sir, I haven't."

"Seven years ago, it was a tennis court. See the fence on each end."

I hadn't, so I leaned for a look. On the far side, I spotted a trampoline full of bouncing kids. Each of them was pounding away with their tongues hanging out, like they'd been at it since sunup. "What's going on over there?"

"Oh, Clayton bought that for the neighborhood kids. Those young'uns belong to Ol' Lady Wilbanks over at number twenty-three."

"She's got that many children?"

"Grandchildren . . . and she does a little daycare on the side."

"I'd like to climb up there and give it a go," I said, enjoying the sight. "Sorry, what were you saying about the tennis court?"

"Residents used to play tennis—mostly at night after work. Then Ol' Lady Wilbanks started raising Cain. She claimed the lights shined in through her front window, putting a glare on the TV. She got a petition going and took it to the board. They sided with her and shut that puppy down. Of course, I heard they mostly did it because of the cost of keeping the lights on at night. But Ol' Lady Wilbanks, yes *sirree*, she set the wheels in motion."

"Now that you mention it, I can see the faded lines around the edges."

"Clayton decided he needed a better place to park his rig. Since the court was just going to waste, I took the matter to the board, and they approved it unanimously. If you need something done, I'm your man."

"Actually, I have—"

"Clayton favors the pad 'cause he don't like getting his tires dirty. He used to park down by the lake, but the rain made a mess of the blackwalls."

"I can see how that would be a problem."

"Let me tell you something most people around here don't know, but you didn't hear it from me," Fate said, leaning closer. "Right over there, where number twenty-seven sits . . . that used to be a swimming pool."

I followed Fate's finger as he pointed to the residence next to the office.

"What happened?"

"People argued day and night about the rules and regulations. It was one thing after another. Then one day, a lady gave the lifeguard a tongue-lashing for sitting her son down for running. "He wasn't running," she screamed. "He was trotting!" That was the day the board of directors ordered up seven loads of topsoil and filled that sucker in. Yes *sirree*, that was about twelve years ago. I wasn't manager back then, but I understand the vote was four-to-one. This cabana—right behind us here—used to sit over by the pool. Now it's the office. It's a helluva shame. Esther Williams once swam in that pool." Fate tipped his Dr Pepper for a long sip.

"I have a question, and I promise it's not a complaint," I said. "Have you seen a white Lexus at my place in the last day or so?"

"A Lexus?" Fate lowered the can, frowning.

"That's right, it's my wife's."

"Is that kind of like a . . . lesbian?" Fate said, his voice pitching.

"No! I mean—it's a car."

"Well, I knew that didn't sound right the second it rolled off my tongue—her being your wife and all. It just wouldn't make much sense."

"Actually, it's a luxury car."

"I'm just messing with you," Fate snickered. "It's a fancy one. Like a Lincoln, right?"

"Sort of . . ." I said, immediately wishing I hadn't.

"Years ago, my brother bought a brand spanking-new Lincoln. Still has it, too. I remember the day he drove that kitten home. She's white, like your wife's car, only with a landau roof. Let me tell you, the seats in that sweet one are the softest vinyl you ever set your ass on. Burgundy interior, air conditioning, 8-track stereo, and electric windows. Under the hood, she has four hundred and sixty cubic inches of get-up-and-go. Now that vehicle is bad to the bone."

"Fate—"

"They should have named it after one of them wildcats, 'cause she is one little hissy-fit. Of course, they did make another car called the Cougar, but it was a bit sporty for my taste. King of the Jungle . . . now that's what they should've called it."

Fate took a sip of his drink, grinning like he had just won the Nobel Prize.

"Fate, have you seen my wife's car?"

"No *sirree*, but that don't mean a thing. See, I always take an hour at lunch, and then I knock off at five. And besides, we're closed on Mondays. If you ever need to pay your rent on a Monday or after five, just slip the check under the door. Only, don't do it if you're paying in cash."

"Got it," I said, sliding off the bench. "I apologize, but I've got to run."

"Stop by anytime. I'm gonna keep an eye out for that Lexus, if you don't mind?"

"That would be great," I said, taking another look at the kids on the trampoline as I walked off.

Behind me, I heard Fate call out, "Could be my eyes playing tricks on me, but I swear you kind of resemble my brother from a distance . . ."

Chapter 15

Midtown Atlanta
Tuesday, October 8th
10:00 A.M.

The stallion stepped out of the van dressed in skintight leather and spiked combat boots, the hair and sunglasses slick and shiny. Although rosy in color, the cheeks resembled chiseled granite. Raising the loading dock door to enter, it was promptly locked as the sound of heels echoed across the warehouse, accentuating a strut that progressed all the way up front where construction was still underway. In a corner office just off the lobby, Gustav sat at a makeshift desk of stacked boxes, talking on a cell phone. As the call ended, the stallion dropped in his lap and planted a kiss.

Gustav recoiled with an annoyed expression. "Trevor Wentworth is AWOL. Clearly, he is unaware of who he's dealing with. We must move forward," he said, taking the stallion's chin in his hand. "Do you have anything new?"

"I hacked into his credit report and checked the most recent financial activity."

Gustav's phone rang, and he swiveled around for a look outside a window, taking the stallion along for the ride. "Go," he said into the phone, continuing after a brief pause. "We need fifty vans . . . Yes . . . I like the ones FedEx drives, only in black . . . No, the smaller version . . . Hold on." He pried the stallion out of his lap. "What's the name of the van?"

The stallion tapped on a smartphone. "The Mercedes Sprinter . . . Five hundred cubit feet."

"The Sprinter with the high roof—five hundred cubics," Gustav repeated into the phone before looking up at the stallion. "We're supplying the interior racks?"

The stallion nodded.

"We supply the racks," Gustav said into the phone, pausing again. "Nonsense . . . We'll pay two-point-five million US, not a dollar more. For that price, you supply the vehicles in two weeks." He nodded. "We will wire the money to the bank of your choosing, but the delivery is for Atlanta. Do we have a deal? . . . Very well, send me the routing instructions."

"The racks arrived yesterday," the stallion said as Gustav hung up. "They will be installed as soon as we have the vans."

"Of course they will," Gustav said. "Now, tell me what our Mr. Wentworth has been up to."

"He hasn't used the AmEx card since the night we met him. To our good fortune, his financial picture remains a disaster."

"Leverage is a wonderful tool. Can you get creative?"

"That depends," the stallion said. Taking off the sunglasses, the big green eyes flashed at Gustav.

"We have everything at stake here, and I'm afraid we're out of time," Gustav said, standing up. "Whatever it takes, just get the job done."

"Then we will start with his automobile."

"The BMW?"

"Trust me," the stallion said.

"We prefer to win him over, so no physical harm—at least, not initially."

"I have the perfect opening."

"Speak to me," Gustav said.

"The lease on the BMW is past due. As it so happens, he's sixty days delinquent on the payments. Lenders are adverse to such behavior."

"How does that help us?"

"For a slight premium of sixty thousand dollars, I offered to buy out the lease." The stallion put on the sunglasses.

"I like it. I may have to give you a bonus." Gustav smiled and popped the stallion's rear. "Do the deal tomorrow . . . and take the funds out of petty cash."

Chapter 16

Suwanee, Georgia
Tuesday, October 8th
11:30 A.M.

The hammering in my head had returned, pounding away like the drum corps at a holiday parade. I popped a couple of aspirin, and then decided to work on a survival plan, starting with an inventory of Parkway 12. I was running short on cash and needed to economize on food, especially since my foray into fishing had failed miserably. Despite the annoying wallpaper, the kitchen and breakfast nook had a touch of hominess about them. Unfortunately, as I turned around there was a sea of blue tarp stretched across the hallway where the family room once opened up. And then like a news flash, reality raised its ugly head. *College football.* The season was in full swing and Saturday was a big game day, leaving me in a quandary without my oversized flatscreen. Returning to the kitchen, I tried to refocus as I began to randomly open and close cabinets.

My phone rang and I froze, praying it was Tracie. When I pulled it out, the originating number was blocked. Without answering, I stuffed it in my pocket and poked at my sore lip. *Gustav will have to wait*, I thought.

Pretty soon I was rummaging through cabinets, pulling out pots and pans. When I grabbed the door over the stove, it popped off in my hand, sending screws rattling across the counter. I laid it on the stovetop and turned my attention to the contents.

Two place settings of dishes sat on the bottom shelf. The first was a rustic sailboat pattern I had bought when I was a bachelor. Tracie didn't particularly care for them, but she knew they were my favorites. To her credit, she served my birthday dinner on them every year. Next to them was a stack of fine china. I ran a finger around the platinum rim on a coffee cup, taking note of the matching dinner plate, soup bowl, and salad dish beneath it. The remaining shelves were empty.

Advancing to the utensil drawer, I looked for anything useful. Sprinkled among the odds and ends was some loose silverware—the real McCoy. *How much is this stuff worth?* I wondered. Wasting little time, I rustled through the pile, searching for more silver. Nothing.

BAM! BAM! BAM!

I jumped, slamming my knee into the drawer. A hailstorm of flatware came raining down on the floor, like shattering glass. I grabbed my knee and started hopping on one foot, knowing for a fact I was in for a nasty bruise. Looking around at the mess, I could feel my blood pressure rising as it dawned on me someone was at the front door.

BAM! BAM! BAM!

I flexed the knee a couple of times and limped into the foyer. As I pushed the door open, a gust of wind caught it and started dragging me outside. I couldn't hold it, so I let go. There was a solid thump just before the door whipped free and banged against the outside of the trailer. Stepping out onto the stoop, my eyes zeroed in on Goldfinger. To my utter shock, Betty Jean was sprawled across the hood.

She raised her head and mopped hair out of her face as I stood there dazed, listening to palm fronds rattling overhead. But then I came to my senses and raced down the steps.

"I'm so sorry," I said, reaching out to assist her. "Don't move, and I—I'll . . ." At that instant, I spotted a dent the size of a dinner plate above Betty Jean's head.

She slid off the hood and raised an arm, examining an imprint of a doorknob in her ribcage. "What the hell's going on in there?"

Tom-toms started beating in my head as Betty Jean poked at her wound, red and puffy beneath a turquoise bikini top. My eyes drifted to the denim miniskirt and cowboy boots, separated by miles of bronzed legs. My brain couldn't get past it.

"Earth to *Trev*," Betty Jean said, staring up at me.

"Oh . . . the, *uh*, noise. I dropped some silverware."

"Is it me or have you fallen on a streak of bad luck?" she said, rubbing her side.

"I wasn't expecting anyone," I said, noticing how the fingernail polish matched the bikini top. "Can I get you something for that injury? I have a bottle of Sea Breeze."

Betty Jean twisted around. "*Aww*, just look at your beautiful car."

I shrugged, doing my best to pretend it wasn't a big deal. "What do you think of her?" I said, slipping over to the driver-side door.

"Can't say I'm familiar with this particular model."

"She's a special edition—with a retractable hardtop. I named her Goldfinger."

Betty Jean gave me a hard look. "Boys and their toys," she said, mostly to herself. Still rubbing her side, she limped over and rapped her knuckles on the roof. "You know, BMW is reporting issues with the motor bearings on these?"

"The hardtop?"

"It was in last month's *Motor Trend.*"

"I have a service contract," I said. "But get this, Goldfinger has the satellite package. And you know what that means?"

"Limited commercial interruption?"

"I'm pretty sure there's a Kenny Chesney channel."

"Oh, that. I've got all his CDs."

"Betty Jean, I'm talking about continuous digital streaming, right at your fingertips. Chicks dig it."

"First of all, I seriously doubt whether you should be digging anything related to chicks, if that's what you've been up to at that golf club of yours. And secondly, they'll get my Kenny Chesney CDs when they pry them from my cold, dead fingers."

"But don't you—"

"And I'd be careful about showing off your hardtop or your satellite package to Tammy Faye Fox next door," Betty Jean said with a nod.

"Who's Tammy Fox?" I said, turning for a look. The place was dark, but I was pretty sure one of the curtains moved.

"Tammy is what you might call the community skank. She gives trailer parks a bad name . . . a *real* bad name."

"Who would name their child Tammy Faye Fox?"

"That's an excellent question to ask yourself from this side of the property line."

I cut my eyes at Betty Jean to see if she was serious, making a mental note to Google the term *skank* later. "Should I lock my car?"

"That's the least of your worries," Betty Jean said. "Anyway, I came over to ask if you wanted to join me down at the lake."

"Are you sure you're okay?" I could make out the silhouette of a keyhole now. "Maybe you should come in and lie down."

"Three inches higher, and it would've been serious business."

"I—I know what you mean. Listen, I'll just meet you at the lake." I raised a thumb toward the trailer. "Do you need anything?"

"You've done quite enough already," Betty Jean said.

Chapter 17

Waynesboro, Georgia
Tuesday, October 8th
Noon

Tracie swung open the double-doors to her dad's utility shed and spotted a stepladder hanging on the wall. She lifted it off a pair of rusty nails, surprised at how light it was. Next, she located a pair of pliers and a mini-flashlight, stuffing them in her jeans. Maneuvering the ladder through the door, she hitched it under an arm and marched off into the cornfield.

When she reached the trailer, there was a protective sheet of black plastic stapled along the backside. She unfolded the ladder and situated it on the ground, using her weight to make sure it was stable. She had to climb a couple of rungs to reach the bottom edge of the plastic.

Using the pliers, Tracie pried out a few staples, making an opening big enough to crawl inside. Sticking her head underneath, she scaled the ladder until the upper portion of her body rested on the floor.

It was dark, and she had to fish the flashlight out of her pocket. When she turned it on, she discovered she was exactly where she wanted to be—in front of the guest bathroom. She rose to her feet and oriented herself. The bathtub was against the far wall and next to it, the toilet. The light skipped across the tile, where she noticed a light dusting of what looked like baby powder. In fact, it was everywhere. She panned the flashlight over to the vanity. Tucked in the corner, she spotted Trevor's leather bag.

Tracie set the bag in the sink and unzipped it. Laying the contents on the counter, she picked up a plastic tube with lights on top, a liter of clear liquid, a prescription bottle, and a Ziploc bag of white powder. Grabbing the prescription, she held it up to the light for a closer look. There was no label, but it rattled when she shook it. *Trevor's precious little treasure*, she thought. *I wonder if he'd be calling if I didn't have this?*

Tracie was packing everything away when her phone rang. Pulling it out, the display read: *Neely*. She had no idea how his name had gotten into her phone, but let it ring several times before answering.

"What do you want?" she said.

"Did you get up on the wrong side of the bed this morning?"

"I'm not laughing."

"Come on, what did I do?" Neely said. "I'm calling to see if you're okay."

"You pumped me full of sake—"

"Now hold on just a minute. I never encourage women to drink on a first date."

"It wasn't a date."

"I hear you. Technically, you were only a substitute. And I believe it was *you* who shanghaied *me*."

"Did I happen to mention that . . . let's see . . . what was it? Oh yeah, I'm married."

"Married, yes. But behaving rather peculiar. Last night, you told me you were going to dump the Rock. Did you mean that, or were you just messing with me?"

"What's that supposed to mean? I spent the day at your pecan orchard to lay low for a few hours. That's all there is to it."

"That sounds a bit fuzzy coming from someone who slept in my car last night."

"Before this goes any further—*Neely*—let me spell it out for you. I'm leaving town tomorrow."

"You're doing what?"

"See . . . that's what I'm talking about—"

"You're in no condition to be traveling. Are you at your parents' place?"

"No, I'm in the middle of a cornfield going through the trailer."

"You're in the doublewide?"

"I came out to collect a few things for my trip."

"You're looking for that bag, aren't you?"

"Why would I be doing that?"

"Because Trevor is desperate to get his hands on it. Are you going to tell me what's going on or not?"

"I found the bag, okay? I'm taking it with me. If Trevor's a good little boy, I might allow him to come to Savannah and pick it up."

"Savannah—what's happening there?"

"None of your pecan-picking business."

"Settle down and listen to me. Pack your stuff, and I'll pick you up and drive you down."

"Are you nuts? I guess you think I should just call my *husband* and let him know I'll be spending a few days at the beach with a strange man. That'll go over well, when he shows up to collect the bag."

"I'm not necessarily disagreeing with you, but tell me this. Did you consult him before driving off with half of the house?"

"That was different."

"You know you're safe with me. Nothing is going to happen as long as I'm around. A girl in your condition shouldn't be roaming all over the state alone. I'll protect you. In fact, I'll be a mediator . . . that is, if Trevor shows up."

"A *girl*? Aren't you the one who keeps shoveling all that nonsense about an older woman? Don't answer that. If it makes you feel any better, I'm staying with a friend."

"That's perfect. I'll drop you by her place and lay low until you're ready to head back."

"Who said anything about it being a *her*? But now that I think about it, a bodyguard may not be a bad idea."

"What time should I pick you up?"

"Not so fast. If this is going down, then I'm in charge. Here's the deal—we'll meet at the pecan stand."

"Should I pack a swimsuit?"

"In your dreams."

"What else?"

"You'll have to find your own place to stay."

"Done."

"And you keep your mouth shut."

"Not a problem."

"*And* no funny business," Tracie said.

"On my word as a gentleman."

"But I do have one question for you."

"Anything," Neely said.

"Aren't you going to ask what's in the bag?"

Chapter 18

Suwanee, Georgia
Tuesday, October 8th
Noon

I circled Betty Jean's lounge chair, pretending to take in the sights and sounds of the lake. It was a clear, blue day, and I even spotted a few ducks out on the water. When I stepped in the path of her sunshine, Betty Jean lifted her head and gave me the head-to-toe, a clear sign she remembered my outfit from the previous night. She sat up, raising the chairback and sliding her boots to one side.

"Have a seat," she said. "This time of year you can't afford to waste a sunny day."

I'd seen a lot of things in my life, but never anyone sunning in a bikini and cowboy boots.

"Wait a minute," Betty Jean said, pointing over a shoulder. "Do you see anyone over at number fourteen?"

I followed the general direction of her turquoise fingernail to a trailer forty yards down the shore. It was just beyond the beach area. A Ford Bronco on lifts was parked next to the front stoop, where a pair of antlers was mounted over the door.

"Looks quiet to me," I said.

"Keep an eye on it," Betty Jean said, signaling for me to sit. "A few weeks ago I was sunning and Ted came out with a deer rifle, wearing a camo—"

"Ted?" I interrupted.

"I call him Ted Nugent because the man's a hunting freak.

"Seriously?" I said. "Oh, wait a minute . . . I think I've seen that guy."

"Are you familiar with Ted's music?"

I shook my head.

"Does the phrase *Cat Scratch Fever* ring a bell?"

"Hold on. What was that you were saying about a firearm?" The lounge chair creaked as I twisted for another look at the trailer.

"Ted snuck up on me one day with a rifle, wearing a pair of camo swimming trunks—at least, that's what he calls them. He scared the crap out of me."

"Sounds like somebody you don't want to mess with."

"Before I knew what was happening, he slapped a hand over my mouth. I was about to bite the fool when he shushed me." Betty Jean fiddled with the lounge chair, reclining into sunning position.

"What do you mean? Where was Clayton?"

"Not important," Betty Jean said. "Anyhow, after Ted made sure I wasn't going to cause a disturbance, he explained how he'd been standing at his kitchen sink and spotted a buck out the window on the far bank. He had his gun handy, so he took a peek through the scope and got all worked-up."

"This guy keeps a weapon in his kitchen? What did he want with you?"

"Let me tell you, Ted is dead serious about his hunting. And he's got a right to bear arms, you know. He asked if I'd seen a buck across the lake. I said, 'Honey, do I look like I'm out here spotting deer?'" Betty Jean gave me a swat and laughed. "It's a good three hundred yards across that lake."

For some reason, I didn't particularly like the story. That's when I realized I didn't much care for Ted either. Without warning the toe of a boot caught me in the backside, and I came off the chair.

"Sorry," Betty Jean said. "Ted scoped out that bank, carrying on about his *Kill It and Grill It* charity the whole time. Did I mention Ted cooks venison for the homeless?"

"The man in *that* trailer runs a charity?"

"Claims he's filing for 501(c) status."

"What's that?"

"It's not a pair of Levi's, if that's what you're thinking," Betty Jean said, wasting a perfectly good joke on me. "It's a tax exemption for nonprofits. Shouldn't you know this, being a consultant and all?"

"I, *uh*, don't work with charities." I studied the lake, peeved that Ted was ruining my day in the sun with Betty Jean. I looked down at her, still not sure of what to make of the boots. "Did you bring me here to ask for help with Ted's charity?"

"Don't be silly, darling. Ted doesn't need your help." Betty Jean raised the chairback, flipping open a cooler next to her. She reached in. "You want something to drink?"

I poked at the sand with my loafer. "I'm good, but thanks."

"Have a seat. I'm not done with you," Betty Jean said. "I have a few questions about Tracie." She waited for a reaction.

I plopped down.

"Do you love her, *Trev*?"

I lowered my chin. "First of all, that's not a Tracie question."

Betty Jean kicked me, this time on purpose.

"Hey, stop—"

She kicked me again.

"If you're going to abuse me, I'm leaving," I said.

"That's more like it. I'd appreciate a little passion, especially when we're talking about matters of the heart."

"It's getting hot out here." I stood up without looking at her. "I'm going home."

Betty Jean aimed a finger at me. "Sit down . . . or I'll scream for Ted."

Chapter 19

Suwanee, Georgia
Tuesday, October 8th
12:30 P.M.

I dropped onto the lounge chair so hard a strap popped loose. Even though I had to sit a little lopsided, I made sure to keep my back to Betty Jean. Out on the lake, the ducks started quacking.

"All right, let's just chill and begin with an easy question," Betty Jean said.

"About Tracie," I added.

"What's her favorite color?"

"Good grief. I'm not in grammar school, Betty Jean."

I heard the boot move behind me.

"Okay, okay. I'll play along."

"So what is it, *Trev*?"

"White."

"*White?* . . . What kind of answer is that?"

"This is ridiculous. I'm not saying another thing if you're going to mock me . . . or kick me. What are you trying to prove?"

"I apologize. It's just—I've never heard that one. So tell me why it's her favorite color."

"That's easy. I bought her a Lexus last year, and she picked out a white one."

"She actually told you it was her favorite color?"

"It's much deeper than that," I said, now turning to face her.

"You seem pretty sure of yourself."

"Betty Jean, she was crazy about that car. She even cried."

"Got it," Betty Jean said. "Let's try another one. What did you do for her last birthday?"

"You're going to love this, you being a Kenny Chesney fan and all. I bought her VIP seats for a Tom Petty concert."

Betty Jean gripped the chair. "You're telling me *your* Tracie is a Tom Petty fan?"

"Hey, you don't even know her."

"That's true," Betty Jean said.

"They were third row seats. Set me back—"

"I didn't ask how much," Betty Jean said, cutting me off. "How long would you say she's been infatuated with the artistry of Mr. Petty and the Heartbreakers?"

"I can't pinpoint the precise moment, but I'd say it started about the time I bought her the *Greatest Hits* CD."

"*Uh-huh*," Betty Jean said. A tongue probed the inside of her cheek. "I'm curious. Do you by chance own any of his music?"

"Only every album he ever released."

"I'm going out on a limb here, so don't take this the wrong way. I don't think I've ever known a woman Tracie's age who swoons over Tom Petty."

"She started—"

"I know, I know. She started crying when you gave her the tickets."

"What about you and Kenny Chesney? You're the only woman I've ever known that gets all worked up over him."

Betty Jean opened her mouth for a rebuttal, but instead reached in the cooler and pulled out a bottle of suntan lotion.

"How did you meet her?" she said.

"It was at the Georgia vs. Vanderbilt homecoming game."

"A date?"

"Not exactly. It happened during the fourth quarter with the score tied fourteen-to-fourteen, and I had to *go* really bad. When I got to the mezzanine the snack line was short, so I stopped off for a Coke. Afterwards, I bolted for the can . . . You're going to love this . . . At the doorway, it was like a bolt of lightning."

"Love at first sight. I knew it," Betty Jean said. "So you spotted her at the snack counter and were moonstruck as you were leaving."

"No. It's even better than that. When I barreled into the bathroom, I collided head-on with Tracie—"

"In the men's room?"

"Actually, it was the ladies'. I was in such a hurry I went to the wrong one. Tracie was coming out, and I slammed into her. The drink slipped out of my hand and soaked her from head to toe."

"And?" Betty Jean said, rolling her hand.

"I told her to wait for me."

"Wait? . . . For what?"

"I couldn't hold it any longer. I had to go really bad."

"Holy cow," Betty Jean said.

"But I went back to her."

"And then you fell in love?"

"First, I had to check the score. Then I did the gentlemanly thing and offered to have her clothes cleaned. As it turns out, I didn't have any cash on me, so she took my phone number to follow up on how much I owed her."

"You didn't offer to call her?"

"You make it sound like a crime. I didn't have a pen, okay? Tracie even told me she had an excellent memory."

"And you were so smitten you couldn't remember anything, except her beautiful face?"

"Betty Jean, didn't you hear what I said? The score was tied and the clock was running."

Betty Jean flashed a folksy smile. "Did she call you?"

"That's right, but the story gets even funnier. The tab for the cleaning was almost twelve dollars, and I sort of . . . *avoided* her."

"You stiffed her with the bill?" Betty Jean's earrings rattled as she snapped her head back. "Never mind, go on. I can't wait to find the silver lining in this cloud."

"Later that semester, one of my fraternity brothers brought her to a party. We had a good laugh, and as it turns out she wasn't sore at me. But here's the magic. I had just won a poker game, and I paid her back for the cleaning."

"And you finally asked her out?"

"She asked me to the spring dance. But I paid for dinner, of course."

"Of course," Betty Jean said. "How old were you?"

"We were both sophomores."

"Now I'm getting the picture," Betty Jean said. "How many years have you been married?"

"Five years on our last anniversary."

"And what did you do on your special day?"

"Can I tell you about our fourth? That was the big one."

Betty Jean lowered her head.

"I bought her a Sundancer 38," I said, giving Betty Jean's thigh a pat.

She shot me a look, so I removed the hand.

"What the hell is a Sundancer?"

"Only the hottest cabin cruiser on Lake Lanier."

"Like a miniature version of the love boat?"

"More like three hundred and seventy-five horsepower of screaming demons."

"You bought her a boat that'll bounce her around on the lake like a ping pong ball?"

"I could have her on her favorite beach in less than fifteen minutes—from anywhere."

"This just keeps getting better."

"Anyway, she prefers not to sun on the deck anymore."

"Go figure—"

"Want to know how much she set me back?"

"No!" Betty Jean said, uncapping the suntan lotion and pointing it at me.

"She loves that boat."

"Okay, tell me why she loves it. And I have to warn you, I've got a bad feeling about this."

"She used to spend a lot of time at the lake. Before I sold it, she'd even go alone and spend the night."

"All by herself?"

"She couldn't get enough of it."

"*Trev*, darling. You met Tracie when you were a sophomore in college. That means you were—what—nineteen when you met?"

"Sounds about right."

"You've been married for five years, so I'd say you were married at twenty-seven. What exactly went on for the interim eight years?"

"We mostly dated. You know . . . did things properly."

"What's the most romantic thing you remember about being with Tracie?"

"Besides buying her the boat?"

Chapter 20

Suwanee, Georgia
Tuesday, October 8th
12:45 P.M.

It might have been me, but Betty Jean seemed agitated as she marched to the water's edge. When she returned, she stretched out on the lounge chair, facedown with her boots on.

"*Trev*, would you mind?" she said, holding up the suntan lotion.

"Can I tell you something, Betty Jean?"

"Shoot."

"If I were Clayton, I wouldn't be too happy about you sunning out here all alone. Not like this. Especially, with the likes of Ted roaming around."

"Nobody's going to bother me. Although, a while back I caught Walt Mobley up on the roof of his trailer with a telescope."

"Which place is his?"

"They live in number eleven, right across the street from you." Betty Jean pointed, without looking up. "Evidently, Walt got a notion to spy on me."

I opened the lotion, squeezing a dab on my fingertips. "Where do you want this?"

"If it ain't covered, it's all yours, darling." Betty Jean twisted for a look at me. "And don't get any ideas."

I touched her shoulder and jumped back, making her laugh.

"Let's see. Where was I?"

"Walt was on the roof," I said.

"Right . . . He was working the knobs on his telescope, zeroing in on yours truly. So when I figured out what he was up to, I got out of the chair and gave him a show."

"You did what?"

"Let's just leave it at that for now."

"Betty Jean, if I didn't know better I'd swear you're one of those wild and salty women."

"Okay, who's telling this story? Do you want to know what happened or not?" She bent her knee and raised a leg up in the air, boot and all.

"I'm all ears."

"It happened so fast," Betty Jean said, rocking the boot. "I heard Walt holler."

"Like a catcall?"

"More like an *SOS*. He stumbled backwards, knocked over the telescope, and plunged headfirst into that big holly bush by the corner. He was wailing like a coyote."

"What did you do?"

"As it turns out, Walt was home alone. So I had to take him to the emergency room." She looked over a shoulder. "And do you know, not a word was spoken between us on the way to the hospital. In fact, nothing has been said about the incident ever since."

"He fell out with you?"

"No, I wouldn't say that. Watch him next time he's around me. Instead of speaking he gives me this little double-eyebrow-pump, kind of like a soldier saluting an officer. It's so cute."

I reached over and gave a tug on Betty Jean's raised boot.

Betty Jean screamed and kicked me squarely in the chest. I fell backwards and landed flat in the sand, not sure what had just happened. She struggled to regain her composure, rolling over to secure the boot as I got to my feet.

"What the hell, Betty Jean?"

"I told you—only if it's not covered."

"It—it's a cowboy boot!" I shouted, almost losing my head.

"Come here," she said, softly.

I dusted myself off and walked over, easing down on the chair.

Betty Jean latched onto my arm. "Can you keep a secret?"

"Like what . . . your favorite color?"

"This is going to sound really, *really* stupid."

"Well, then I'm your man."

"Don't make me laugh. It's about the boots."

I stared at them.

"I don't, *uh* . . . Help me, Kenny . . ." she said, pressing her hands prayer-like under her chin. "I don't take them off in public."

"Is there something wrong with your feet?" I said, looking at her boots.

"It's nothing like that."

"I don't know, Betty Jean. The way you dance, I'd say everything seems to be working just fine."

"That's what Clayton says."

I reached down and slipped off one of my loafers. "Show me yours, and I'll show you mine."

"See—you're making me feel silly."

"Do you want to know what I'm thinking right this second? I'm wondering if there's turquoise polish on your toenails." I looked her in the face. "You're blushing."

"I never talk about it." Betty Jean dropped her head on my shoulder.

"And I thought I was screwed up."

"You're the only person I've ever told, other than Clayton." Betty Jean raised her head, flashing a nervous smile. Her earrings jingled in the breeze.

It was a moment to savor. Forever. I looked straight into her eyes for the longest time.

"You're really something," I said under my breath.

Betty Jean just sat there quietly, batting her eyes.

They were blue . . . my favorite color.

Chapter 21

Burke County, Georgia
Tuesday, October 8th
2:30 P.M.

Neely parked the Grand Prix in front of the office at the pecan stand and climbed out, circling around to pop the trunk. Inside, there was an open suitcase. The contents were a bit tousled, so he folded a few things before zipping it shut. Leaning into the trunk he lifted the spare tire, retrieved a Glock from underneath, and slipped it in a side pocket of the suitcase. He noticed the Coke-stained shirt from the previous night lying to one side. With a snicker, he reached in and tossed it behind the spare, slamming the trunk.

Turning around and walking over to the first bay he gave the door a tug, and it rattled open. Moments later he flopped down on the lounge chair in the office, pulling out his phone.

"Hey, Neely here," he said into the phone. "I only have a minute, so listen up. We've got a new game plan. She's heading to Savannah and I talked her into letting me tag along."

Neely paused for a lecture on the other end of the line, getting words in where he could.

"I know it's a risk . . . I had every intention of sticking around here . . . No, that won't work . . . I found out she's taking the bag with her," Neely said, pulling the phone away from his ear as the sparks came rapid-fire. He waited for the rant to finish.

"The bag is going to Savannah, and there's nothing I can do about it," Neely continued. "So unless you have a better idea, that's where I'm headed . . . No, I haven't seen it . . . She trusts me and that's what's important. I'll call with an update when I have something."

Neely ended the call, stood up, and started pacing. He grabbed a sack of pecans and took it behind the station. Then he returned several more times, cleaning out a portion of the inventory. When he was done, the office looked like it had seen some activity since Tracie had last been there.

Around three, Tracie pulled into the pecan stand with the top down. With a little coaxing, Neely talked her into taking his car and had her pull the Lexus into the open bay. She examined the casual flair of his cap and sunglasses as he retrieved a suitcase and the leather bag from her car. He lugged them over to the Grand Prix and tossed them in the backseat. Without skipping a beat, he slid into the passenger seat.

"I'm the tag along, so you're driving."

"I see you haven't bothered to shave this morning," Tracie said, taking the driver's seat and buckling up. After adjusting the mirrors, she turned the key. The engine roared to life, and then settled into a rumble.

Neely buckled up and toyed with the recliner button, lowering the seatback. "I'm holding my own . . . that is, for someone who spent the night in the backseat of a car." He scooted lower in the seat. "You, on the other hand, are a sight for sore eyes."

"You're along for the ride because I'm weak and vulnerable, so just keep that tucked under your hat and we'll get along fine." Tracie hit the gas and they peeled out.

“No arguments here,” Neely said, pulling the cap low over his forehead. “None at all.”

Chapter 22

Suwanee, Georgia
Tuesday, October 8th
4:30 P.M.

I pulled my head out of Goldfinger's trunk and caught a first glimpse of Walt Mobley acting suspicious over at his place. He appeared to be working in the yard, but I wasn't so sure. Hefting a golf bag out, I propped it against the bumper, examining each club like I was conducting an annual physical. When I was finished, I noticed Walt had wandered out to the street, studying me from a distance. His eyes dropped promptly to the ground.

"Good morning," I called out.

Walt spun around without speaking and slipped off to study a patch of grass.

Back in the trunk, I grabbed a pair of golf shoes and a canvas bag. Then I pulled out a green Masters cap, checking the logo before dusting it against my leg. My phone rang, and I dropped everything next to the golf bag.

"This is Trevor . . . Yeah, I'm polishing them up right now. That's right, it's the full set." As I talked on the phone, I stepped away from the car, only to discover Walt had returned to his observation post. "Graphite shafts . . . No, there's just a pitching wedge . . . *Uh-huh*. The golf bag's a hundred dollars extra . . . It's a Ping. I'm asking . . . What? . . . Three hundred and seventy-five for everything? Are you kidding? I've got two grand invested . . . Precisely, so you know what they're worth." I pressed the phone to my shirt and snarled, then lifted it to my ear. "All right, it's a deal. I'll meet you in the Publix parking lot in thirty minutes." I hung up and spun around.

Walt's head went down, but this time he didn't walk off.

"Mr. Mobley," I said in a raised voice.

Walt took his time, looking up and down the property line before tucking his hands inside the pockets of a tan windbreaker. Finally, he eased across Lakeview Circle. Without making eye contact, he came within an arm's length of Goldfinger, peeking inside her trunk before inspecting the golf bag. "*Dr. Mobley*," he corrected, nudging the canvas bag with his shoe.

"My mistake," I said, offering to shake.

Walt pulled a hand out, rubbing it across his shiny forehead before sticking it back in the jacket.

"My friends call me Walt."

"I'm Trevor Wentworth."

"*Uh-huh*. Who was that you were yelling at just now?"

"Walt, listen. I'm sorry—"

"Dr. Mobley," he interrupted, raising his chin. "Did you steal this merchandise, son?"

"No—it's mine. Look, I didn't mean to disturb you."

"I'll let you know when you're being a pest." Walt gave me the once-over. "You're a bit high-strung, aren't you?"

"Well, not exactly," I said, angling to change the subject. "So—you're a physician?"

"Who told you that?" Walt looked down, this time into the top of my golf bag.

"You just said—"

"What do you do for a living, Wentworth?"

"I'm a management consultant."

"Are you married?"

"Yeah, but I'd rather not get into that right now."

"Figures," Walt said, leering. "If you must know, I'm a retired professor."

"I'm a college man myself," I said, somewhat uneasy with Walt's quirkiness.

He reached into the trunk and extracted a golf club that seemed to extend forever. The oversized head came out last.

"What kind of college graduate sells sporting goods in a grocery store parking lot?"

"It's a long story, and I'd rather not—"

"Figures," he repeated. "What's the story with this one?"

"That's a Big Bertha," I said. "The shaft is bent, so it's not worth much."

Walt took the club by the grip and ambled over to a grassy area, taking a practice swing. "I've thought a time or two about taking up golf."

"That wasn't bad. But you want to keep your head down."

"Why's that?"

"You have to make contact with the ground. Leave a divot."

Walt held the club up in front of him, examining the shaft with one eye. "How much do you want for her?"

"Who?" I said.

"Big Bertha. I'd like to buy her, only I can't offer much."

"Do you have any idea how much a club like that costs?"

"You didn't answer my question," Walt said. "I'll give you twenty bucks, but only if you come clean."

"About what?"

"What happened to your trailer—that's what."

"Listen, it's got nothing to do with this."

"Twenty for both," Walt haggled. "I watched Clayton put up the tarp. That's more curious than anything I ever saw when Leland and Sarah lived here."

"Just take it." I unzipped a pouch on the bag and handed him a glove. "That's a genuine Arnold Palmer . . . And take these." I grabbed a handful of golf tees before tossing him the canvas bag.

"What's this?" Walt said, catching it in the crook of his arm.

"Golf balls. Here's a cap . . . and a pair of spikes."

Juggling the loot, he hoisted the shoes in the air, examining the soles. Then he sniffed inside each.

"What are you up to anyway?"

"Just being neighborly, Walt."

"Hey, Trevor," Clayton called out from the back door of his trailer. "Happy hour on the dock in thirty minutes."

"You seem to have warmed up to the Beasleys mighty fast," Walt said to me.

"Clayton is a good man, and that Betty Jean is something else."

Walt's eyebrows did a double-pump.

I thought my eyes were deceiving me. "What was that you just did?"

"I didn't do anything."

"Yes, you did . . . You made an expression with your eyebrows," I said.

"Must have been something in my eye."

I studied his face. "You know Betty Jean, don't you?"

Like magic, Walt gave a repeat performance.

"Do you want to join us?" I said, cocking my thumb in the air.

"*Uh* . . . me and the wife . . . we usually have an early dinner.

I stuffed the golf bag in the trunk and slammed the lid. "Then if you'll excuse me, I have a deal to close before cocktails are served."

"Much obliged for the goodies," Walt said.

Chapter 23

Tybee Island, Georgia
Tuesday, October 8th
5:00 P.M.

Tracie hopped out and rounded the front of the car by the time Neely started fumbling with the door handle. He seemed obsessed with straightening his cap and sunglasses, and somewhat distracted by the street-side parking.

"Stay," Tracie said, leveling a finger at him through the windshield. She headed up the short driveway to a beach house and climbed a set of graying steps to a second floor screen porch.

Neely watched as an attractive woman with dark, shoulder-length hair stepped out and hugged Tracie. They had a good laugh before Tracie motioned in Neely's direction, then retraced her steps to the street.

"I knew it. Your friend *is* a she," Neely said, stretching as he got out of the car.

"That's right, and she doesn't care to meet you."

"What did I do to deserve that?"

"Okay, here's how it's going to be. I appreciate your offer to look after me, but I'm going to need a little space tonight."

"I get it," Neely said, leaning against the car. "You girls want to catch up."

"Something like that. Listen, tell me where to find you, just in case I need anything."

"Hey, I'm here for you, babe," he said with a grin. "I spotted some motels on the way in. I'll find a room at one of those."

"Just don't take off without me." Tracie handed over the keys.

Neely leaned into the backseat and retrieved her suitcase.

"All of them," she said, pointing at the leather bag.

"Cool your jets," Neely said, shaking the suitcase at her. "I was waiting for permission to touch it."

Tracie shoved him aside and scooped up the bag. Then she had him follow her past a drive-under garage to a door next to the stairway.

"Drop it here," Tracie said, looking up at the stairs.

Brenda was at the top, waving. Neely flashed his million-dollar smile and raised a boot to the first step.

"Oh no you don't," Tracie said, lowering an arm in his path.

"Are you gals all alone in this big house?"

Just then a guy on a Harley rumbled into the drive across the street. They looked on as he removed his helmet, shook out his long hair, and tied a bandanna around his forehead. The biker's sleek sunglasses looked up at Brenda, offering a five-finger wave when he spotted her.

"I forgot to mention the neighbors are real tight around here—they sort of look after one another," Tracie said. "There's also a man of the house, but don't expect an introduction."

"Who's the dude on the bike?" Neely said.

"He's the one who's going to pound your pretty face, if you don't do as I say."

"In that case, I'll be in touch."

Chapter 24

Suwanee, Georgia
Wednesday, October 9th
6:30 A.M.

I fell out of bed and landed flat on my face, dumbfounded. It seemed like I was three years old again. I lay there in a semi-comatose state for the longest fifteen seconds of my life before realizing where I was. Coming to my senses, I looked up at the bedroom door, not sure if I had been dreaming or someone was actually prowling around the trailer. Then I heard a couple of familiar sounds. A car door slammed, and an engine started.

Goldfinger?

I scrambled to my feet and sprinted into the hallway with my socks slipping and sliding on the laminate as I rounded the corner, racing to the foyer. Crashing into the front door, I nearly lost my balance as the wind got ahold of it and sucked me out onto the stoop. I stopped just short of taking a nasty tumble down the steps. When I regained my balance, I spotted Goldfinger—the apple of my eye—sitting on the shoulder of Lakeview Circle with her fuel-injected cylinders revving. Suddenly, she peeled out for the highway.

"Hey!" I yelled, leaping off the steps. I dashed to the end of the driveway, waving my arms in the air. Still in shock, I was surprised when the brake lights came on at the top of the street. The engine fell into a soothing idle. That was the moment I lost it. The driver—*the thief*—had the arrogance to lower the hardtop and flip on the radio. It sent me into a rage. "Hey!—Hey!—Heeey! You sorry . . ." I tore out toward the Parkway entrance, just as the motor's hum gave way to screeching tires fishtailing onto the highway. I stopped in the middle of Lakeview, wheezing as I reached for the pocket where I kept my phone. Instead, I felt only the silkiness of my boxers. Drawing my hands higher, I patted my bare chest, and then instinctively stomped my foot. The cold asphalt delivered a biting sting through a hole in my sock that brought tears to my eyes. Exhaling in disgust, my breath wisped into the morning chill like a puffball.

I lifted the injured foot for a diagnosis. Even though my heel was numb and bleeding, I felt the first warm rays of sunshine on my back as a breeze rippled the hems of my boxers. I detected movement out of the corner of my eye and turned to my neighbor's trailer. I was pretty sure it was the front door, but it was closed now.

I hobbled over and climbed the front steps, in no mood for decorum. *What was her name?* Before I could knock, the door popped open. But only an inch.

Tammy Fox, I remembered.

"I like those cute little shorts," someone said through the crack.

I looked down at my boxers and strategically lowered my hands. "Someone just stole my car. Did you see anything?"

"I had this dreadful karma all night long . . . I saw men coming."

Did she just say what I thought she said? It was impossible to see much, but I spotted a mountain of hair and a flimsy negligee that cut just above her knees.

"There was more than *o-one*?" I said, starting to shiver. I stepped closer and felt warm air blowing through the slit. The woman had dark shiny hair that was the color of a raven and a waxy buildup of lip gloss.

"They both had bad aura, I tell you."

"Did you see them snooping around my house?" I said.

"They used to visit Leland and Sarah."

"*G-G-Good* . . . so you recognized them. Listen, I've got to make a phone call, but I may need you to speak to the police." I was freezing, so I bounded down the steps and charged next door, spotting snoopy-eyed Walt across the street. At the top of my stoop, I heard footsteps and turned to discover Tammy Fox coming up the driveway. In the sunlight her hair seemed bigger, and the eyebrows had been penciled-in. What's more, the sunshine left little mystery about her physique. *Thirty-six, twenty-four, thirty-six* shot through my scrambled brain. It was from one of those old movies, probably James Bond. I shook my head to root out the insanity. "Was there *s-s-something* else?" I said, through chattering teeth.

"I'm Tammy Fox," she said, pressing a hand to her chest.

"I know . . . Trevor . . . honored to meet you," I said, reaching for the door.

"I get that a lot."

"Excuse *m-me*?" I replied, turning to face her again.

"People frequently admire me from afar before they get the nerve to introduce themselves."

"Actually—"

"What happened to your lip, honey?"

I checked Walt's place, and he had thankfully disappeared, so I gave Tammy Fox my best distressed look. "I'm *s-s-sorry*, but I'm freezing and someone just stole my car."

"What line of work are you in?"

I noticed a hint of crow's–feet at the corners of Tammy Fox's eyes and tried hard to focus.

"Tammy—"

"Word around Parkway is you lost your job."

"Okay, *l-listen* . . ."

Tammy Fox raised a hand in the air, and her body started shaking all over. "Wait, I'm sensing something."

I cut my eyes over at Walt's place. There was no one in sight . . . *Thank You.* "Hold on. It's true. I am a consultant, and I *g-got* downsized."

The shakes stopped instantly. "Oh, you poor baby," Tammy Fox said. "You know, we're practically in the same line of work."

Goose bumps had invaded every square inch of my body, forcing me to fold my arms across my chest and hunch over. "*T-T-Tammy*, did the men say anything?"

"It was actually a man and a woman."

"But you said there were two men."

"I was referring to the apparition . . . from last night."

"*Jeez*, I'm freezing here. So it was a man and a woman?"

"Most people wouldn't have noticed. After all, she sometimes dresses a little masculine for my taste."

"I really can't *g-get* into this right now—"

"It's probably the reason they both came to me as men last night."

"But did either one say anything?" I repeated.

"The woman asked if Trevor Wentworth lived here. But I could tell she already—"

"Where did she *c-c-come* from?"

"The man dropped her off."

I did a double-take, noticing she was wearing fluffy earrings the size of tennis balls. *How the hell did I miss those things?* I opened the front door.

"This might help," Tammy Fox said, slipping something from her negligee.

"What is it?" I said, tip-toeing down the steps.

"A business card."

"The *t-thief* gave you her card?" I said. "Wait a minute. This is the number for my lease company."

"Did I say she was a thief?" Tammy Fox said.

"Excuse me. I have to make a phone call."

Chapter 25

Suwanee, Georgia
Wednesday, October 9th
9:00 A.M.

Doing my best to warm up in the kitchen, I dialed the number on the business card Tammy Fox had forked over minutes earlier. It smelled like perfume. While I was working my way through a series of voice prompts, I filled a pot with water and set it on the stove, turning on a burner. The flames licked around the bottom of the pot as someone came on the other end of the line.

"Hello, this is Trevor Wentworth."

I stepped into the hallway, making my way to the master bathroom. I turned on the light and grabbed a robe off the back of the door, examining my lip in the mirror. "Okay, I'll hold." In my state of mind, I tried to imagine a car thief with an answering service. "Yeah, it's a BMW . . . . Okay, I'll hold." Cradling the phone on my shoulder, I dug inside a drawer and pulled out a tube of ointment. I unscrewed the cap and squeezed a dab on my finger, working it into my upper lip. "That's right . . . a gold BMW. Yeah, two months past due . . . I thought we had an understanding . . . Yes, I'll hold." Turning on the faucet, I washed my hands before returning to the mirror.

"Yes, this is Trevor Wentworth." I raised a hand in frustration. "What? You're transferring me? . . . Okay." Music began to ooze over the line.

Finishing up with the inspection in the mirror, I lifted my nose and sniffed the air. Then I reached over and flipped on the exhaust fan. Back at the counter, I noticed the ointment and remembered my foot injury. I closed the toilet lid and sat down. Reaching over, I squeezed out a marble-sized glob and started massaging it into my foot. The smell wafted in again. I raised my finger and sniffed . . . It wasn't the ointment.

Going back to wash my hands a second time, I heard a disturbance outside and turned off the faucet, praying it wasn't Tammy Fox.

BAM! BAM! BAM!

"Please, no." I crouched down on the toilet, cringing as I heard the front door rip open and stomping in the foyer.

"Trevor Wentworth?" a voice said over the phone.

"I'm here," I said, losing my train of thought as pandemonium broke out down the hallway. I heard a hissing that sounded like bad news. "*Uh*, could you hold for one second?" I lowered the phone and stuck my head out the bathroom door. There was a gray fog rolling down the hall in my direction. It felt cool, but with a distinct smoky aroma.

I limped toward the kitchen, where the fog only grew thicker. Fanning the air, I was startled by a second wave of hissing, and then a blast in the face that went straight up my nose.

"Mr. Wentworth, are you on the line?" I heard someone say on the phone.

Disoriented, I stumbled into the breakfast nook, where a masked man appeared out of the fog.

I tried to turn and run, but he grabbed me. The phone slipped from my hand, clattered to the floor, and disappeared. I managed to pull free and drop to my knees, searching like a blind man.

The intruder vanished into the fog, only to return with a charred mass that was still smoldering. I looked up at his mask, and then recognized the cowboy hat. He lowered a respirator.

"You okay, *Trev*?" Clayton shouted.

"What have you done?" I said, batting at the fog.

"I was coming to get you for breakfast, when I spotted a cloud rolling out of your window." Clayton pulled off the hat, wiping his forehead. "I grabbed a fire extinguisher and ran over as fast as I could."

"What's that?" I coughed to clear my throat.

"It's what's left of a cabinet door," Clayton said, holding it up. "Someone put it on the stove."

I wanted to scream, but lowered my head in disgust.

"Any idea what happened?" Clayton said.

"I don't want to talk about it."

"Let me guess. It's a long story?"

I looked around the room, where the fog was beginning to lift. There was a powdery residue clinging to every visible surface. "Look at this carnage. It's like a blizzard hit in here."

"These extinguishers can be a bit taxing on the cleanup crew."

"Just shoot me," I said.

"Forgive me, but I have to ask," Clayton said. "You wouldn't be trying to burn this place down, would you?"

Snatching the door from his hand, I slung it across the room and heard it bounce off the cabinets. Squaring off with Clayton, I said, "You think I want to kill myself?"

"The thought never crossed my mind," Clayton said, resting a hand on my shoulder. "You're way too smart for something like that."

"What then? Let's hear it before I do something *really* stupid."

"You know how me and Betty Jean think the world of you. We admire the fact that you're taking responsibility for this awful setback."

"Get to the point."

"I was . . . thinking about the insurance money."

My mouth dropped open. "The cabinet door fell off. That's all there is to it. Maybe I'm an idiot, but I'm not an arsonist."

"Hang on just a minute." Clayton stepped out to the foyer. "Honey Bunch," Clayton yelled.

"What's keeping you?" Betty Jean called back.

"Grab that pot of coffee and get over here." Clayton sat down next to me in the breakfast nook.

"Don't mess with me, Clayton," I said.

"I swear . . . I wish you could catch a break."

"That's it. Just get out," I said, not really meaning it.

"Hold your horses," Clayton said. "Listen, now's probably not a good time to bring this up, but I checked with my buddy, like I told you I would. No one in his circle seems to know who hauled your trailer out of here. And I'm telling you, he knows everyone." Clayton's eyes stared into mine. "It's like—it vanished into thin air."

"Clayton?" Betty Jean said from the front door.

"In here."

I heard Betty Jean's boots coming our way and turned to Clayton, suddenly feeling a load lifting off my shoulders. "That can mean only one thing. It's an amateur job, and she's not serious about leaving me. Tracie may be mad, but she's probably just hiding out—embarrassed. I wouldn't be surprised at all if she's looking for a way to save face. I'll bet she's been balling her eyes out, wishing she could come home."

And then . . . I smiled.

Chapter 26

Tybee Island, Georgia
Wednesday, October 9th
7:00 P.M.

Tracie could feel the rhythm of the guitar deep down in her toes. It was one of those twangy, foot-stomping vibes that makes you tingle all over. She closed her eyes and raised a hand in the air, swinging her hips like no one else was watching. There was laughter, and then she realized it was *her*, cutting loose as a cute guy took her by the hands.

He wrapped her in his arms, and then launched into a half-spin. Tracie's head went back, and she stared into the rafters where a ceiling fan flapped beneath the bamboo roof. He turned loose, and they both twisted in perfect tempo until they touched the floor, just before leaping in the air. Their bodies bumped as they landed with clasped hands. This time Tracie let out a whoop, closed her eyes, and rocked her shoulders. Her hair whipped freely as a bongo player pounded away on stage. She peeked at her partner and screamed with delight, moving in nose-to-nose.

As the song came to an end the crowd cheered, and Tracie planted a kiss on Carver's cheek. He returned the favor, cupping her face in his hands.

"Miss Tracie, my daddy has a name for women like you," Carver said, his mischievous grin defying him. He took her by the hand to a nearby table.

"Well-well-well," Brenda said as they strolled up. "You guys are perfect together."

Tracie smiled as Carver pulled out a chair for her. "I think I'm in love," she said to Brenda, looking over at Carver. "Are you sure you're only eight?"

"Yes, ma'am," Carver said, patting her on the shoulder. He turned. "Brenda, would you like to dance?"

"Why don't you take Bailey while I talk to Tracie?" Brenda said, looking at the six-year-old sitting next to her.

"Yippee!" Bailey shouted, climbing out of a chair. She snuggled in close to Brenda. "Then can we visit with Mr. Don?"

"You have to wait until he takes a break," Brenda said.

"Okie-dokie," Bailey said, bouncing off to the dance floor.

"I'm leading, Bailey," Carver said, trailing behind as the music cranked up again.

"Those two are so sweet," Tracie said. "You're about the luckiest woman alive."

"I wish I could take credit for the little angels, but I have to say Jon's the one who brings out the best in them."

"Don't be silly," Tracie said. "Look at how they love you. You're going to make a wonderful stepmom. When is Jon coming home anyway?"

"He's flying in tonight."

"See what I mean. He goes out of town, and the children fall right in step with you, like it's nothing. You're doing great," Tracie said, leaning closer. "Is their mother being a pill about all this?"

"Every once in a while she gets a streak in her, but she's so busy spending the divorce settlement she rarely makes an appearance," Brenda said. "It's sad, but probably best."

"Let's hope so," Tracie said. "What's the plan with you and Jon?"

"He's wrapping up an assignment at a medical device company, Johnson Medisys. But recently he filed paperwork to set up a new investment firm. I'm still working for Stone & Associates in town and living in my condo, but I come out to Tybee on weekends or when Jon's away."

"What do the children think about that?"

"Jon and the kids live upstairs, and I've laid claim to the downstairs apartment ever since the previous owners moved out. That's the arrangement until after the wedding."

"Tell me everything," Tracie said. She pushed aside an empty margarita, grabbing a second.

"Aren't those wonderful?" Brenda said, not waiting for a reply. "Okay, hold on to your swizzle stick because you're not going to believe this. Jon talked me into getting married on a catamaran in the Virgin Islands."

Tracie's eyes got big. "Wow. That's awesome. You know what that reminds me of? Blue Hawaii . . . You're living in an Elvis movie."

"Not exactly. At least, I don't expect Jon to show up in a sequined jumpsuit." Brenda giggled. "But the scary part is flying in a seaplane to this teeny-tiny harbor to pick up the boat. From there, the four of us will be cruising the islands for ten days."

"You're taking the kids on your honeymoon?" Tracie nearly came out of her chair.

"It's a huge boat," Brenda said, motioning for Tracie to settle down. "Anyway, there are two master cabins. We've hired a nanny for a few of the anchorages, and the kids get to spend a couple of nights at a special tropical camp while we explore a few exotic beaches on our own. But I have to tell you, it took a bit of coaxing to convince Jon to take them along."

"It was your idea?" Tracie said. "You just may be my hero. That's about the bravest thing I've ever heard. You're not getting married by one of those voodoo priests, are you?"

"A local magistrate," Brenda said. She picked up her drink. "And as long as it's official, I'm standing by my man."

Tracie looked around to Carver and Bailey hopping around on the dance floor. "I envy you."

"So is it too soon to ask why you're here with this Neely guy?"

"No-no-no. Don't even go there. He just caught a ride."

"Does he know that?"

Tracie sipped her margarita. "It's like this. You've got Elvis, and I'm living with Tarzan the Ape Man. The thing is I'm tired of his nonsense, doubly-so now that I hear you're sailing off into the Caribbean."

"Got it," Brenda said. "But how do you really feel about the Ape Man?"

Tracie toyed with the straw in her drink. "My mother says I'm still in love."

"That's not what I asked you."

"I don't know . . . Do you remember when Trevor and I met you guys up at the lake? We were sailing and laughing and enjoying the sunset. I watched how you and Jon were into each other. You both just savored every moment."

"And you don't have that with Trevor?"

"He bought me a floating rocket ship that's faster than a text message, whether I like it or not. I've got bruises on my behind to prove it. It's not exactly romantic."

"So you're saying he's selfish?"

Tracie laughed to keep her emotions in check, grabbing a napkin to dab a tear. "He's the most insensitive pain in the *you-know-what* known to man . . . or ape."

"For real? What do you guys have in common?"

"Let's see, he likes fast cars . . . and I don't. He likes Tom Petty . . . I like country music. He's into tailgating, and I dream of a table-for-two in a French restaurant. He likes beer and speed boats . . . and me? . . . I want to share a bottle of wine and sail off into the sunset."

"Clearly, you've given this some thought," Brenda said. "Isn't there something you love about him . . . anything?"

"Well, he once knocked me off my feet in the ladies' room—"

"What?" Brenda interrupted.

"It's how we met, but that was a long time ago. Trevor used to be so innocent and loving, like he needed something . . . *someone* . . . to complete him. Silly thing is I thought it was me."

"And it wasn't?"

"No . . . I mean . . . yes . . . *maybe*? It used to be, but something's changed. I think Trevor left the building when he started making money. Maybe I did, too."

"But you guys live in a trailer park—not that there's anything wrong with that," Brenda said. "When you hear about people blinded by success, there's usually not a mobile home involved."

"I hate to admit it, but I actually like Parkway Community."

"I'm listening."

"At first I thought I'd be embarrassed. But to be honest, the place has a certain charm. It's surrounded by palm trees, grassy areas, and a lake—nothing like where we used to live. There are no pretenses. I was starting to think of it as a private island where we could rediscover ourselves."

"What happened?"

"He didn't get it."

"Get what?"

"He never wanted to talk about what happened. He just went into overdrive, worrying about his job, houses, cars, and the boat . . . all the *stuff*. It's like he didn't care about *us*."

"Yeah, but somewhere deep down, don't you think the passion is still there?" Brenda said. "It may be hard to see, but the real thing doesn't just disappear over hard times. Mind you, we *are* talking about the weaker sex. He'll always have that urge to swing from the vines. It's wired into his brain."

"That's a good one," Tracie said, raising her margarita. "To the weaker sex."

The music stopped, and Brenda turned to check on the children. Tracie watched as Carver and Bailey scampered off the dance floor and up on stage. Brenda gave a little wave, and the performer winked at her. Tracie's jaw dropped.

"That hunk just winked at you."

Brenda giggled. "His name is Don Vegas."

"Don Vegas! Are you serious?"

"*Shhh*. The kids will hear you."

"I'm sitting here in a tropical bar listening to a hunk named Don Vegas, who plays music that drives me wild . . . and you're shushing me?"

"It's not what you think."

"You've got Don Vegas, Elvis, and a wedding in the Virgin Islands. It's not fair!"

"Stop it." Brenda glanced over as Don hefted Bailey into his lap. "Calm down and I'll explain. Only, you can't tell Jon."

"Spill it, or I swear I'll start dancing on this tabletop—"

"Tracie, it's family night," Brenda said. "Hunky Don—as you call him—is our new neighbor."

"If that guy's your neighbor, I'm checking into the downstairs apartment when you move out," Tracie said, taking a gulp of margarita. "Wait, that's the guy on the motorcycle."

"Don's pretty tight-lipped about where he's from, but he moved in across the street and struck up a friendship with Jon. One thing led to another, and now they're comparing notes on home remodeling."

"I need another drink."

"Tracie, no. You've had enough. Anyway, Don is sort of a modern-day John Wayne. The guy drives a Jeep, rides a Harley, surfs, jogs, and plays football on the beach."

"Hunky Don," Tracie repeated.

"So I enjoy talking to him on weekends."

"Yeah, but talk is cheap," Tracie said.

"*Shhh.*"

Tracie's eyes lingered. "From this distance, I'd say there's nothing but beard stubble and muscle on that *bod.*"

"You're married."

"So why can't I tell Jon?" Tracie said, propping her elbows on the table.

"Because I said so."

"So behind door number one we have Hunky Don . . . and behind door number two we have Elvis," Tracie said. "So Brenda, which door do you choose?"

"Jon, *of course.*"

"Do you mind telling me what tips the scale in his favor?"

"He's the man I'm spending the rest of my life with. That's all you need to know."

"So—Hunky Don is available?"

Brenda snatched Tracie's glass. "Okay, young lady. Two margaritas is your limit."

Tracie waved at Don.

"Listen to me," Brenda said. "Forget about Don. We have to figure out what to do about Trevor."

Tracie sank down in her chair. "Oh, yeah. The Ape Man."

Chapter 27

Suwanee, Georgia
Thursday, October 10th
7:30 A.M.

BAM! BAM! BAM!

I shot up in bed, sucking in stale air that reeked of smoke. Before I could wrestle free from the covers, I grabbed the pillow and pressed it to my nose. The smell reminded me how everything now had a barbequed bouquet.

BAM! BAM! BAM!

"I've got to get a doorbell," I said, falling back on the bed. I grabbed my phone, noticing a giant crack across the display. I checked the time, and it was 7:30 A.M. *This better be good.* Not bothering to get dressed I climbed out, wrapped a sheet around my boxers, and headed down the hall.

When I opened the door Fate was standing out front, propped against the palm tree. It was the spot where Goldfinger had been parked only twenty-four hours earlier. He wore the same green flight suit as the last time I had seen him and was sipping on a Dr Pepper.

"Isn't it a little early to be making house calls?" I said. The street was quiet, and I glanced over at Tammy Fox's place to see if we were being watched.

"Not for official business," Fate said. "If you wait too long most folks leave for work."

"So what's up, Fate? Did you find out something about the Lexus?"

He shook his head and grinned. "No *sirree*. I'm researching that on my own time. This is official Parkway business." His demeanor stiffened up. "You mind if we take a walk around back?"

I descended the steps, noting a chill in the air. "Whatever you've got to say, just give it to me right here . . ." When I looked up, Fate was already halfway to the backyard.

I took off after him, panicking as I remembered my little secret lurking in the ductwork. He marched past the garage and did an about-face in the middle of the lawn, studying the trailer. The blue tarp flapped in the morning breeze. To the left was Tammy Fox's place, and to our right the dock's tin roof was visible through the trees.

"Okay, we both know what this is about, so let's just head inside where it's warm," I said. "I'll make a pot of coffee."

"This'll only take a second."

I gestured at the trailer. "Come on, the tarp is only temporary. Besides, Clayton is the one who put it there."

"And I'd say he did a fine job," Fate said. "But we've got bigger fish to fry here."

I cut my eyes at the duct hanging in the shadows. A piece of insulation stuck out like a wad of cotton candy. Fate unzipped a pocket and unfolded a piece of paper.

"When you moved in, the welcome package included a copy of the Parkway Community covenants and regulations. Do you so acknowledge you received such paperwork?" Fate sounded official, but then paused for a sip of soda.

"I think . . . Tracie may have it."

"But do you acknowledge receipt?"

"Yeah. It's just . . . I didn't have a chance to look it over—"

"Ignorance isn't an acceptable defense—"

"Hold on, Fate. Are you saying I'm ignorant?" I said a bit too loud.

"I'm referring to legal terminology—"

"That may be true, but I wouldn't go around calling people—"

"And unfamiliarity with the aforementioned paperwork."

"Do you have any idea where I went to school or who I've worked for?"

"It's only pertinent to the case if it relates to a mental incapacity, which is highly unlikely under the circumstances."

"The case? What case?" I glanced over at Tammy Fox's place. She had just made an appearance on the back stoop in a nightie and a pair of earrings that perfectly matched her fluffy marabou mules. I pulled the sheet tighter around my midsection.

Fate turned for a look, and then gestured with his head. "Is *that one* the reason your wife made off with the Lexus?"

"Are you crazy?" I said, raising my voice again. I suddenly realized losing my cool wasn't going to help matters.

Tammy Fox blew one of us a kiss.

I turned my back to her. "Listen, just tell me what's on your mind and let's get this over."

Fate kept an eye on Tammy Fox over my shoulder as he returned to the paper in his hand.

"Do you so acknowledge that you hold the title to unit number twelve at Parkway Community?"

"Yes, Tracie and I own it jointly."

"I only need one owner present to conduct my business."

"Fire away."

"I've got a petition, here, that is being circulated by one of the residents. It's presently got thirteen signatures on it. If they get fourteen, then the board of directors will be required to take a vote on the case."

"Back up. What case?"

"Are you familiar with paragraph ten in the covenants?"

"We've already been through this . . ." I began, but changed my mind. "Why don't you explain it to me?"

"Paragraph ten, as so amended in nineteen hundred and eighty-nine, states that only doublewides are allowed within Parkway Community."

I stood, deep in thought, as the tarp continued to billow and pop.

Fate gave an approving nod. "That Clayton sure knows his way around a toolbox."

"Let me get this straight. Are you suggesting my home is now considered a singlewide?"

"Measured it myself, right before I knocked on your door. Paragraph ten specifically defines the dimensions—"

"Fate—"

"We've got a clearly marked sign over at the office: *No Singlewides Allowed.*"

"I'm not arguing with you, but isn't there something in the covenants about extenuating circumstances? You've got to admit this wasn't intentional."

"Sorry, but the rules are pretty black and white. Your trailer dimensions are out of *spec*, and the residents are entitled to redress the matter before the board of directors by presenting a petition signed by a majority of the homeowners."

"So what are my options?"

"Besides putting the trailer back together?"

"Yes."

"You mean, like a loophole?"

"Heaven forbid," I said, under protest. "No, I'm just looking to buy a little time until I find the other half."

Fate started fiddling with the zipper on his flight suit. *Zip . . . zip-zip.* "That's an easy one he said, like it was nothing. *Zip-zip . . . zip.* "Make sure they don't get that fourteenth signature."

Chapter 28

Tybee Island, Georgia
Thursday, October 10th
10:00 A.M.

Tracie relaxed on the beach, digging her toes into the cold, damp sand. The spot had been secluded for the better part of the morning, with only an occasional jogger breaking her train of thought. Behind her, the second floor of Jonathon Browning's beach house peeked above the dunes. Just beyond the surf in front of her was a shrimp boat trawling the shoreline.

She picked up a paperback, and then tossed it on the towel. What had seemed like an open and shut case on Monday, now appeared to be a bit more flimsy under cross-examination. It was almost like the man who showed up to haul the trailer had read her mind, or better yet listened in on her phone calls. Who recommends a place to hang out, and then waits around all day so you can park a trailer in a cornfield? Especially when that someone says he'll send you a bill later. He clearly appeared at the right place at the right time—nothing but accommodating.

Then on the way into town, she stops off at Neely Pecan Orchards and meets a local who takes an immediate interest in her predicament. Her mother had expressed doubts that Tracie was serious about leaving Trevor, and then Neely charmed his way into tagging along for the ride, only to have Brenda express what true love was all about. It wasn't fair. After all, Trevor *was* an ape.

Moving to Parkway Community had been an unexpected bump in the road, but a welcome safe harbor for her. After moving to Atlanta, Trevor had gotten the big head . . . no, make that a bigger head. The promotion had turned him into an animal. All he cared about was new stuff—houses, cars, boats, golf . . . anything with a shiny veneer. Not that she had a problem with those things. It was mostly the way he prioritized them over everything else, including their marriage and her dreams.

Parkway was symbolic, a place where the material things didn't have quite the same sheen. The neighborhood seemed nice and cozy, kind of an oasis in the middle of an affluent desert. But that ended all too soon, with Trevor doing everything he could to cling to the past. They had jointly made the decision to move to Atlanta, and when misfortune raised its ugly head they should have been thankful to have one another to figure out the next chapter. She had hoped the setback would be a defining moment. But Trevor couldn't see past the embarrassment.

"Fancy meeting you here."

Tracie looked up to find Neely standing over her. "How long have you been there?"

"Long enough to realize you were in a place far, far away. What were you thinking about?"

"Nothing that would interest a man on his way to Chicago."

"Now that response has . . . How would I describe it? . . . A hint of jealousy. Maybe you'd like to come along?"

"How is it that a guy with such specific plans has the flexibility to just up and leave on a beach trip at the drop of a hat?"

"I take it—you're not into spontaneity?"

"Answer my question, and just maybe I'll tell you what I'm—"

"If I didn't know better, I'd say you're trying to change my plans. Does Trevor even know you left town?"

"That's between me and him," Tracie said. "Where did you stay last night? And where's your car?"

"It's parked in the driveway, and I stayed a little ways down the beach at a motel. I left you a voicemail last night. What do you say we take a walk, and I'll show you my room—"

"Says the man on his way to Chicago," Tracie said, reaching for a pair of sunglasses."

"Humor will get you everywhere."

"How's this? I love spontaneity, just not at the moment."

Neely spread his hands out wide. "Hey, what did I do? Besides, I have a more important question." He dropped down on the towel and gazed into her sunglasses. Their noses touched. "What's in that bag?"

Tracie shoved him. "You're kidding, right?"

"What's the big deal?"

"If I didn't know better, I'd say you followed me here for that bag. Did Trevor put you up to this?"

"Never met the guy, but you've got to admit it's sort of odd."

"You're the only odd thing on this beach."

"Really? First you run away with half a trailer, and then you ditch it, only to remove a mysterious bag before leaving town. Every time I ask you about it, you get all defensive—like I'm trying to steal your purse or something."

"You touch my purse and they'll find you at that pecan stand in a burlap bag."

"You know what I'm saying. Why can't you tell me what's going on?"

"Because you're acting strange."

"Is it that obvious?"

"I'm sitting on the beach with a man I met three days ago in a pecan orchard. What do you think?"

"I think you're absolutely perfect."

"Brother!"

"I'd kiss you right here, that is, if you promised not to smack me."

"You've got a fine case of Jekyll & Hyde syndrome. One minute you want to know what's in the bag, and the next you move in for a kiss. That doesn't work with me."

"Okay, so I haven't earned your trust. Tell me what it's going to take."

"For a chance to find out what's in the bag, you can start by explaining why you're here."

"You're asking for my entire life story." Neely leaned in closer. "Let's assume I'm willing to share my most intimate secrets. Where do you see this going?"

"Nowhere. So back off. And what's that aftershave you're wearing?" Tracie foiled Neely's advance by planting a hand in his chest. "Need I remind you, Don Vegas is only a scream away?" She pointed.

Neely glanced over at the house. "Who's Don Vegas?"

"The neighbor you saw on the Harley."

"I *will* earn your trust," Neely said. "And I want you to feel safe when you're with me. Only, this is no place to foster a new relationship."

"It's the beach."

"Yeah, but I know a great restaurant in Savannah where we can spend the entire evening getting to know one another."

"It's not sushi, is it?"

"Just the best seafood in town. How does that sound?"

"I'm afraid Brenda already made arrangements for dinner."

"Tomorrow works for me," Neely said. "I'll take care of the reservations."

"I'll agree, but only if you promise the fish is cooked."

"You can take it to the bank."

"Would you check to see if they serve French wine?"

Neely raised an eyebrow. "Let's do this right. Do you have a nice dress?"

Tracie blushed. "I will by tomorrow."

"Now, as for the matter of a kiss . . . what's that gonna take?"

Tracie looked out at the Atlantic and ran a hand through her hair.

"How about this? You walk on water, and just maybe I'll think about it."

Chapter 29

Tybee Island, Georgia
Thursday, October 10th
11:00 A.M.

As Neely disappeared over the sand dunes, Tracie's phone rang. She picked it up, pausing to study the name on the display: *Trevor Wentworth*. "The Ape Man," she said out loud, convinced it was his new title. She wondered if there was a ringtone suitable for him.

The phone rang two more times as she weighed her options.

"You've got one minute," she said, pressing the phone to her ear. "If you say anything stupid, you'll be disconnected at once."

"Tracie?"

"What do you want?"

"Tracie, what's going on?"

"Okay, that's no way to begin this conversation. But it's not really stupid, so I'm going to give you one more chance."

"I'm sorry . . . Where are you?"

"Fair question, only I'm not going to answer at the moment. Was that the only reason you were calling?"

"What has gotten into you . . . wait . . . I'm sorry. What I mean is—are you all right?"

"Feeling much better, thank you. How about you?"

"*Uh*, not so good. I really don't know where to begin."

"Then perhaps you'd like to call back at a better time—"

"No! Please don't hang up. I've been trying to reach you for . . . I've called a hundred times. Clearly, I did something wrong. I screwed up. I'm an idiot."

"You're an ape man."

"Yes . . . that, too. Tracie, can you tell me what I did to deserve *this*?"

"There's not enough minutes on our phone plan to get into it at the moment."

"I'm trying to find another job. I know I made a mess of things, and I'm going to get everything on track . . . for both of us. I won't give up until our credit score is back in the eight hundreds."

"Our what?"

"Our . . . never mind. It would really help if you could give me something to go on here."

Tracie allowed a few strategic seconds to tick by, adjusting her sunglasses and loosening a couple of buttons on her shirt. She dug into her purse for a tube of sunscreen, and then kicked back to take in the sun.

"Where were you the day I left Parkway?" Tracie said.

"You know I go to the driving range on Mondays, and—and when I came home you had vanished with half of our home."

"And where were you the evening before?"

"I—I had an interview. I told you about it."

"And this interview lasted until one-thirty in the morning?"

"You see . . . I never got to tell you about it. It's turned into a huge opportunity . . . different from anything I've ever considered before."

“We agree on that point. I checked the American Express account and guess what I found? A concert ticket and bar tab big enough to choke an elephant.”

“I can explain—”

“Did you get the job?”

“Not yet, but that’s precisely why I’ve been trying to reach you. There’s a bag in the hall bathroom that contains a device. I was supposed to do a demo for the second interview. Only you took off with it, and I haven’t been able to set up the interview. And it’s a really great job.”

“You already said that.”

“If you can tell me where you are, I’ll stop by and pick it up. While I’m there, we can talk. I’ll tell you about the job and we can work out the future from there.”

“Explain the credit card charges.”

“I was really nervous about the interview—and well—I needed to de-stress after everything I’d been through.”

“Who was with you at the concert? There’s no way you drank that much alone.”

“You should have been there. It was the Old 97’s, and you know how crazy their shows get. They’ve just released—”

“I’m about to hang up,” Tracie interrupted.

“Okay, okay. I went alone after the interview, but I made some new friends over drinks.”

“Trevor, we just lost our home, and you think you’re entitled to throw a four hundred dollar pity-party?”

“I bought the place at Parkway. Doesn’t that count for something?”

“Do you think for a second that half of the doublewide would be missing if everything was okay? The trailer was fine by me, but everything else is all wrong.”

“I’m sorry I had to sell your boat, but look at it this way. I just sold my golf clubs, and the lease company came and . . .”

Tracie listened as the words fizzled mid-sentence, like he was about to cry. "They came and what?"

"Tracie, I can make this right, if you'll give me the bag. I'll buy another house, a bigger boat . . . whatever you want."

"Try this on for size. I don't want any of those things—at least, not right now. I want to fix *us.*"

"That's easy—"

"Hey, do you remember what I said about acting stupid? This isn't about a job or any of our stuff. I'm talking about ground zero."

"Anything you want, just tell me where you—"

"Not so fast, buster. What's in that bag anyway?"

"It's a prototype of a drug detection device."

"There's a bottle of pills and a Ziploc full of white powder. In fact, it was all over the bathroom. Those aren't real drugs, are they?"

"It's not like that. They're only there to test the device."

"Who else knows about the bag? Did you shoot your mouth off at that concert?"

"Tracie, I swear—"

"Don't say it. I've heard all the excuses I care to hear from you." Tracie sensed someone approaching and turned. It was Neely.

"Hey, I forgot to ask you—"

Tracie raised a finger to her mouth, warning Neely to zip it. He raised his shoulders. *What?*

"Who was that?" I said. Then I heard birds cawing and something else in the background. The sound had been there throughout the conversation, but I hadn't given it any thought.

"It was only a stranger being friendly," Tracie said. She pressed the finger to Neely's lips, and then shook it at him.

"I don't think so. Whoever it was, knows you. He was about to ask you a question." I listened again. The birds faded in and out, but then I picked up on a distinct sound. “I hear waves crashing. You’re at the beach. You’re at the beach with a man!”

“Don’t be silly.”

“But you admit you’re at the beach.”

“Let’s suppose I am.”

“Then you’re at Tybee. You’ve run away to visit Brenda. Where’s the trailer?”

“It’s not here. I dropped it off in Waynesboro.”

“You left it with your parents? What are you trying to do to me? Now I have to deal with them.”

“Wait-wait-wait. You’re not going to see anybody. I have the bag with me.” Tracie looked over at Neely, who was intrigued with the conversation. In fact, the topic made his eyes grow bigger.”

“Why did you leave the trailer and take the test kit? Is there something you’re not telling me?”

“I couldn’t very well haul a trailer to the beach.”

“Who is the man with you?”

“Look, I removed the bag because you sounded desperate. I figured it was important, so I wanted to make sure it was safe.”

“Then you *have* been thinking about me.”

“I can’t talk about that right now.”

“I have some things to take care of, but after that I’m coming down. And you tell that weasel who’s with you to watch out.”

“When are you coming? I can’t have you barging in on Brenda and Jon.”

“It’ll take a couple of days. I should be there by Saturday.”

“And you’ll take the bag and leave, right?”

“I’ll do what any red-blooded ape would do.”

Chapter 30

Suwanee, Georgia
Thursday, October 10th
Noon

I was reeling from my conversation with Tracie as I crawled out from under the trailer with one of the Ziplocs tucked in my pants. By the time I got around to the driveway, I was fiddling with my phone when the cab pulled up. I had a few logistics to take care of before I could take off for Tybee, so I wasted no time in setting *Plan A* into motion. It started with a short ride over to my old golf community—the one Clayton referred to as *The Springs*. When we arrived, I told the driver not to wait.

Inside the clubhouse, I checked the premises from one end to the other—the pro shop, locker room, and restaurant. There wasn't a familiar face anywhere, even though it was lunch hour. After pacing the front entrance for a spell, I stepped into the parking lot to do a little soul-searching.

I had played it over in my mind a dozen times, hitting upon the notion of talking to a couple of our former neighbors. I was certain if they heard my story they would be willing to lend me enough cash to get to Savannah. Of course, I had called everyone I knew on our old block, but had yet to hear back from anyone. *These are the same people who came to our backyard cookouts and drank wine in my hot tub*, I recalled. If all else failed, I had brought along a Ziploc to explore potential cash transactions with a couple of the shadier types.

"Son-of-a—" I stopped short, lowering my head as I noticed a security guard stretched out in a nearby golf cart. I remembered him from my days as a resident. He was tapping on his iPhone, probably checking e-mail. I looked away, seriously not wanting to make eye contact. Chances are he had been briefed on Monday's incident, when the pro caught me sneaking out on the driving range and threatened to call the police.

These people all have cases of the Johnny-come-latelies, I thought. "I always paid my dues," I fumed out loud. Not wanting a repeat of Monday, I headed across the parking lot toward one of the fairways next to the clubhouse. When I reached the edge of the grass, I cut a trail toward a row of homes that ran along the golf course.

Slipping past a stand of pine trees, I made a beeline for the nearest house. There was a wrought-iron fence in the backyard, with pointed spikes on top that resembled a mouthful of snarling canines. I took a deep breath and hoisted myself up. Just as I was about to clear the top, I heard the whir of a golf cart approaching. Without thinking, I looked around, and at that moment something grabbed my shirttail.

"Halt!" I heard the guard yell.

I gave a final push, and my shirt snagged, letting loose with a giant rip as I muscled my way over the top. I thought I was clear and let go of the fence, when all of a sudden one of the spikes grabbed my waistband. But it was too late. Plunging headfirst on the opposite side, I slammed into the wrought-iron, dangling upside-down. But only for a moment. A button popped, and I landed flat on my back in a bed of azaleas. A puff of white powder shot up in the air, like a mushroom cloud.

"I've got a *perp* fleeing on foot and headed for Golden Bear Drive," I heard the guard bark into a walkie-talkie. "Continuing pursuit."

"I sprang to my feet and tripped over a shrub. It snapped as I stumbled, losing a shoe in the process.

"You're on private property!" the guard yelled. He pulled up on the other side of the fence only six feet away and started climbing to the roof of his cart.

With no time to worry about my shoe, I cut out across the yard with a plume trailing behind me. I rounded a mound of pampas grass and found myself next to a sculpted swimming pool. I had to steer wide, noticing the on-again, off-again clop of my lone shoe on the stone deck. That was when it dawned on me it was time to ditch the cocaine.

The guard landed with a *whomp* behind me as he dropped over the fence, but I figured I had a good fifty feet on him. Thinking fast, I zeroed in on a side yard just beyond the house. It looked like the perfect escape route, offering cover once I negotiated past an oversized holly bush at the corner. I slowed and spun around, pulling out the bag without skipping a beat. With every ounce of energy I could muster, I hurled it into a Cyprus hedge next door. It sailed through the air, leaving a powdery tail as the foliage engulfed it. I didn't have time to worry about where it landed, so I resumed my flight.

Fifteen feet and I'm home-free!

Coming alongside the bush, I spotted an unidentified object out of the corner of my eye. Still sprinting, I felt a pair of arms wrap around my midsection and drag me to the ground in a patch of Bermuda. We slid to a stop, branding a grass stain on my right cheek.

"That's the last time you vandalize my pool, you bastard!" a voice screamed from on top of me.

I couldn't move, but managed to look back at the pool. A frothy head of bubbles overflowed a Jacuzzi in the far corner.

"You've got the wrong guy!" I shouted, on the verge of freaking out. "I used to be your neighbor."

The man wrenched my arm behind me. "You've still got soap powder all over you. You're going to clean up this mess. You got that?"

Just then, the guard huffed around the corner.

"It's about time," the man said. "I apprehended the vandal singlehandedly."

"He slipped in from the golf course," the guard said, dropping to his knees. "Give me a second, and I'll take it from here."

A couple of hours later, I stepped out of the security vehicle at Parkway Community and leaned inside the window.

"I apologize for the misunderstanding, officer," I said.

"Well, you should feel better now that you've returned that man's pool to working condition," the guard said. "A little honest work just may do the trick for you."

"But like I said, I didn't vandalize the pool."

"Yeah, yeah. Innocent until proven guilty. Let's just call it even, okay?"

"I used to live down the street."

The guard panned his head around, taking in the trailers. "Sure, pal." He reached in the floorboard and tossed out my shoe. "You might need that."

"Come on, even the homeowner believed me. Look, he gave me fifty bucks for cleaning up." I pulled the cash out of my pocket.

"That's for food, not drinking, mind you."

"Is there any way I can get in to see my neighbors?"

"I'm afraid you've paid your last visit to our fair community. We welcome most anyone, but your name is on the watch list. Next time, you'll be dealing with the sheriff."

I looked over at the Beasleys' place and spotted Betty Jean coming out.

"Now I know how it feels to be the poor boy at the zoo," I said to the guard, hanging my head low.

"How's that?"

"Everybody's got bananas for the monkeys, but nothing for a kid down on his luck."

Chapter 31

Suwanee, Georgia
Thursday, October 10th
3:00 P.M.

Betty Jean strolled over and joined me next to the palm, accessorized to the nines with her silver and turquoise jewelry. The security guard's jaw fell open as he pulled away, his eyes taking a long look all the way down to her boots. He gave me a thumbs-up and sped off down the street.

"What's the deal with *The Springs* security guy dropping you off?" Betty Jean said.

"He was just being neighborly."

"Clayton filled me in on the Beemer getting snatched. Have you heard anything from the police?"

"I'm—*um*—working on it," I said, anxious to change the subject. "So what's up?"

"Come with me."

Betty Jean led me by the hand over to her trailer. Inside, she fixed us both a cup of coffee before sitting me down at the table, where there was a stack of pink flyers.

"What do we have here?" I said, pulling one off the top.

"It's a response to the petition being circulated around the neighborhood."

"Can you believe that? Fate dropped the news on me this morning." I froze. "You didn't sign it, did you?"

"You know, sometimes you can be pretty thick. Has it not registered in your brain that the Beasleys are on your side?"

I glanced at the flyer.

ATTENTION PARKWAY NEIGHBOR

My name is Trevor Wentworth, and I live at Parkway 12. I would like to personally apologize for the appearance of my home, which has been impaired by events beyond my control. I want to assure you that the present condition is only temporary and will be remedied over the next few days. I hope my humble gesture of putting your trash out by the street this evening will serve as a symbol of my goodwill, and you will allow me time to make this right. Should someone ask you to sign a petition, I will be eternally grateful if you JUST SAY NO. Clayton and Betty Jean Beasley have offered to serve as character references, if you have any questions.

Kind Regards,
Trevor Wentworth

"What do you intend to do with these?" I said.

"I'm not doing anything. But you, on the other hand, are going from one end of this neighborhood to the other and roll every stinking trash can to the street for pick-up in the morning. While you're at it, you'll knock on doors and hand out these flyers. And you're going to be a gentleman about it, no matter what happens."

"Why did you have to go and make them glow-in-the-dark pink?"

"Seriously? Didn't they teach you anything about marketing at McKinsey?"

"I can tell you one thing. It never involved insanity like this." I smacked the flyer with my hand.

"Well, tuck your tail between your legs and get over it. It's your chance to *love thy neighbor*."

"Oh, *jeez*. They're going to think I'm a pansy."

"Listen to me. The men are already sympathetic to your plight. It's the women we've got to work on. They need to know you're sensitive to their concerns."

"By taking out the garbage?"

"I'd sign you up for the garden club if I thought it would do any good."

"Why don't you just plant *me* in a garden?"

Betty Jean shoved the flyers at me. "I suggest you get started."

It was dark by the time I finished up with the trash cans. Everyone I had spoken to offered only tight-lipped responses, with the exception of Tammy Fox. She invited me in for tequila shots, but I graciously declined by pointing out I had more house calls to make.

When I reached the front stoop of my trailer, an unidentified object zipped past my ear and ricocheted off the siding. I hit the deck, my first thought being I might have ticked someone off during the trash can tour. About half the trailers had no answer at the door, but Betty Jean had equipped me with a roll of Scotch tape for leave-behinds. Clearly, someone didn't appreciate my neighborly gesture.

Just then, I spotted a golf ball in the flowerbed next to the steps. Behind me a whirring sound started up the driveway. When I turned, a golf cart skidded to a stop, and Walt Mobley hopped out with Big Bertha slung over his shoulder. He went straight to the ball, poking at the pine straw with his shoe—*my golf shoe*.

"Lucky for me your house was here."

I slowly got to my feet. "You put a dent in my trailer."

"Golf is like life . . . It's part skill, part luck."

"Which part almost took my head off?"

"Doesn't really matter. In the end a scorecard doesn't know the difference."

"Very Zen, Walt. What are you doing in my yard?"

"You're number twelve."

"Of course, I am . . . Parkway 12. Is this about the flyer?"

"*Nah*—forget about that. You're the twelfth hole on my new course." Walt used Big Bertha as a pointer, gesturing at my side yard.

I leaned over the railing for a better angle.

"Is that a flag?" I said.

"Number twelve is a dogleg par three. In case you didn't notice, I sliced that last shot, which leaves me with a rather difficult lie in your zinnias."

"Wait a minute . . . Fate allowed you put in a golf course?"

"Nope."

"But you did it anyway?"

"The board of directors said it was okay."

"How many holes?"

"Eighteen."

"I don't get it. Aren't there rules against constructing a golf course in a man's front yard?"

"I should say not."

"Well, there should be. It's a safety hazard."

Walt eased over to the cart and exchanged Big Bertha for a wedge—*my pitching wedge*? He sized up the flag before approaching the ball.

"Where did you get that?" I pointed at the club.

"I bought the entire set from a fellow at Publix. And he gave me a sweet deal on the cart."

I cut my eyes and spotted a golf bag in the cart. "Why didn't you buy them from me?"

"I prefer not to get mixed up in a neighbor's business."

"But you put a golf course in my yard."

"Parkway has a proud history of supporting outdoor activities."

"They closed the tennis court and the pool."

"Those were entirely different matters."

"Why would they allow you to put the course so close to the houses?"

"That's an easy one," Walt said. "According to the board, it's good for property values."

Chapter 32

Suwanee, Georgia
Thursday, October 10th
9:30 P.M.

It took a couple of beers and a hot shower to clear my mind of the encounter with Walt on number twelve. Now sitting in the breakfast nook, I finished licking the bowl clean from a can of clam chowder I had nuked in the microwave. Without a television for entertainment, I picked up the soup can and started reading the label, making a mental note to address the golf course lunacy with Fate next time I saw him.

BAM! BAM! BAM!

"Just shoot me!" I shouted, dropping the can on the table. Fresh and clean from the shower, I lifted my beer and shook it. It was empty. I pried myself out of the chair and ignored the fact that I was in my boxers, slipping on my loafers.

Strolling to the front door, I turned the knob and gave it a push. The stallion barreled in and delivered a swift punch to the gut. I doubled over and heard my bottle hit the porch and clink down the steps. With my brain screaming for air, I dropped to my knees, gasping for breath. Looking up, I spotted Gustav's Mercedes idling in the driveway. Then I blacked out.

I awoke to the glow of blue lighting at the Arts Center warehouse. The air was cool and filled with a mechanical hum that was coming from the shadows. I raised my head for a bearing, noticing how the place had been transformed since my last visit.

A woman came out of a doorway, one that hadn't been there before. She wore a sequined evening gown and strutted over to my chair like a Broadway chorus girl. There was something familiar about her.

"Darling," she called out over a bare shoulder.

I did my best to sit up straight. "Wait . . . You're—"

"Has Mr. Wentworth decided to join us?" Gustav said, now appearing.

The woman . . . *or should I say* . . . the stallion opened a purse and stuck something under my nose. I jerked back and coughed.

"What is that?" I said.

Gustav walked over and kicked a chair that slid across the floor, screeching to a stop in front of me. He moved in and sat down.

"I believe you have something that belongs to me," Gustav said.

I tried to size up the situation, but my eyes kept returning to the woman. She puffed out her chest, snorted, and paraded over to the door and disappeared.

"The stallion is . . . *a girl*?" I said, mostly to myself.

"A lady," Gustav corrected. "And a fine assistant."

"She hits like a man."

"Yes—a trained bodyguard. One of the reasons you should never make her mad." Gustav got up and pressed closer, taking my chin in his massive hand. He inspected my face, and then turned loose. "I see no permanent damage. Ariana has done well."

"Remind me to thank her later," I quipped.

Gustav ignored the comment, returning to his seat where he crossed his legs.

"I wish to know the whereabouts of my test kit."

"The bag?" I said, stalling for time. I was hoping for some inkling as to why our relationship had deteriorated so rapidly. *Most people don't tie you to a chair in a warehouse, and then ask questions*, I thought.

"You know very well I have been trying to reach you."

"It's a great product, and I have a few thoughts that might be—"

"I want the bag!"

"I understand, but you see there's this funny story."

Gustav snapped his fingers and the stallion reappeared. "Humor is precisely the type of nonsense that does not sit well with Ariana in times like these."

"Your kit is safe, so let's not ruffle any feathers," I said, my voice cracking. "You see . . . I know you've been calling . . . like we agreed . . . but my wife accidently left town with the bag."

"You're saying your wife took my property—*accidently*? The bag is fairly unique, not something one would mistake for a piece of luggage."

"That's the funny—" I stopped short when Ariana popped me on the head. "That's the interesting part of the story. You see, she didn't take luggage. She took half of our house on this trip."

There was a confused expression on Gustav's face as he glanced up at Ariana. "What is he talking about?"

"This is true. The back of his house is missing. I could not believe my eyes when I first saw it." Out of the blue Ariana slapped me again. "Tell the man what he wishes to know." She stepped away.

"I'm having marital problems, but everything will be patched up soon," I said.

"Why would your wife leave with half a house?" Gustav said.

"She's angry—quite put out with me actually."

"That's your answer? She's mad, so she steals a house?"

"Half a house," I corrected. "And technically, she didn't steal it. It's joint marital property."

"Then why did she take my bag?" Gustav cut his eyes at Ariana to see if any of this made sense to her.

"You lie!" Ariana said, glaring at me. She started circling my chair.

"The bag was in the bathroom. Tracie didn't know it was there," I said.

"Is Tracie an addict?" Ariana said.

"*A what?*" I said, unbelieving. "You mean . . . like, drugs?"

"No, gummy bears," Gustav snipped.

"How did you know about the drugs?" I said, thinking he was referring to the Ziploc.

"Ariana put something in the test kit by mistake."

"But I put . . ." Looking down, I closed my eyes to retrace my steps. *I took the cocaine out of the duct at the trailer. I hid it in Goldfinger. I did the test in the parking lot with Gustav's kit after our meeting . . . stuffed it in the bag.* Then it hit me. *The oxycodone tablets?*

"Ariana mixed up the prescription bottles, and now your Tracie has the evidence. Who does she work for?"

"Tracie? . . . *my* Tracie?" I couldn't process the logic.

"Just a minute," Ariana said to Gustav, directing the next question my way. "Are you saying *you* put something in the bag?"

"I, *uh* . . . I don't know how it got there, but I found some cocaine at—"

"Parkway 12?" Gustav interrupted.

I was amazed at how fast he rattled off my address. *He asked about Parkway at our first meeting.*

"The man is waiting," Ariana said, drawing back her hand.

I looked up at her, and then at Gustav. "I found cocaine in the house after we moved in. But I didn't actually know what it was until the night we met. I took a chance I would be able to test it with your prototype and brought it to the meeting. You let me take the kit, so afterwards I tested it and put it in the bag. The next morning Tracie made off with the trailer."

"Does she know about the oxycodone?"

"I didn't even know about it—until now."

"Tell me about the cocaine," Gustav said.

"I figure the previous owners were dealers—or something. But everyone at Parkway talks about them like they're saints."

"Really?" Ariana said.

"They refer to my house as the Dorsey Place."

"And what do you intend to do with these drugs?" Gustav said.

I hesitated, but then thought it best to come clean. "I'm going to tell you the truth, and then maybe we can forget this entire mess. Look, I was desperate for money. There was a little voice inside my head that kept telling me to sell the stuff and get the hell out of Dodge. My problems would be behind me . . . and I . . . *we* could start over."

"Tracie knows nothing?" Ariana said.

"Of course not. I'm the one responsible for the bag," I said. "If you'll give me a little time, I'll drive to Tybee and retrieve it. I'll do it tomorrow."

"And you will return my property?" Gustav said.

"Absolutely. And I'll hand over the cocaine to the authorities. Then everything will be on the up-and-up."

"I don't think so," Ariana said.

"I want *all* of my property," Gustav said.

I was a bit fuzzy about this last statement, and then all at once I was even more confused about the job interview. *Did the polished résumé trick Gustav into meeting with me, or did he come after me because I lived at Parkway 12?*

"Where exactly is Tracie?" Ariana said.

"At a friend's beach house . . . Jon Browning. I swear I'll go down, get the bag, and return everything to you. Then we'll call it even."

"If you notify the authorities, you will die," Gustav said.

"Along with Tracie and your beach friend," Ariana added.

I couldn't believe my ears. Not wanting to say anything stupid, I closed my eyes and lowered my chin. I wanted the world to go away. When I finally opened my eyes, I noticed a fleet of vans in the rear of the warehouse. And sitting in the far corner . . . like a kidnap victim . . . my beloved Goldfinger.

Chapter 33

Suwanee, Georgia
Friday, October 11th
10:00 A.M.

I barely slept at all after my near-death experience with Gustav and Ariana the previous night. Now standing in front of the counter at the Nifty-Thrifty, a local consignment shop, I waited as an associate sorted through a bag of clothes I had just lugged in. She was barely twenty years old and dressed to the hilt in a vintage ensemble, propped up against an old NCR cash register. An eight-track player sat on a stool in the corner, thumping out Rick Derringer's *Rock and Roll Hoochie Koo*. Behind me was an eclectic retail space filled with circular clothes racks that were organized by size with little plastic dividers. On the walls were eye-catching displays of outfits—very nicely done, actually.

When finished, she looked up. The dollar store earrings jingled against her neck. "You've got fifteen items," she said, giving me her best Valley Girl accent. "These aren't hot, are they?"

"Hot?" I said, missing the point. "Oh . . . you mean, like stolen?"

Her eyes lit up as she examined one of the labels.

"Absolutely not," I said. "They belong to my wife." I gave myself a gold star for this stroke of genius. I had cleaned out a selection of Tracie's things from the closet, knowing full-well they would fetch more than my stuff."

"Fill out an information card, and you can stop by once a week to collect your cut of the sales."

"I was hoping for an advance."

She ogled over another label before responding. "This is really good stuff. It'll move in no time."

I noticed a glimmer in her eye. "You wouldn't happen to be size five, would you?"

She didn't look up, admiring the stitching on a sundress.

"What will they sell for?" I said.

"For all of the items—four-twenty-five. We split the proceeds, so your share will be—"

"I'll take a hundred dollars on the spot. The rest is yours when they sell."

"The owner has a strict policy." She glanced in the back room.

I had already noticed that the owner had stepped out, so I leaned across the counter. No one was around, and I detected a sparkle in the associate's eyes.

"How about this . . . Penny?" I said, peeking at her name-tag. "I'll take these little treasures outside and stow them in the vehicle of your choice, all for the cool, low price of seventy-five bucks."

"Are you nuts?" She started to pace, biting a drugstore fingernail. "I lied . . . we'll sell them for six hundred, easy."

I bucked up. "So now we're getting somewhere."

"The dresses, alone, cost her two grand."

"And lucky for you, I'm extending this offer for . . ." I looked at my bare wrist. ". . . another thirty seconds."

"Does she have any idea you're doing this?" Penny fanned with her hands, like she was having a hot flash.

"What's it to you?" I said. "Listen, this is a common law state. Do you know what that means?"

"Not exactly."

"It means . . . you've hit the jackpot. Do you have seventy-five on you?"

She settled down and lowered her voice. "I do," she said, excited and ashamed all at once. Then a naughty smile surfaced.

"I'll take them out to the car before your boss returns."

I paid the cab driver and hopped out in front of the house. Standing in the driveway, I decided the time had come to review my financial situation. After starting the week with thirty dollars in my pocket, I had taken in three-seventy-five for the golf clubs, fifty for pool cleaning, and seventy-five bucks for Tracie's wardrobe. Of the five-thirty, I had already spent fifty-three at Publix, twenty for cab fare to *The Springs*, three hundred to American Express, thirty bucks for a phone battery, and forty-five for the ride to Nifty-Thrifty. This left me eighty-two in cash and roughly one hundred and twenty available on my credit card. I stuffed the cash in my wallet and started up the driveway.

Nailed to the palm tree, I noticed someone had taken my *Beware of Dog* sign and replaced it with the *No Singlewides Allowed* from the office. "Nice neighbors," I huffed, as I snatched it down, did an about-face, and marched directly up the street. Passing the tennis court, a Lincoln sat in the spot where Clayton normally parked his rig. On the other side of the fence, the kids were going at it on the trampoline, tongues and all. I spotted Fate kicked back on the pew at the office. He seemed starry-eyed, admiring the car.

I tossed the sign down next to him, and it landed with a thud. The chain rattled as it slinked off the seat.

"I want to know who's responsible for this," I said.

"Ain't she a beaut?" Fate said, unfazed.

"Someone vandalized my property. What's the board going to do about it?"

Fate didn't respond at first, resorting to the zipper on his flight suit like he might be studying the question. *Zip-zip-zip . . . zip-zip*.

"Have you filed a report?" he said.

"I left an hour ago and returned to find *that* on my tree."

"Mighty peculiar," Fate said.

"Did you see who did it?"

"I noticed the sign was missing when I came in this morning. That's a fact. So I notified my superiors about the theft right before I washed my brother's car."

Taking another look, I noticed puddles all around it.

"So what do we do?" I said.

"I can retract my notification, seeing how the property's been returned . . . or you can add your report to mine, and we'll build a case."

"I just want to nail whoever's behind this."

"That makes two of us. Only, I don't want the board getting the wrong idea. Now that you've shown up with the smoking gun, they just might think it was you that did the stealing."

"Fate, that's insane. Why would I take the sign?"

"Mind you, I didn't say you did. A man's innocent until proven guilty. Of course, with the circumstances as they are, some might speculate you did it to make a mockery of our policy."

"What policy?"

"The one about singlewides."

"I'm sick and tired of hearing about . . ." I lost steam mid-sentence, suddenly distracted by the Lincoln. "How much would your brother charge to rent his car for a couple of days?"

"Now *that's* crazy talk. My brother don't let anyone drive that one, except me."

"How about I hire you and the car?"

"Not possible. I've already used up my vacation."

"I'll pay you a bonus."

"Where do you need to go?"

"Savannah."

"You're talking road trip. I can't get mixed up in that kind of nonsense."

"Fate, I have to get down there."

"Then you might want to check with Greyhound."

"A bus? I'm not—"

"Do you know I've never missed a day of work? They give me a certificate every year for perfect attendance."

"Are you positive your brother won't make an exception?"

"*Yes sirree*. He's pretty sweet on that kitten. You'd just be wastin' your time."

I kicked the pew and stormed off.

"Hey, *Trev*," Fate called out. "What about my notification?"

I raised a fist in the air. "Retract it!"

Chapter 34

Savannah, Georgia
Friday, October 11th
9:00 P.M.

I woke from a deep slumber on a Greyhound bus with my head resting against a window. The bus was only half full, and surprisingly more comfortable than I had imagined. Who knew they had recliners and free Wi-Fi? I rubbed my eyes, wondering if I had dreamed about the stopover in Macon. I strained for a look at the darkness outside, figuring we were traveling somewhere along I-16 in central Georgia.

Betty Jean had stopped by the trailer earlier in the day, following my fray with Fate. She gave me an update on the petition, and in the scheme of things it turned out to be pretty good news. She and Clayton had visited every trailer in Parkway. None of the residents had admitted to actually signing the petition, so naturally no one offered to take their name off. She had to explain it twice before I understood why I should be so happy.

They still don't have the fourteenth signature, she said. *The next board meeting isn't for a few days, so you've got time to save yourself.* I could still hear her voice and see those flashy earrings bobbing as I reached for a brown paper sack in the seat next to me. Pulling out a Dr Pepper and peanuts, I reclined in the seat and caught a reflection of myself in the window: day-old beard stubble, denim jacket, and a button-down flannel Polo. I looked at my wool slacks and Italian loafers, realizing it might have been a good idea to put a little more thought into my attire. A pair of socks wouldn't have hurt. Glancing up at the window, I spotted the gold chain around my neck and stuffed it in my shirt.

I cracked open a few peanuts and tossed the shells in the aisle.

"Hey!" someone yelled from behind me. "This ain't no pool hall."

"Sorry," I said, cleaning up the mess.

The bus fare set me back forty-seven dollars, and the snack was purchased from a vending machine. I put the ticket on AmEx and used two-fifty in loose change for the food. Cash flow was no small matter now. I calculated my cash position to be a little over seventy-nine dollars, with seventy-three in borrowing capacity left on the card. Suddenly, I wondered how Tracie had managed to bankroll a trip to the beach. *Must be her parents*, I thought.

Returning to my meal, I replayed the plan I had hatched in the waiting area of the Atlanta bus station. Once I got to Savannah, I would hail a cab for Tybee Island. When I reached Jon's house, a nice walk with Tracie on the beach would take care of our marital woes and secure the bag—two birds with one stone. After that, we would enjoy a "makeup" night at the beach and return to Atlanta in the morning. I would contact Gustav to let him know he could pick up his property at Parkway Community. Arrangements for the return of Tracie's half of the trailer would have to wait until Monday. I had a good feeling everything was about to fall into place. My marriage would be saved, Gustav erased from my life, Fate could call off the petition hounds, and me and Tracie . . . *well* . . . we could set sail into the future.

Ariana turned off Butler Avenue onto 7th Street. There were parking meters running down both sides, obviously for the Tybee Island tourists. The street dead-ended at an arched boardwalk that spanned a sand dune over to the beach. She checked the address on the last house to her right. Bingo.

It was a white clapboard cottage, with a short driveway leading to a park-under garage. The longer side of the house ran parallel to the street, where a lower-level entrance and a window gave off a soft glow. Next to the door was a weathered set of steps that clung to the exterior and climbed to the second floor. She had to lean forward to see the top. There was a landing next to a screen porch looking out over the beach.

Checking the street, she saw no signs of activity anywhere. No people, no dogs, no cars—deserted. If she parked close enough to keep an eye on things, the car would stick out like a sore thumb—after all, someone was bound to recognize the BMW, especially since Trevor was expected to show up at some point. She examined the neighboring house across the street. It was dark with no one at home.

Ariana lowered the roof on the Beemer, and then backed into the neighbor's driveway. It felt a little too conspicuous, so she pulled into the garage where the shadows provided cover. She made sure the angle to the Browning house suited her before turning off the ignition. In the peace and quiet, the sound of crashing waves drifted in over the dunes.

There were no lights in the Browning upstairs windows. Although the garage was a double, no cars were parked inside. She popped open the console and pulled out a Beretta, loading a round in the chamber. *It's Friday night, and this neighborhood is like a monastery*, she thought. Her phone displayed 10:20 P.M. as she dialed.

"Hello, darling," she said, pausing to listen between sentences. "I've just located the address with no sign of Mr. Wentworth . . . I checked out this Jonathon Browning, and apparently he is a man of means, but his house belies him . . . No, there's no trailer park in the area . . . I plan to watch the place for a while, just to see what I'm up against . . . I understand . . . I'll retrieve the bag with minimal collateral damage . . . I promise . . . Did I mention my new outfit? . . . You're a devil! . . . No, I don't want his car, but a night on the town will suit me fine."

Chapter 35

Tybee Island, Georgia
Friday, October 11th
Midnight

The cab driver had been kind enough to swing by the Arby's drive-thru after picking me up at the Savannah bus station. The ride was a good fifteen miles to Tybee, so I had plenty of time to enjoy a roast beef combo en route. The cab fare was fifty bucks on my card, and the dinner was six-seventy-five from cash. I didn't bother to run the numbers. It was too depressing.

The street in front of Jon's beach house was dark, except for a buzzing light pole. I knocked on the downstairs door, but nobody answered. Checking the garage, I confirmed there were no cars at home. Upstairs, everything was pitch-black.

After a bit of soul-searching on the beach, I returned to the arched boardwalk spanning the dunes, where I had a clear view of the ocean and house. Someone had left a broken lounge chair nearby, so I hauled it up top to get comfortable. It worked, and before long I dozed off.

Around one in the morning, I heard a car door slam and sat up. Jon and Brenda were climbing the stairs to the second floor, each carrying a sleeping child. *Carver and Bailey,* I recalled. The lights came on, and I considered heading in, but then realized Tracie wasn't with them, and her car was nowhere in sight. *She specifically warned me about crashing in on them.* After weighing the options, I settled back to see what came next. The boardwalk was close enough to hear movement and conversation in the house, only I couldn't understand a word being said.

I had no trouble staying awake this time, especially since it wasn't long before things started to happen. A car turned onto 7th Street, and from my vantage looked as if it might rocket straight out onto the boardwalk. The engine rumbled toward me like an old muscle car, and as it pulled up next to the curb the driver killed the engine. He parked under a street lamp about fifty feet from where I was seated. I almost fell out of the chair when he turned out the lights. It was the classic lime-green Pontiac from the Arts Center—a Grand Prix.

"What the . . ." I said, a bit shaky getting up.

The driver's door opened, and a man straight off the cover of *GQ* made his way around to the passenger side. My eyes were deceiving me. I stumbled back into the chair as Tracie got out all polished up in an eye-popping dress. *A new dress.* I watched as they laughed and disappeared inside on the ground floor.

Upstairs, I heard Jon and Brenda talking, and from the sound of things didn't appear to be expecting anyone. Then I remembered yesterday's phone call, and it hit me. *The man on the beach.*

"Wait a minute," I said under my breath. "*GQ*'s car can't be the same one, can it? We're three hundred miles away. But maybe it does make sense. Tracie was fishing for details about the interview, accusing *me* of stepping out of line that night."

The house was only feet away, so I charged for the door. When I was within striking distance, I changed course as a lighted window caught my eye. There was movement, and I heard voices. The curtains were pulled tight, except for a tiny slit. I leaned in for a closer look.

Tracie seemed to know *GQ* pretty well. In fact, the way they carried on was nothing short of chummy. Yes, it was a barrel of laughs. Tracie was waving her hands, all animated. And the guy was making a move. Tracie flopped down on a sofa, messing with her hair. Then he did it. *GQ* dropped next to her and planted an arm on the cushion above her shoulder. I gripped the windowsill, feeling splinters dig into my fingertips.

As my eyes opened wider, Tracie hitched up the hem of her dress, holding it between her fingers. Her words were barely audible, but I could swear she said, "This dress smells like lobster bisque. Excuse me, while I slip into something else." And with that she floated out of the room. I couldn't see where she went, but I distinctly did *not* hear a door close. *What the hell's going on?* I thought. I rested my head against the glass, struggling to think clearly. *I'm going in.*

Before I had a chance to budge, I sensed movement again. When I raised my eye to the slit, *GQ* had crossed the room to a chair. And then I spotted it. *It* . . . being the leather bag. He unzipped it and carefully examined the contents, like he was taking inventory. I saw the cocaine, the tester, the chemical, and the oxycodone. He held up the pill bottle and shook it. Then he jumped, like he was startled.

Barely in my field of vision, I spotted Tracie in a silky robe . . . the flowered one I gave her for Christmas. It was too much. The door was only inches away, and I wasn't thinking straight. *Maybe this is what they mean by temporary insanity.* Pacing between the window and door, I harnessed enough brainpower to realize I'd better not screw this up. Tracie had been edgy last time we spoke, and now here I was faced with the reality of a cheating heart. I looked down at my clenched fists. *Who is this home-wrecker? I'll strangle him.*

When I stepped to the window for the last time, there was only one thing I could come up with. I had to take *GQ* out of the equation. With my eye glued to the slit, it was obvious he was good-looking, confident, and riding high. All of a sudden, Tracie snatched the bottle from his hand, and her face turned red. I heard the tone in her voice. She was scolding him . . . it was shrill . . . *a glorious shrill.*

And then the nightmare began. *GQ* pulled out a pistol.

I took a deep breath.

Sweet Moses, I'm going in.

Chapter 36

Tybee Island, Georgia
Saturday, October 12th
1:25 A.M.

I lunged for the door, grabbing the knob so hard I thought it would rip off in my hand. Then suddenly I remembered *GQ* had a gun. Turning loose, I made a detour into the garage and stumbled around in near-darkness for what seemed like an eternity, searching for a makeshift weapon. Against a side wall, I came across a two-by-four nearly three feet in length. Doing an about-face, I was making for the scene of the crime when something bizarre happened. Not once, but twice.

Someone called my name. But it came from across the street. I snapped to attention as a silhouette stepped out of the neighbor's garage. In the same instant, a Jeep appeared out of nowhere and screeched to a stop in the middle of 7th Street. To my surprise, a surfer dude jumped out and bolted toward this mysterious figure who was vying for my attention. The next word I heard clearly.

"Halt!" the silhouette shouted.

The voice was vaguely familiar, only I was too baffled to process it. Surfer dude barreled ahead, even as his opponent raised a pistol. He was within striking distance, but the command didn't seem to dampen his momentum. First he dipped, and then he leaped in some kind of a pretzel-like twist, unleashing a kick squarely to his assailant's chest. I could almost feel the impact as the limp body launched backwards into the garage, followed by the sounds of shattering glass and crumpling metal.

Surfer dude reached into the darkness and retrieved the pistol. His hands moved rapid-fire, disassembling the weapon as ammo and pieces of metal clanked to the driveway. When he was done, he pulled out a cell phone and dialed.

Half-dazed, I figured the entire episode had taken only seconds. That was when I remembered my own predicament. I pulled up my bootstraps and retraced my steps. Inspired by surfer dude, I squared off with the door and kicked it with every ounce of energy I could muster.

There was a crash as the door slammed into the wall. I rushed inside just in time to witness Tracie snatch the bag from *GQ*, let out a scream, and bolt past me. That left the two of us in a stare-down.

"Don't do anything stupid," I said, raising the two-by-four.

GQ seemed to take pleasure in the remark and stepped toward me. I responded by backing up.

"I'm warning you." I gripped the board like a Louisville Slugger.

He raised the gun, shoulder-high.

I retreated once again, stopping in the doorway.

GQ pointed the pistol at my head, raised a thumb, and cocked the hammer.

"I'm not kidding," I said, with all the nerve of a frightened chicken. I inched back, just outside now.

Before my next heartbeat, I heard the shrill of a madman and glanced over a shoulder. I spotted a mass of wild hair and mangy beard leaping off the stairs toward me. He drew back a brass spyglass in mid-air, cracked me over the head, and delivered a full body-slam. The two-by-four slipped from my grasp and took a couple of bounces down the driveway. That was the last thing I remembered before blacking out.

I wasn't sure if I was dreaming, but someone had ahold of me. I tried to fight back, but they pinned me to the ground.

"Trevor," he said, shaking me.

It was a familiar voice, only different this time.

"How are you doing, buddy?"

I felt pounding in my head, and then replayed the madman's attack in my mind. With a jolt, I tried to break free, but only managed to get my eyes open. I was lying on my back outside the beach house, with Jon Browning on top of me.

"Say something or I'm putting you in the ambulance," Jon said.

Raising my head, I looked past him to the stairs, making sure the coast was clear. Next, I checked the doorway. No one was there. Then I spotted blue and red strobes flashing against the clapboards. I twisted around, eyeing an ambulance and patrol car sitting in the middle of the street. An officer was stuffing *GQ* in the back of the cruiser.

Jon took me by the arm and hefted me to my feet. Then he walked me over to the driveway. I couldn't take my eyes off the commotion in the street.

"What happened?"

"The police arrested a man who attempted to rob Tracie."

"No, I mean . . . who hit me?"

"We think it was the same guy that took down the robber."

"The madman?"

"The what?" Jon said. He turned me around, starting toward the house.

"A maniac dove off the stairs and tackled me. He had this . . . old telescope."

"Take it easy. You may have a concussion," Jon said. "They also apprehended a woman across the street. The neighbor's silent alarm went off, and he came home and caught her prowling around."

"Have they identified her?"

"That—I'm not sure about," Jon said. "We should get you checked out at the hospital."

"No insurance," I groaned.

"Then let's get you inside."

"I could use a couple of aspirin."

Jon helped me over to the door. "Wait here, while I run upstairs."

"You're certain no one else saw the wild man?"

Jon gave me a funny look as he turned and started upstairs, shaking his head.

"I'm not crazy, you know," I called out. "I saw him with my own eyes."

"Walker," Jon said, holding back a smile.

Chapter 37

Savannah, Georgia
Saturday, October 12th
2:40 A.M.

An hour later I stepped out of Jon's car and was ushered inside an old building in the historic district. It was late, so there were no tourists on the cobblestone street as we passed through a pitch-black entrance. He guided me up a crooked flight of stairs that turned ninety degrees at a landing, halfway up. When we reached the second floor, a jaw-dropping view of the river opened up.

Overhead lights flickered to life, and we crossed to the center of the room where there was a desk and chairs. I hadn't noticed it until now, but Jon slipped Gustav's bag off his shoulder and tossed it on the desktop.

"Tracie told me to give you that," he said, his heels echoing off the hardwood as he headed over to a corner. "How about a cup of coffee?"

The second story was pretty much open space. I didn't bother with the bag or a response. Instead, I lost myself in the surroundings, starting with the back wall. It was an impressive display of oversized casement windows, probably a hundred years old. The combination of vintage glass and woodwork was stunning. The other three walls were solid masonry. I recalled hearing about a special type of brick called Savannah Grays on a tour years ago, and from the looks of things these were originals. Overhead, exposed beams supported the underside of a gabled roof. The floors showed years of wear and tear, probably ancient pine. Suddenly, I was uneasy. My last encounter in a warehouse hadn't gone so well.

Stepping up to the windows, the Westin rose up from the riverbank like a tropical oasis. Upriver, I noticed the Talmadge Memorial Bridge shimmering against the sky in a ghostly apparition.

"Is Tracie meeting us here?" I said, making my way to the desk.

Jon set a coffee cup in front of me and dropped into a swivel chair. "She said she couldn't do this right now."

"What is this place?"

"The future offices of Browning Ventures. A long time ago, it housed cotton factors. We're gutting the interior to give it a facelift."

"Tracie told me you were setting up an investment firm—life sciences, I believe?"

"That's right. Now about your situation, tell me what's in the bag. We've managed to keep it out of law enforcement's hands, but I'm still in the dark about what's going on. And I have to tell you, I don't like the looks of that powder on the flap."

"First, let's talk about Tracie," I said.

"Tracie's biggest worry seems to be the contents of that bag."

"Who was the guy with her?"

"He claims to be a detective, only he wasn't carrying ID or a warrant. The sheriff will have to sort that out."

"That means the cops will be onto me soon. What's Tracie got to do with all of this?"

"Listen, Trevor. Tracie has been talking to Brenda. She hasn't said much, so maybe you should lay it out for me."

I sat down across from Jon, poking at the lump on my head—thinking. Then I reached for the coffee. "I screwed up bad," I said. "That's probably never happened to you."

Jon let out a breath. "What planet are you from? I'm not exactly what you call an expert on women, but I have had my share of extenuating circumstances."

"Tracie left me."

"That kind of stuff, I know about."

"Oh, yeah . . . your divorce," I said.

"So why did Tracie leave you?"

"For starters, I lost my job."

"There's no way you could have seen that coming. Cal Hunter is a friend of mine and told me the entire Zuritech story, including how he uncovered the illegal activities after taking the CEO position."

"True. But then I lost the house and everything else we own. It's not exactly the lifestyle of the rich and famous. I don't blame her for leaving."

"Taking off with half a house, that's pretty creative. Some might call it an attention-getter," Jon said with a smile.

"Why didn't she just stick it out with me? I know I can fix this—"

"*You* . . . can fix this?" Jon leaned forward. "Do you hear what you're saying?"

"Is there something wrong with taking responsibility?"

"Last time I checked, you weren't flying solo."

"Tell that to the Bozo who had his hands all over my wife," I said. "Besides, Tracie doesn't talk to me anymore."

Jon's cell phone rang, and he paused to take the call. After listening for a moment, he said, "Thanks for the update," and hung up before looking at me. "Based on what I understand,

Tracie has felt—empty—since she's been away from you. But given the circumstances, the prospect of facing you seems even worse at this juncture. The good news is the passion is still there."

"And I'm still here . . . in a gutted warehouse."

"Are there any pressing legal issues facing you?"

"You tell me."

Jon stood up. "In that case we're both tired, and it's late. Let's find you a place to bed down. In the morning, you can head home."

"Unless you're taking me to Tybee, I prefer to stay right here."

"There's nowhere to sleep," Jon said.

I took a swig of coffee, and then stood up to face him. Since I couldn't bear to look him in the eyes, I took another glance at the Westin across the river.

"I'm a bit low on funds," I admitted.

"Not a problem. I'll take care of your lodging and airfare to Atlanta in the morning."

I winced, then held up the bag. "Airport security might be a problem."

For as long as I had known him, Jon had always been a decent guy. But the current circumstances made me a little nervous, given that he had grown up in the same town as Tracie. That meant one thing. Even though he was a bit older, he was first-and-foremost *her* friend. Of course, I was beyond exhausted, so my options weren't good. I knew some sleep would buy me a little time—just to be sure my mind wasn't playing tricks on me.

It was just after noon on Saturday, when Jon picked me up at the River Street Inn for lunch. Afterwards, we strolled beneath a canopy of mossy oaks down to his office. I was traveling light, carrying only the leather bag on my shoulder. Parked on the street in front of Browning Ventures, I got a nice surprise.

Goldfinger.

"How did she get here?" I said, quickening my step. I suddenly stopped. The windshield was smashed, and the hood had been crushed in. "What the hell?"

"The lady arrested at my neighbor's place last night was driving your car."

"Ariana?"

"You know her?" Jon said, giving me the eye.

"Not exactly. At least, not in the way you're thinking. Let's just say she has an interest in this," I said, tapping the bag.

"What was she doing with your car?"

"There may be a slight issue with the title."

"Then I advise you to deal with it as soon as you get to Atlanta," Jon said, tossing me the keys.

"You have my word."

"One more thing. Until we're sure about the guy with Tracie last night, you may want to dispense with the contents of that bag."

"As fast as I can get down the expressway," I said, patting Goldfinger's roof. "Can you clarify one thing for me? Last night when I asked you about that freak who attacked me, I could have sworn I heard you say *Walker*—like you knew the guy."

Jon hesitated, pulling out some cash. "Walker is the ghost of a drifter who lived at the beach decades ago, but I'll deny it if you tell anyone. You've got enough problems, so let it go." He peeled off two hundred bucks, handing it to me.

"I'm not sure when I'll be able to pay you back," I said, opting not to press about the spook.

"Tracie has an open invitation to stay with Brenda for as long as she wants, but I suggest you find someone up your way that she'll feel comfortable connecting with. She needs a woman's ear at the moment, and it's better for both of you if she's closer to home. I'm willing to help facilitate the transition."

A tear came to my eye, and I embraced Jon in a bear hug, just to keep from losing it.

"I owe you, man," I said.

Chapter 38

Savannah, Georgia
Saturday, October 12th
4:00 P.M.

The open road was as good a place as any for reflection. The ribbon of I-16 between Savannah and Macon offered nothing but eighteen-wheelers, bugs, and clear skies. The world had a different look as I eyed it through Goldfinger's broken windshield—one of those feelings that transports you to another galaxy. For the first time in days, I had a glimmer of hope. I was beginning to realize there was more to life than memories of jobs and the frills that fly the coop when the music stops playing. I didn't like the way it felt . . . but then again, I didn't have to. Of course, there was one thing I did have to do. *Change my way of thinking*, I thought.

Tracie opened the door at the beach house, beside herself when she discovered who was standing there. "I'll give you until the count of three, and then I'm calling 911," she said, leaning on the jamb.

"Hey, that's a perfectly rational response to what went down last night," Neely said, holding up his hands.

"Maybe a restraining order will do the trick."

"I'm sorry," Neely said, pasting on a puppy-dog face. "I can explain everything—I swear."

"Do the police know you're here?" Tracie looked up and down the street. Neely's Grand Prix was nowhere in sight.

"Trust me . . . They're okay with it."

"If that's an apology, then we're done here." She grabbed the door, with every intention of slamming it in his face.

Neely stuck out a foot, cutting her off at the pass. He reached into his jacket, where a pistol was strapped to his waist. Extracting a cardholder, he flipped it open.

Tracie stared for a moment, as her eyes popped wide-open. "That's a fake, just like the man carrying it," she stammered.

"Actually, it's standard Bureau issue."

"Give it to me." Tracie pulled out her phone. "I'm sick and tired of your little games." She dialed before speaking again. "Yes, this is Tracie Wentworth. I'm staying at the Browning residence on 7th Street. Can you confirm the identity of the man you arrested last night? . . . That's right . . . I see . . . And he's licensed to carry a weapon? . . . *Uh-huh* . . . No problem . . . Thank you." She snatched the phone away from her ear, fuming.

"Like I said, I'm sorry for the misunderstanding," Neely said.

"That was no misunderstanding. It's nothing short of deception."

"I'm on assignment—"

"Am I some kind of suspect? You'd better start talking and get to the point, real fast. Otherwise, I'm about to scream."

"Okay, okay," Neely said. "Is it all right if I come inside?"

Tracie stepped out and closed the door behind her. "We're doing this in broad daylight . . . over there by the stairs." She slipped past him and sat on the bottom step.

"I'm after the bag."

"Obviously."

"It's actually the people behind it that interest me." Neely walked over and rested a hand on the rail. "That bag came out of a warehouse we have under surveillance in Atlanta. The men responsible for it—actually, a man and woman—gave it to Trevor. We followed him to Parkway Community last Sunday night."

"I was there that night."

"What I mean is we staked it out. Then something strange happened." Neely leaned down, looking into Tracie's eyes.

"What happened?"

"You took off with half the trailer."

"Hold on just a minute. You were selling pecans at a stand outside of Waynesboro that same morning. How could you have been watching our house?"

"I have a partner. He kept an eye on Parkway while I headed south."

"That's not possible. You couldn't have known what I was up to or where I was going." Tracie said. "And in case you haven't figured it out, I have nothing to do with that bag."

"I know that now," Neely said, hiking a boot up on the step. "But it's like this. After we ID'd Trevor at the Arts Center, he met with our suspects and later attended a concert that he paid for with his credit card. We intercepted the transaction—"

"You did what?"

"We verified Trevor's identity and checked him out."

"So you're suggesting Trevor is involved in what—*exactly*?"

"He was never really on our radar until Sunday." Neely scratched his head. "Oh, boy. You're not going to like the next part."

"And it's been going so well up to now."

"When we ran the check on Trevor, oddly enough he had a Parkway address. During the process, we discovered the trailer was scheduled to be hauled to Waynesboro the next day."

"He didn't do that, *I did* . . . And what's odd about Parkway?"

"Let's just say there have been reports of someone running drugs out of the neighborhood. It's an ongoing investigation. We got a break when we came across Trevor's activity and your sudden plans to skip town. We figured he was about to make a run for it."

"I was leaving town, not Trevor. How did you . . . what's with the pecan stand?"

"Once we found out about the move, we had to act fast. We contacted the transport company and secured the logistics. They were happy to cooperate with the FBI."

"I had been having second thoughts and almost canceled the whole thing. Then he pulled that all-nighter on Sunday, so I cut the cord. What would you have done if I had called it off?"

"Sit around in that pecan stand and wait. Of course, my partner would have tipped me off."

"So the trucker was your partner. Now it makes sense. He's the one who convinced me to stop at the pecan stand in the first place. I knew that station was abandoned a long time ago."

"We had to cover all our bases. There was a possibility the drugs were in your half of the trailer, and we were right."

"So I'll repeat my earlier question. Am I a suspect?"

"That depends. Do you have the bag?"

Tracie slid off the step and started backing up the stairs. She pointed at him. "You're trying to trick me, aren't you?"

Neely let out a snicker and did his little head-bob, like he thought she was funny.

"Stop it."

"I'm not tricking you . . . I like you."

"Wait a minute. All that stuff about the family orchard and going off to Chicago, it's a pack of lies."

"It was my cover," Neely said. His expression turned serious. "And for the record, I intend to clear your name."

"Well, I'm reporting you to the authorities. Maybe even call in one of those investigative reporters. The FBI has stepped over the line on this one."

"I said—I'm going to clear your name."

"So why are you really here?"

"Hopefully to convince you of your civic duty," Neely said. "I need you to help me nail the felons behind that bag."

Chapter 39

Suwanee, Georgia
Saturday, October 12th
9:15 P.M.

After a quick stop at Publix for beer and essentials, I turned off Highway 141 into Parkway, well after dark. I was munching on a chicken finger from the deli, when I pulled alongside Tammy Fox's trailer and slammed on the brakes. A red neon sign in the shape of a hand with the word *Psy-Chic* flashing across the palm hung in the front window. Even from the street, I could hear a buzzing sound.

I pulled Goldfinger into my driveway, just when the bottom fell out of a nasty weather system passing through the area. As I pulled in close to the house, I noticed the "Check Engine" indicator blinking on my dash. Taking her out of gear, I revved the engine a couple of times, hoping the problem would go away. Next door, I could still see the glow of Tammy Fox's sign. The rain started coming down harder, so I gauged the distance to the steps before making a run for it. That was when something caught my attention. I turned on the windshield wipers for a better look.

I must have left a light on, I thought.

There was a break in the downpour, so I jumped out and grabbed the groceries from the backseat. With a sack in one hand and beer in the other, I closed the door with a knee and felt an unexpected tug. Looking down, my blazer had caught in the door, and I gave it a yank with my full body weight. *Riiiiip.* The breast pocket went limp, flopping down to my waist with only a thread holding it in place. A gaping hole yawned up at me.

Change my way of thinking, I reminded myself, bolting for the house.

Inside, I found the culprit. The light over the stove was burning. I set the sack on the table and stuffed the beer in the fridge. The breakfast nook was much cleaner than I remembered. In fact, there was no longer fire extinguisher residue on the floor. *Betty Jean strikes again.*

Heading into the master bath, I took a shower and pulled on a fresh pair of boxers. Glancing over at the tarp where the bedroom once stood, a yearning for my pillow-top mattress nipped at me. It was a bit chilly, so I slipped on the blazer.

Returning to the kitchen, I grabbed a beer and picked up the grocery sack to put a few things away. On the counter was a disposable clamshell—the kind for fresh fruits and vegetables. Next to it was a corkscrew, and in the sink a mixing bowl filled with chocolate icing. I looked around, and everything else was spic-and-span. *Nothing wrong with a person having a little snack after cleaning house*, I thought. I made a note to return the favor.

Lifting a *Sports Illustrated* out of the sack, I felt good about the events of the day, bouncing down the hallway for the spare bedroom. *Polish off a beer, catch up on football standings, and drift off to sleepy-land.* The floor was cold, and for good reason with the tarp flapping, not to mention a dampness in the air. I came to an abrupt halt when I reached the bedroom door. It was closed, but I distinctly caught a whiff of something spicy. *A female fragrance.* Stepping back, there was a hint of light spilling out from under the door.

Betty Jean? I thought, suddenly a bit nervous. Then I slicked back my hair, spilling beer in the process.

Temptation had never been a rare vintage for me. I sipped of her nectar most every day. After all, it was the twenty-first century, and we're entitled to life, liberty, and the pursuit of happiness. *Isn't that how it works? . . . Betty Jean Beasley in my bed . . . Nice! . . . The only fifty-something to ever do it for me.* I felt a twinge of admiration for her.

Stuffing the magazine under an arm, I buttoned my jacket and reached for the door, nudging it open. The light floated into the hallway like fairy dust, but I suspect it was mostly in my head. On the dresser, a portable Bose stereo crooned out a classic song by none other than . . . *Barry Manilow*? Next to it was a bottle of wine and my sailboat plate, covered with a supple arrangement of chocolate-covered strawberries. Even the wineglasses were brimming.

"Holy Toledo," I whispered.

I was so nervous I had trouble opening the door the rest of the way. At the same time, I was anxious to get a look at this Venus who had come to orbit my solar system. "May the Lord grant us peace and gravy," rolled off my lips. I don't know why, because it wasn't like me. In fact, I suddenly wished I hadn't. It was Clayton's blessing.

"And strawberries and vino," I heard a voice chime in from the bedcovers.

"No," I said, reversing course. "Change my way of thinking."

"You just leave that to me, honey."

"I—I—I . . ."

"Those are mighty cute boxers you're wearing," she said.

At once, my knees started knocking.

"Have you gone totally insane?" I said, gripping the beer bottle.

"That's not what you were thinking when you opened the door."

"Don't get me wrong. I appreciate your being neighborly and all. But this is a little sudden, don't you think?"

"We have so much in common, and now we have tonight."

"That *m-may* be true, but . . . like what?" I couldn't get my knees to stop.

"Next door neighbors . . . lost jobs . . . divorced . . . same profession."

The *Sports Illustrated* slipped out and landed on the floor.

"You're divorced?"

"I can tell you're surprised," she said.

"What exactly is your profession?"

"I'm an advisor, like you."

"The sign at your place says you're a *Psy-Chic* . . . What's that supposed to mean?"

"I'm a graduate of the Psychic Tea Room. It's a certificate program on the Internet that offers degrees in palm reading, tarot cards, and crystal balls."

"That's totally unrelated to what I do."

"You advise businesses about the future . . . I divine for individuals. We're both into helping people. Of course, *you* don't have a job at the moment."

"Is hopping in the sack with clients one of the *Psy-Chic* services?"

"It's included in the premium package."

"Wait a minute . . . I'm not divorced," I said.

Tammy Fox fluffed the pillows on my bed, in no particular hurry to dispute my claim. Her hair was actually quite lovely, curling across her cheeks like a flamenco dancer. She wore new earrings, and from the looks of things, a new negligee.

"Do you know *s-something* you're not telling me?" I said, taking a deep breath. *Change my way of thinking.*

"I'm still working the bugs out of my crystal ball, but what you need is a palm reading. They're much more reliable."

"Please tell me what you're doing in my bed."

"I was hoping you'd like to be my first client—at a preferred rate, of course."

"I—I'm tempted . . . but you see, I can't afford it right now. Let's get back to this matter of divorce—"

"Would you mind passing the strawberries?" Tammy Fox said, raising a pinkie.

I slammed the beer bottle on the dresser, soaking the front of my jacket. Desperate to get out of this trap, I handed her the plate. As she sampled a plump one, I noticed a fresh manicure and whitened teeth. After just a nibble, she set the plate aside.

"A certain someone paid me a visit with a petition about a certain person that we are both quite fond of."

"Oh, no," I moaned.

"With everything we've been through—being close neighbors and all—I thought we could work things out, if you know what I mean."

Tammy Fox wiggled her toes, and I couldn't help but notice they matched the fingernails.

Change my way of thinking.

"Being next door, I'm actually the one most affected by these horrific conditions," Tammy Fox said. "That tarp is an eyesore from my place. It could be bad for business, not to mention property values."

"Tammy, in case you haven't figured it out, *I'm* most affected by all this."

"That's nothing but consultant gibberish."

"You've got a neon sign in your front window."

"That's not the point."

"You can't hang a commercial sign in a residential community."

"Paragraph nine in the covenants specifically allows non-industrial services. It also permits Clayton to park his rig on that old tennis court. Didn't they explain it to you when you moved in?"

"Oh, *jeez.* Somebody put me out of my misery." I grabbed my head.

"See . . . that kind of attitude is probably what got you fired. If I were you, I'd put this argument to bed." Tammy Fox flashed her cow eyes, patting the sheets.

Change my way of thinking.

"How much for the premium package?" I said.

"Two hundred and ninety-nine dollars. That's less than twenty-five a month."

"I, *uh*, don't have that much on me."

"*Psy-Chic* accepts all major credit cards." Tammy Fox whipped out her smartphone with a card-reading device on top.

"My credit's maxed out," I said, hanging my head.

She slid out from the sheets and wiggled into her marabou mules. I hadn't noticed it until now, but she removed a robe from the bedpost, draping it over her shoulders.

"Give me a few days, and I'll raise the money," I said.

Tammy Fox slinked over and pressed her body against mine, cupping my chin in her hands. We locked eyes.

"Honey, I'm willing to wait."

Chapter 40

Suwanee, Georgia
Sunday, October 13th
7:30 A.M.

Tammy Fox chased me out of the bedroom and into the hallway. Turning the corner I bounced off the tarp, narrowly escaping a nasty spill. My feet squeaked against the laminate, like I was making a fast break on a basketball court. Behind me, I could hear her marabou mules pounding like a racehorse. Just past the breakfast nook, I spun around for a bearing on her position. I realized I had made a mistake as she barreled headfirst into me, sending us both airborne. We came to a sliding stop in the foyer, with Tammy Fox on top of me. "I'm willing to wait," she panted, smothering my face in kisses.

I woke up with a jolt, facedown on the floor with my nose throbbing. Lifting my head, I inspected a mass of sheets tangled all around me. There was a noise that at first sounded like someone at the door. Only, it wasn't the BAM! BAM! BAM! I had grown accustomed to, but more of a monstrous VROOM! I sat up on the laminate, rubbing my nose and trying to remember falling out of bed last night. Of course, the good news was—Tammy Fox had left the building.

VRRROOOOM!

The sound revved louder, suddenly coming to me. Clayton was warming up his truck out on the tennis court. Jumping up, I slipped on my blazer and a pair of jeans. Then sprinting down the hall, I grabbed my loafers and bounded outside. When I reached the street, Betty Jean called out from her back door, waving me over. I checked the rig, and Clayton wasn't in the cab, so I made a detour.

"What happened to you?" Betty Jean said, taking a look at my torn jacket as I followed her inside.

"Backlash from the petition," I said, still trying to catch my breath. "Listen, I was hoping to have a word with your husband."

Clayton appeared in the hallway, doing a double-take. He shook his head. "I don't even want to know."

"I'll explain later, but right now I need to talk to you."

"Betty Jean's heading to church this morning, and I've got to run to the office. You're welcome to walk me out to the truck."

"Here's a coffee to go," Betty Jean said, herding us toward the door.

As Clayton and I made our way out to the tennis court, the trampoline was a beehive. It wasn't even eight o'clock, and the venue was wall-to-wall kids.

"Where have you been all weekend?" Clayton said.

"Meeting up with Tracie."

"I hope she wasn't the one that got ahold of your jacket."

"Never mind that, I have an important question for you."

"Fire away."

I lowered my head, digging deep for courage. "What would you do if another man was chasing after Betty Jean?"

"Tracie's run off with a man?"

"No-no-no. Listen to me, Clayton. This is important. I'm talking about Betty Jean."

"I wouldn't do a thing. That woman's sailed through many a storm. She can take care of herself. Besides, she always tells me everything I need to know."

"So you're saying . . . you don't think she could ever be wooed?"

Clayton scratched his chin, like he was thinking it over. "In the vast scheme of things, that's exactly how I feel."

"But what if it was me?"

He let out a snicker. "Sorry. I didn't see that one coming, sport. Now, look at me. You're telling me you've got a log on the fire for Betty Jean?"

"Only, there may be a little more to it than that. You see she told me . . ." I stopped mid-sentence, just as I was getting ready to spill the beans about the boots. For some reason I had a change of heart, pumping my eyebrows as I took a gulp of coffee.

Clayton's eyes leveled on me, and then bounced around like pinballs. "What the devil's gotten into you? You're doing that thing Walt does with his eyebrows," he said. "But go on. She told you what?"

That was when the skies opened up for me, and I realized Clayton was my friend. Maybe the only true friend I had in this world, besides Betty Jean.

Change my way of thinking.

"To be honest, this isn't about her," I said. "It's just . . . I don't trust myself around her."

"So you're confessing it to me?"

"I honestly don't know what I'd do without you . . . because I seriously need help with this marital fiasco. I know it sounds strange coming from me, but I value your advice."

"So you're sort of looking for a mentor?"

I took another slug of coffee and swallowed hard. "That's precisely what I'm saying. Will you to do it for me?"

"Well now. That's a horse of a different color."

"And if it's okay with you, I'd like to ask Betty Jean to spend some time with Tracie. I know she's a good sounding board, and that'll allow the two of you to compare notes."

"We'd be honored," Clayton said, sticking out his hand. "Something told me you were going to be all right. I've got to take care of a little business, but when I get back I want a complete update on Tracie and the trailer. Are we square on this issue with Betty Jean?"

"Totally," I said. "That story about Walt and the telescope kind of drove me nuts."

"Puts me in stitches every time I hear it."

"Betty Jean mentioned she had never told anyone, other than you. I didn't want it between us."

"Vulnerability, they call it. That woman sure knows how to get a person to open up. I wouldn't be surprised if she has Tracie talking in no time at all."

"That would be great," I said.

My cell phone rang, and Clayton headed for the rig.

"That Tracie's a lucky gal," Clayton said over his shoulder.

Chapter 41

Tybee Island, Georgia
Sunday, October 13th
8:00 A.M.

Tracie paced back and forth at the beach house as she counted the number of rings. "Trevor?" she said, when he finally answered. "Can you talk?"

"Only for the rest of my life," I said, still pumped up from the conversation with Clayton. I stepped off the tennis court, heading toward the trailer. A dog was barking down at the lake.

"Where are you?"

"Just strolling through the neighborhood and wishing you were here."

"I was calling about Friday night. Jon filled me in on the details."

"Boy, I really owe him—"

"That bag of yours has caused nothing but trouble."

Please, God, I said to myself, clasping my hands. I stared up at the sky. *Pretty please*? Returning the phone to my ear, I did my best not to panic.

"Jon told me the police arrested a woman over at Don's house, and I'm getting a little paranoid. What do you know about her?"

"Ariana? . . . Wait, who's Don?"

"Don Vegas is the next-door neighbor—"

"So all of a sudden you're on a first-name basis with *another* guy?"

"Trevor, a woman—who you refer to as Ariana—aimed a gun at his head. Clearly she's mixed up with the drugs, and now it turns out you're connected to her."

"That's not exactly true. But hey, what do I know? You see, when I first met her I thought she was a dude. I had no idea she would show up at Tybee."

"Why was she driving your car?"

"Goldfinger was stolen a few days ago, and somehow Ariana followed me here. But Jon managed to get her back, and I'm eternally grateful."

"So the two of you weren't together?"

"Tracie, I took a Greyhound."

"A bus?"

"I did it for you," I said, adding icing to the cake. It suddenly occurred to me I was walking in circles around the front yard, waving a hand in the air. Assuming a less aggressive posture, I headed over to the steps.

"Are you involved with her?" Tracie finally said.

"Of course not. Ariana's boss owns the bag and drugs. For some reason he needs my help, which obviously involves an illegal business," I said, exhaling. "But to be honest I was tempted just a *wee bit*, when I figured out what he was up to. You know, because of our financial situation. But I came to my senses. And I had every intention of returning the bag, only you ran off with it."

"And that's everything?"

"Tracie, it's the truth. I want you to come home. There's a couple, here, that wants to help with this plague I've brought upon us."

"You've made new friends at Parkway?"

"As miraculous as it sounds, yes. And things are starting to happen."

"Brenda mentioned it might be a good idea to find someone to talk to up there. Can you give me names?"

"Betty Jean and Clayton Beasley. Betty Jean leans a bit to the salty side, but she's totally down to earth. You'll love her."

"Do they know about the drugs?"

"Not yet. The Beasleys are good neighbors, so I'd rather not drag them into that right now. They've been extra-nice to me ever since they noticed part of the trailer was missing. I promise to make a full disclosure, when the time is right."

"What is the drug boss's name?" Tracie said, switching gears.

"Gustav? . . . *Why*?"

"I'm just curious. I've never been around this sort of thing."

"Give me a chance to make everything right, and then we'll sit down and talk. You'll do that for me, won't you?"

"Are you sure you're not in over your head?"

"My next meeting with Gustav will be the last."

"Hold on," Tracie said, pausing. "Trevor, where is the bag right now?"

I looked over in the driveway. "It's in Goldfinger's trunk."

"And when are you returning it to Gustav?"

"That depends. He has a private number, so I'm waiting to hear from him. But I'll take care of it as soon as he calls."

"Will you let me know *before* it happens . . . so I'll know where you are?"

"You do worry about me, don't you?"

"Yes, but I'm still mad."

"Please come home and talk to Betty Jean."

"Get this done—safely—and we'll see."

"I'll call you the instant I hear something. And you've got to believe me. I don't like being separated from you."

"That makes two of us," Tracie said, hanging up. She turned to Neely. "The name is Gustav."

"Do you think Trevor is dirty?"

"According to him, no. I swear I don't understand how he got mixed up in this mess."

"Yeah? Well, just so you know, Gustav is better known as Dr. Frederick Gustafson. We've been trying to nail him for years. This could be our lucky day."

"Are we done here?"

"We're just getting warmed up, babe," Neely said.

Chapter 42

Suwanee, Georgia
Sunday, October 13th
Noon

I know, I know. I shouldn't have, but an urge to kick back at the local sports bar got the better of me. This reconciliation business with Tracie was beginning to feel like a roller coaster ride. And with professional football calling my name, a few quarters of action would be just the trick to ease my worries and rekindle that awesome gridiron fire in the belly. Tracie had made off with the television, but the Macho Taco down the road had dozens, broadcasting every NFL game imaginable in high-definition. Besides, I had made a lot of progress over the past week, so I deserved it.

The entire experience lasted until half past six, at which time I settled a few wagers up and down the bar. I netted a thirty-five dollar loss, and somehow racked up a fifty-seven dollar bar tab. On the way home, Goldfinger flashed her "Empty" warning, so I stopped off for five bucks of premium.

Pulling into the driveway, I parked under the palm and used the vanity light to assess my liquidity before getting out. I counted one hundred and thirteen and change. With my phone, I checked the available credit at American Express—

twenty-three dollars. As I was putting away my wallet, I heard Betty Jean call out.

"*Tre—vor . . .*" Her voice drifted up from the lake.

It was just after dusk, and I could make out the string lights all warm and inviting, glowing their little hearts out down at the dock. The scent of charcoal was in the air, and I heard music . . . Kenny Chesney, to be sure. Then Clayton piped in, letting out a hoot.

"Be right there," I shouted.

After running inside to freshen up, I slipped around back to check the ductwork. All the Ziplocs were accounted for, so I struck out for the lake. Along the way, a question nibbled at me. *What was the cash value of the cocaine I ditched at The Springs a few days ago? Don't even think about it*, I told myself.

"What were you doing in the backyard?" Clayton said, as I stepped out on the dock.

"Hiding from Tammy Fox," I said, trying to stall. Surprised Clayton had been able to see me, I had to think fast. "I was checking the tarp. The flapping kept me awake last night."

"You just can't get good help these days," Clayton said, letting out a cackle.

He rose from an Adirondack to shake my hand. Betty Jean snuck over for a hug.

"We've got leftover shrimp on the hibachi, if you're hungry," she said.

"And there's a nice Bordeaux in the cooler," Clayton added.

"I'm only here to bask in your charming company."

"Well now, you're in fine spirits," Clayton said. "Sit down and join us for a spell."

I leaned on a rail and took in the lake. There was a chill in the air, but I liked the serenity.

"Hard to believe it's only been six days since we met," Betty Jean said. She tossed it out, like she might be fishing for something.

"Seems more like a lifetime," I said, caught up in the moment.

"The Good Lord crafted the entire universe in six days," Clayton said. "I'd say we're doing pretty good."

"And on the seventh, he rested. That's the day he wants you in church," Betty Jean said.

"We're having church right now, Honey Bunch."

"*Trev*, I understand you've located Tracie," Betty Jean said, shifting gears.

"She's at Tybee, visiting a friend. But I'm hatching a plan to get her home to iron things out. I'm hoping you'll help with the reentry."

"Darling, point her in my direction and us girls will get along fine. Was there anything in particular on your mind?"

"You're a good judge of character, so I have no doubt you'll know exactly what to say. Just calm the waters, even if it means letting her rip into me. I think it's only fair to do unto me as I've done unto her."

"Amen," Clayton said. "I like a man with a sense of humor."

"I'm serious, Betty Jean. Whatever the two of you dish out, I can take it."

"Now that we have that settled, how're you doing financially?" Clayton said.

I looked across the lake where a crescent moon glistened atop the ripples, noticing a breeze beginning to stir. "To be quite honest, I've barely got my head above water."

"What's the story with your car?" Betty Jean said.

"Goldfinger? Someone stole her, but she came back to me. A little worse for wear, but she's still running."

"I'd be honored if you'd allow us to help out," Clayton said.

"Not a chance," I said, wagging a finger. *Imagine me taking charity from trailer park people*, I thought, instantly wishing I hadn't. *Is this what I've come to? Belittling my friends who are only trying to help?*

"Ted's got a boatload of wild game over in his freezer. I'm sure he'd be happy to feed you. That's sort of his passion," Betty Jean said.

"I'd rather not. I'll tweak the budget a little, just until things turn around."

"Are you open to suggestions?" Clayton said.

"Do I have a choice?" I joked.

"The way I see it, Betty Jean can hook up with Tracie and delve into the relationship issues. That's the most critical part. But I can tell you from experience, financial problems can set you right on your ass. I'd attack fast and furiously . . . Jump on it."

"What do you mean?"

"I'm talking lean and mean," Clayton said.

"But not when it comes to Tracie," Betty Jean clarified. "She requires investment."

"Absolutely," Clayton said. "But beyond that, discretionary expenditures are fair game."

I looked at Clayton sideways, and then retreated to my comfort zone—gazing at the moon.

"Such as . . ." I said after a pause.

"I'd start by canceling the weekly trash pick-up and Internet service."

"You can't be serious. My garbage? . . . And how am I going to look for a job, if I'm not online?"

"Put the trash in our can," Clayton said.

"And we've got a good signal, so you can tap into our Wi-Fi," Betty Jean said.

“Next, there’s the cable service,” Clayton said. “Seeing how you don’t have a television, it makes perfect sense to shut that sucker off. If you’ve got any of those premium packages, nix ’em.”

I swallowed hard at the reference to *premium package*. Then I said, “It’s football season.”

“*Trev*, we’re dealing with matters of the heart here. I think it’s better to sit the season out for once,” Betty Jean said.

“But I’ve barely seen—”

“We’re on a mission, darling,” Betty Jean interrupted. “And we have to focus.”

“Video streaming is less than ten bucks a month. Am I *that* desperate?”

“Do you remember what you told me about those biotech companies?” Clayton said.

“Yes, but that’s different.”

“You went on and on about how you give them strategic advice.”

“Still—*different*.”

“Tell me who you came to for advice? Did you run to those so-called friends at *The Springs*, or maybe a big shot at McKinsey?”

I gave him the silent treatment, looking around for something to throw in the lake. They had no inkling of my field trip to *The Springs*.

“Well?” Clayton said.

“Okay, I get it!”

“Simmer down,” Betty Jean said.

“Unless one of your old buddies wants to collaborate, I’d suggest you tuck tail and get with the program.”

Change my way of thinking, I mused. The reality stung. “Clayton, I’m sorry. I’m just not used to being the client.”

“And I apologize for the pain you must be going through, but it’s gonna get better. Just wait and see.”

“Why don’t you come over next Saturday for the big game?” Betty Jean said. “Kenny Chesney’s announcing his picks for the bowl games.”

“We’ll have pizza and beer,” Clayton added.

Suddenly, the turn of events was making me queasy.

“Only, let’s not forget we’re working on a deadline,” Clayton said. “We’ve got to get that trailer of yours back together before the Parkway residents evict you.”

Chapter 43

Suwanee, Georgia
Sunday, October 13th
9:00 P.M.

Crossing the shore to a stand of pine trees between the lake and my house, I was pretty steamed over the advice Clayton had just dished out at the dock. The wind picked up, and I was suddenly engulfed in a bizarre tempest that nearly knocked me down. When it had fully surrounded me, a whisper beckoned out of the eerie calm in the eye of the storm, stopping me in my tracks. Then I heard a distinct tinkling of music, like an ice cream truck coming down the street. My eyes drifted to the dock, where Clayton and Betty Jean were kicked back in their Adirondacks, laughing and carrying on like always. I closed my eyes.

I heard music again, only this time it was in my head. I felt my feet lift off the ground, and suddenly my mind was swept up in a whirlwind. At that very instant, I felt ashamed of everything, and how this circus was nobody's fault but my own. A strange feeling overtook me, an uncontrollable urge for a treat. Images of Pavlov's dogs flashed through my head. They were salivating. Then a bell rang, but instead of dogs I saw myself down on all fours ripping into a frozen treat, gnawing it to shreds and licking gooey fudge from around my mouth. Without warning, the tempest lifted and released me from its clutches.

When I opened my eyes, I was shocked to find myself curled up on the ground, chewing on a pine cone. *Did I just black out?* I felt my lip, and there was a trickle of blood. Then I gagged and spit out shards of wood. Coming to my senses, I remembered where I was, but not really sure about what had happened. I got up, lightheaded at first. Looking around, I made sure no one had witnessed this insanity. My eyes cut back to Clayton and Betty Jean at the dock.

"Repent!" I shouted, like I had lost my mind. I thrust a fist in the air and turned for the house.

Once inside, I headed straight to the kitchen. My stomach let out a growl, but was still raw from the pine cone experience. "It wasn't real," I said out loud, trying to convince myself. I opened the refrigerator for a beer and sat in the breakfast nook, rustling around in a grocery sack until I came up with a strip of beef jerky.

My friends had just offered me money, and I pretty much gave them the cold shoulder—like they had offended me. *Where did I get off with such an attitude?* Here I sat with sixty-seven dollars in my pocket, acting like best in breed. All this after Betty Jean graciously agreed to take Tracie under her wing, someone she has never met . . . to help salvage our marriage. And then to top it off, Clayton proposed tips on saving money. But all alone in the opposing corner, there's arrogant little *me* who can't bring myself to spill the beans to either of them about the hundred bucks I've just blown in a bar. I won't confide in them about Tammy Fox blackmailing me in my own bedroom, the stash hidden under the trailer, or the impending wrath of Gustav. *What is it with me?*

My cell phone rang, and I answered.

"King Plow Arts Center in one hour," the voice instructed, hanging up.

I couldn't raise Tracie on her phone like I promised, so I left a message as I backed out of the driveway. Next door, I spotted a Jaguar basking in the glow of Tammy Fox's *Psy-Chic* sign. You could have landed a 747 in the street with all the light.

Forty minutes later I pulled up in the parking lot at the Arts Center, where Ariana was pacing out front by the gate. She was decked out in a suede jacket and matching riding boots. The makeup seemed heavier than usual, and the look in her eyes was a dead ringer for a rabid jackal. I grabbed Gustav's bag out of the trunk and followed her inside.

The lobby had been outfitted with European-style furniture, hardwood floors, and a sleek reception desk. On the rear wall, raised stainless steel lettering spelled out the company name: *TestEZ.*

Ariana whisked me through a door, down a hallway, and then used an optical scanner to access a set of steel doors that opened like an elevator. We passed through the front of the warehouse and entered a lab. The place was immaculate.

I jumped as Gustav cleared his throat. I hadn't seen him at first, but he was sitting at a lab bench in the corner. Ariana gestured for me to sit, so I tossed down the bag and sat on a tall stool, a good ten feet from Gustav.

"So you finally return my property," Gustav said. "As you may have deduced, Ariana is not so happy to see you."

"What happens in Savannah stays in Savannah," I said.

"You left her stranded far away from home—in a jail, no less. I had to personally go down to retrieve her."

"I had nothing to do with it . . . I swear."

"But you took her car."

"*Actually* . . . it's my car."

"Enough!" Gustav said. "Now, who have you told about the contents of the bag?"

"I would be out of my mind to do such a thing." I leaned against the bench, hitching my elbows up on the Formica top.

"Perhaps your wife?"

"I already told you. She's not involved. She took the bag by accident."

"Then let us consider this. It takes a professional to take down Ariana," Gustav said.

I looked her over. In the fluorescent lighting, I noticed the outline of a nasty bruise on her cheek. "She was trespassing on private property. That's all I know."

"And how did you come into possession of the BMW?"

"The professional, as you refer to him, is Jon Browning's neighbor. He's the guy with the beach house. Anyway, he recognized the car and returned it to me. I needed a ride home to deliver the goods, so here I am."

"Does Browning or the neighbor know about the bag?"

"I thought we just covered that. Look Gustav, I went to Tybee on a Greyhound bus—no less—for one purpose only. To retrieve your test kit. I did my best under the circumstances, so I'm a little fuzzy on why you're upset."

"Idiot!" Ariana hissed, starting to circle the bench. I had once seen a movie where a panther stalked its prey in similar fashion.

"Now-now," Gustav said, feigning to calm Ariana. "Do you have any suggestions on how we might thank our friend?"

"I'm for calling it even—"

"He's lying," Ariana snarled. "When he arrived at the beach, he cased the house. He didn't want to be seen."

"There's a good reason for that. My wife isn't exactly pleased with me at the moment. I told you how she took half the trailer. It had nothing to do with the bag."

"But why all the cat-and-mouse?" Gustav said.

"I had to retrieve your stuff without drawing suspicion. She wouldn't agree to see me, so I attempted to get in and out, unnoticed."

"There was a man arrested with Ariana. He was inside the house with your wife."

"Exactly," I said. "So you can appreciate the tension."

"Does this man know about the bag?"

My mind did a flashback. *GQ was snooping through the test kit when Tracie left the room.* I had forgotten this little detail, but clueless as to what it meant.

"No one knows about the bag, okay? The goon was hitting on my wife and things got a little rough," I said. "Surely you understand that."

"What is his name?" Ariana said.

"You're asking me? You're the one who spent the night in jail with him."

"Why was he there?" Gustav said.

"I have no idea. I just went down for the bag."

"We should keep Mr. Wentworth on a short leash," Ariana said. Without warning, she leaped up and pinned my shoulders to the bench with her knees. Her forearm pressed against my throat, and I could feel the countertop cutting into my back.

"I returned everything . . . I swear . . . I thought that's what you wanted," I gasped.

"You must learn to never dispute Ariana's intuition," Gustav said.

"Let me go, and you'll never see me again," I said, barely above a whisper. "You have my word."

"So, I will play nice and loan him the car," Ariana said to Gustav.

"My car?" I said, immediately regretting it.

"My car!" she retaliated.

"Okay-okay . . ."

"Please accept our gratitude," Gustav said.

Ariana hopped to the floor, but got in my face. She popped the cuffs on her jacket. "The car is to be returned . . . once we're done with you."

Chapter 44

Tybee Island, Georgia
Sunday, October 13th
10:30 P.M.

Tracie had just hopped out of the shower after a visit with Brenda, when she discovered her phone was missing. Pulling on her robe, she headed upstairs.

The porch was dark, but she managed to locate the phone without a problem. There were two voicemails from Trevor. The first had come shortly after nine and reported he was on his way to meet Gustav. The second confirmed he was headed home, ending with Betty Jean Beasley's cell number.

Tracie bit down on a fingernail. *Neely wanted advance warning about the drop-off.* She hesitated, wondering if she should call Trevor or Neely. She dialed.

In the darkness outside, she heard a phone ring. It was coming from the beach.

"Neely here," he answered.

"Where are you?" Tracie said, walking over to the screen.

"On the 7th Street boardwalk."

"Are you spying on me?"

"Can we do this in person?" Neely said, waving his hands in the air.

Tracie marched down the stairs, fast-walking behind Neely as he headed for the beachside of the boardwalk. There was a sand dune between them and the house, with only the roof visible by the time they stopped.

"What are you doing here?" Tracie said, shoving Neely.

He tripped and fell in the sand.

"Hey, what's the big idea?" he said, climbing to his feet.

"I ought to let you have it." Tracie kicked sand on him.

"It's a felony to strike an agent. And for the record, I'm one of the good guys."

"You're a creep who's been spying on me."

"Don't flatter yourself. I'm just making sure we've seen the last of the lowlifes," Neely said. "So why did you call?"

"I didn't see your car in the street."

"Tracie, what's up?"

"Trevor returned the bag."

"The meeting already went down? You were—"

"I know. I was supposed to call you, but I just found out."

"What happened?"

"He drove to the Arts Center to meet them."

"Now my stake-out is blown," Neely said. "That's exactly where I wanted to nab these guys."

"Including Trevor?"

"I'm a professional. If he's guilty—"

"A professional con artist."

"Are you mad because I wasn't really falling for you? Is that what this is about?"

"Keep dreaming, Mr. Pecan Man. I've been trying to brush you off since we first met."

"So that's what you were doing at dinner the other night? Fancy dress, high heels, Marilyn Monroe smiles."

"I was doing no such thing."

"Well, tell that to the crazy chemicals in my brain."

Tracie smiled.

"According to his second voicemail, he dropped the bag off and headed home. Based on that tidbit, I'd say Trevor has cleared his name."

"You hope that's the case," Neely said. "Sometimes these things are meant to throw us off the trail."

"Did it ever occur to you I might have shown up at the Neely Pecan Orchards to divert your attention?"

"Not a chance. I know how to read women."

Tracie drew back and slapped him. "Can you read that?"

Neely smiled and bobbed his head, like he thought she was being funny.

"That's what I love about you."

"Quit saying that. This has nothing to do with love."

"I'm the one scaring you back into the arms of that goofball husband of yours, whatever you call that."

"What do you want from me?"

"We've got a situation here. Given that the exchange has already gone down, we have no choice but to take our sting operation up a notch."

"Tracie?" Brenda called out from the screen porch.

"I'm down here," Tracie said.

"Are you okay?"

"Nothing to worry about," Tracie said, turning to Neely. "Now, listen to me. There is no *our* from this point forward. Tell me what you want, and then we're done."

"If that's the way you feel about it . . . Let's see . . . I need you to return home and keep an eye on Trevor. That way you can report any suspicious activities from the inside."

"Does that mean you're still on the case?"

"It's my job."

"What makes you think I want to see him?"

"I thought we already covered that territory," Neely said.

Tracie inched up the boardwalk with her head down. Then she stopped and looked back at Neely.

"I'm not ready to move back in, but I'll help you. That is—if it means clearing Trevor's name."

"All the better," Neely said. "So what made you change your mind?"

She smiled. "A dream and a prayer."

"As you wish."

"But I do have one condition."

Neely stepped closer. "Give me your best shot."

"When I give the word, you haul my half of the trailer to Parkway Community."

"Deal."

Chapter 45

Suwanee, Georgia
Monday, October 14th
5:05 P.M.

Reclining in the breakfast nook, I heard someone coming up the front steps. I tried to ignore the distraction, having developed a phobia about uninvited guests. Outside the window, I could make out the top of the palm tree in the yard. The sun was setting in the west, and there was a golden glaze shrouding the fronds.

BAM! BAM! BAM!

I sank low in the chair, but it only took seconds for worry to get the best of me. I popped out of my seat for another look, easing back into place once I spotted Goldfinger nestled in the driveway.

Betty Jean and I had spent the entire morning together. She didn't exactly spell out why she had rolled out of bed with this particular mission in mind, but after breakfast we had a powwow right here at the table. The overall discussion had gone smoother than our *Q&A* at the lake last week. I could tell she was pleased with the outcome, mostly by the tone in her voice, not to mention the hug she unleashed on me when she left.

I picked up a pen and read through the points listed on a notepad in front of me:

<u>TREVOR'S DAILY Rx</u>

1. Pay a compliment
2. Do a nice deed
3. Let her know you love her

I was rather proud of the title at the top: *TREVOR'S DAILY Rx*. It was my contribution to this morning's heart-to-heart. I smiled, remembering how Betty Jean had ruffled my hair, proud I was taking the process seriously. *You can't go wrong starting out with these three simple actions*, she said. *But it's going to be up to you to fill in the specifics, each and every day. I suggest you start the minute she comes home.*

Recalling how emotional she had gotten about it all, I found myself in the deep end of the pool again. A tear rolled down my cheek, prompting me to do the only man-thing possible. I swiped it away before somebody walked in and got the wrong idea. But then I flashed back to Savannah, where Jon Browning had inspired that same feeling. *Why?* I thought. *Why do these people care*?

BAM! BAM! BAM!

I had forgotten about the door, almost wishing I didn't have to leave my comfort zone. Dragging myself into the foyer, I took a deep breath. To my surprise, I found Fate on the front stoop with his arms crossed.

"Fate," I said, a little perplexed. "It's Monday . . . your day off."

"The board authorized eight hours of overtime. Sometimes you have to go above and beyond the call of duty to maintain smooth operations in a community. It's in the bylaws."

"If you're here about—"

"This isn't what you call an official visit."

"So it's not about the petition?" I said.

"Nope. I officially clocked out at five. Are we perfectly clear about that?"

"Wait a minute. Something else happened?"

"It's about the car."

I stepped past him, giving Goldfinger the once-over. She glistened in the afternoon sun right where I had parked her, staring up at me like she was licking her wounds.

"Not that one," Fate said.

Fear suddenly gripped me. *Was Gustav back?* I looked up and down Lakeview Circle, with the sun blinding me as I squinted toward the highway. "Is it a black Mercedes?"

"The white one," he said.

I heard a noise and turned to Fate. He had lapsed into the zipper routine with his flight suit.

Zip . . . zip . . . zip-zip . . . zip.

"Your brother's Lincoln?"

"Heck no."

Zip-zip . . . zip.

"Then what?" I said, grabbing his hand.

Fate gestured at the Beasleys' place. I followed his line of sight, but saw nothing out of the ordinary. Then he shook his finger at the far corner, where the driveway snaked behind the house. There . . . just barely visible . . . was the rear end of a car . . . a white Lexus!

"How long has it been there?" I said, leaning over the rail.

"Well, now. Let's see . . . I took lunch at one-thirty . . . Walked over to the Rib Shack. Mind you, I typically brown bag it. But it wasn't my normal working day."

"Fate!"

"I returned at two-thirty on the button, and that fine one was parked exactly where you see her now . . . You ever tried the Shack Sampler Platter?"

I let go of Fate's hand, scrambling down the steps. Behind me, I heard *zip-zip-zip . . . zip.*

Sixty seconds later, I was pacing in front of Betty Jean's range, all jittery and broken out in a sweat. "Where is she?" I said.

"Just pull in the reins," Betty Jean said, pointing a turquoise fingernail at me. "I had every intention of calling you as soon as Clayton got home."

"You didn't say a word about any of this earlier. When did it happen?"

"Ever heard of a woman's intuition?"

A rabbit ran across my grave. *Never dispute Ariana's intuition,* Gustav had warned last night. It felt like I was living in parallel universes.

Change my way of thinking.

"Okay, fair enough. What gives?" I said.

"Tracie called last night and told me how you had left my number for her. By the way, that was an excellent move on your part."

"I did that . . . I absolutely did that—"

"Simmer down. She apologized for not being neighborly when you moved in, but more or less gave me the same picture you painted . . . in her own words, of course."

"Is she still mad at—"

"Down boy."

"Betty Jean, when can I see her?"

"Sit!" Betty Jean said, pointing at the table.

I followed orders and dropped in a chair.

"We're dealing with a delicate matter here, so I need you to trim back on the adrenaline."

"But I can't stand it . . . This is my moment. I can fix everything. Rip off the Band-Aid."

"Listen to yourself. A Band-Aid? . . . *Seriously?*" Betty Jean hitched her hands on her hips.

"What's wrong with that?"

"Does the Beatles' tune, *I Me Mine,* mean anything to you?"

"You're losing me," I said.

"I've only known Tracie for a few hours, but I can assure you of one thing. That beautiful woman, the love of your life, isn't built for speed."

"Betty Jean, I've been married to her for four years and I know her a lot better than you."

"Anything you say, *Trev.* But for starters, you've been married five years."

"I—I know that."

"Then think about this. We're on a journey and driving down a long, open road. The sky is blue and filled with big, fluffy clouds. The trees are green and birds are singing. Tracie wants to slow down and take in the scenery. She longs to experience a full life and savor every moment the two of you share. And all of a sudden, you zip her onto the expressway to some unknown destination, a place that doesn't hold the same magic as the scenic drive."

"Why do you have to make this into some kind of touchy-feely thing? Roads are designed to get you places. Who even cares about the sky and stupid birds that poop all over your paint-job? Why don't we get all bent out of shape about the weather forecast while we're at it? Oh, my goodness. It's going to rain today," I mocked.

"Where's a real man when you need one?" Betty Jean said.

"Life is more complicated than some cute little bird analogy."

"Would you like me to simplify it for you?" She gave me a hard look with her big, blue eyes.

The offer sounded tempting, but I knew for a fact it was a trap. So I just nodded.

"Forget about Tracie."

I stood up to protest, letting Betty Jean know she had crossed a line. "Aren't you supposed to be—like—fixing things between us?"

"How straight do you want it, *Trev*?"

"Right here," I said, pointing between my eyes.

"You're unfixable."

"Does Tracie know you're talking to me like this?"

"We had a nice chat, and she asked if she could stay with us a few days."

"She's not coming home?"

"You're not ready, believe me."

Change my way of thinking, I reminded myself.

I sat down and pulled out **TREVOR'S DAILY Rx** and took a dose of my own medicine. "I'll do better, Betty Jean. From this moment forward. I promise. But I have to see her, if only for a second. Then I'll leave . . . I just need to look into her eyes and see if she still believes in me. She's all I've got."

Betty Jean must have pitied me because she seemed to melt right then and there. She stepped to one side, and standing in the hallway behind her was Tracie.

My Tracie.

"Hi," she said.

Chapter 46

Atlanta, Georgia
Monday, October 14th
11:00 P.M.

The Mercedes pulled into the Arts Center warehouse as the loading dock door lowered behind it. Gustav climbed out and strolled around to the passenger side, playing the perfect gentleman as he took Ariana by the hand.

"How does it feel to be chauffeured around in style for a change?" Gustav said. He surprised her by doing a little two-step.

"I just wonder why it took so long," Ariana said. She wrapped an arm around Gustav's waist, her stilettos echoing off the brick architecture as they swayed. The sequins on her gown sparkled in the blue light.

"We must have music," Gustav said, in the moment. He took her in his arms, humming a bar of *Moon River*.

"That's nice, but don't think for a second this makes us even."

"The night is young, my darling."

"I spent time behind bars for you. Do you have any idea why I do such things?"

"It's your job?" Gustav said.

"I do them for you. Perhaps now you can clearly appreciate my devotion."

"From tonight forward, there's a new rule," Gustav said. "It's all for *us*." He took her by the hand and strolled over to the lab.

"Why did you interrupt our celebration to bring me here?" Ariana said.

"I forgot to lock away the bag. It will only take a second."

"I'll open the storage area for you."

As they entered the lab, Ariana crossed the room to a supply cabinet. She leaned around one side, swinging it open like a door. Reaching in, she flipped on a switch, lighting up wall-to-wall shelves stockpiled with bags of cocaine.

"I see the inventory has arrived for the initial wave of new clients. Our first Fortune 500 delivery is scheduled for next week," Ariana said, stepping back into the lab.

"An exciting phase of our new business model," Gustav said, unzipping the leather bag. "The preliminary drug testing turned up a vice president, three directors, and fourteen managers. We will report three of the managers to human resources. The remaining will be offered deals they cannot refuse."

"How significant of an opportunity do you foresee?"

"This company, alone, has thousands of employees. We could easily secure a few hundred users by the time the vans are in full operation."

"And how many will refuse our offer?"

"None . . . if they wish to retain their jobs. In this market, blackmail is but a small price to pay for saving one's career. Besides, they are all users. We are simply requesting they buy from us. If they do not wish to take advantage of our excellent services, then the true test results go to HR." Gustav finished emptying the bag, and then turned it upside-down, shaking it. "*Hmm.*"

"What's wrong?"

"That's funny. There is only one bag."

"The cocaine? How many were you expecting?"

"Based on our accounts with the Dorseys, I'd say there should be nine."

"But the police seized two on the night we shut them down," Ariana said.

"An unfortunate setback . . . It slipped my mind. But that leaves seven, so we have six missing."

Ariana slipped up behind Gustav and massaged his shoulders. "After everything that has happened, do you think Mr. Wentworth could be so foolish as to steal from us?"

"You know him better than I do."

"He's not a dealer, if that's what you're suggesting."

Gustav picked up the bag and stuffed the paraphernalia inside. "A woman's intuition comes with a price."

Ariana smiled. "Does this mean what I think it does, darling?"

"I had hoped to continue our distribution at the Parkway 12 address. It was one of our largest hubs outside the city. With the Dorseys out of way, the authorities would not suspect the location to re-open under new management. But I'm afraid we must suspend our activities there—permanently."

"And Mr. Trevor Wentworth?"

"Based on what is missing, the liability is too much to ignore. I'm afraid he has run out of excuses. Next time we meet, he will be begging for mercy."

Ariana retrieved the bag and stowed it in the secure area. She turned out the lights and locked up. "Are we done here?"

"For tonight, yes."

Taking Gustav's hand, Ariana said, "Then we have unfinished business at the Ritz."

Chapter 47

Suwanee, Georgia
Tuesday, October 15th
7:30 A.M.

I was beside myself for a couple of reasons. Instead of the usual wake-up call at the door this morning, I received a text from Tracie inviting me to meet her at the lake. I promptly hopped out of bed, brewed a cup of joe, and was presently kneeling in our walk-in closet rustling through a pile of clothes.

All indications from the air seeping in around the tarp suggested we were in-store for a perfect day. I pulled out a pair of red shorts Tracie had given me last spring, an Alice Cooper t-shirt, and a wool sweater to cover up the *No More Mr. Nice Guy* slogan. I slipped on my loafers, grabbed the coffee, and scrambled out the door.

When my shoes hit the dock, Tracie was already kicked back in an Adirondack with what looked like her well-worn Bible in her lap. She was sipping from a Kenny Chesney mug, one I recognized from Betty Jean's kitchen.

"Can you get over this place?" Tracie said, twisting for a look at the lake. Then she sank down in the chair.

A smoky layer of fog hovered above the water's surface. Every few seconds a swarm of ducks would swim into view, quack, and disappear. The palm trees next to the beach rattled in a light breeze, and across the lake a gabled roof peeked out amongst the tall Georgia pines. On the beach just past the dock, the yellow sailboat basked in the morning light.

"Some trailer park, *huh*?" I joked.

"It's like being on a tropical island."

For some reason, even the rush-hour traffic on Peachtree Parkway had taken a holiday, bowing in reverence to the occasion.

"As it turns out, we acquired a spectacular view of the lake," I said, looking up the shoreline at our demi-doublewide. "Of course, I can't take credit for the selection."

"You did good."

"*I did?*"

"Tell me everything you know about Parkway Community."

"There's not much to it. You've met Clayton and Betty Jean. They're here because of a financial setback, but I don't know much about it. Next door to them are Walt and Jess Mobley. They're retired academics who have an observatory on top of their trailer."

"You mean . . . one of those giant telescopes?"

"We'll get to that later. Thanks to yours truly, Walt has most recently taken up golf. And the neighborhood now features a par three course. Around the bank over there, you have Dabney Chalker, aka Ted Nugent. He's into hunting and runs a charity that donates fresh game to the needy."

Tracie laughed. "Nugent's the rock 'n' roll guy, right?"

"Where did that come from?" I said.

"There are things you don't know about me."

"A word of advice—you might want to steer clear of Ted. Next there's Ol' Lady Wilbanks across from the office. Word is she single-handedly shut down the tennis court. That's where Clayton parks his rig now."

"Clayton drives a truck?" Tracie said.

"According to Fate, it's six hundred horsepower of raw muscle."

"Who's Fate?"

"He's the property manager. You may not remember him, but he's an absolute nut-job when it comes to enforcing rules and regulations. And don't tell anyone, but I kind of enjoy listening to his stories. They're like windows into another time and place."

"I can't wait to meet him."

"That's about all I know," I said, pausing. "Oh, I almost forgot one."

"You're turning red."

"Wait until you hear about our next-door neighbor."

Tracie's back stiffened as she looked up at the street.

"Get this . . . Her name is Tammy Faye Fox," I said.

"So she's a southern girl?"

"That—and a palm reader."

"A real one?"

"She graduated from something called the Psychic Tea Room. Isn't that insane?"

"Has she read your fortune?"

"Oh, no," I said.

"How well do you know her?"

I weighed my words carefully. Bobbing my head, I laughed like she had said something funny. "You see—she's got this neon sign shaped like a hand in her front window. You'll get the picture after dark tonight."

"Why did you just do that head-bob thing?" Tracie said, studying me.

"I don't know, but get a load of this. The name of her business is *Psy-Chic*, with a hyphen. Get it?"

"I think I'm beginning to," Tracie said.

"You might want to stay away from her as well."

Tracie raised an eyebrow. "It sounds like you're afraid of her."

A woman's intuition, I thought. At the moment it had about as much charm as a deadly weapon. Changing the subject, I said, "This is my favorite spot in the neighborhood. Of course, with twenty-seven residents scattered up and down the street, there's still a lot of unexplored territory."

"Wow," Tracie said, mostly to herself. A smile appeared on her face.

"Okay, so I'm going out on a limb here, but I vaguely remember that look."

"Just listen to yourself. You haven't talked like this . . . since forever. You actually care about these people and seem to know something about each one. How did that happen?"

"*These people?*" I said.

"Trevor, it's like you're home. You're living an adventure, and just maybe you're discovering something important about yourself."

I scratched my head, somewhat amused. *Tracie seems to be warming up to Parkway. More importantly, she likes me here.* Looking over at her, I gritted my teeth and wondered if what I was about to say was going to hurt. "You know, I hated this place when we moved in. And I particularly didn't care for the neighbors, even though I didn't really know them. But that was before everything happened. As it turns out, the community is special, and the residents all have character."

"Including Tammy Faye Fox?" Tracie said.

"There's an exception to every rule," I said, counting on humor to get me through the next part. "I'm about to take a risk and admit something you may not like, but I'm going to say it because . . . I've changed my way of thinking."

"It's going to take a lot to spoil all this."

"Don't say that. Just let me get it out, and then you can be the judge."

"*Uh-oh.*" Tracie gripped the armrests on her chair.

I looked away to avoid eye contact. But after that I just let it fly. It came out like a dam bursting.

"There's a quarter of a million in cocaine under our trailer."

Chapter 48

Suwanee, Georgia
Tuesday, October 15th
9:00 A.M.

"Two hundred and fifty thousand dollars!" Tracie screamed, coming straight out of her chair. The Bible slid off her lap and plopped open on the dock.

"*Shhh,*" I said, planting my hand over her mouth. "The neighbors . . ."

Tracie slapped it down. "Don't neighbor me," she said. "You're involved in this—this—drug ring."

A drug ring? I thought. Before I could reply, Tracie picked up the Bible and shoved it at me.

"Give me your hand," she said.

I didn't hesitate, and she pressed it flat on the Bible.

"Do you promise to tell the truth at the risk of losing everything near and dear to your heart?"

"Of course, I do. But please . . . sit down."

Tracie studied the chair, then opted for the railing instead. She was clinging to the Bible, like it was a life preserver. I kept my distance, just in case she decided to throw it at me.

"It was the day before you took off—"

"Don't even try to pin this on me," Tracie said.

"You want the truth, so I'm giving it to you—no matter how crazy it sounds." I waited for her to settle down. "Last weekend I discovered a bag of white powder crammed in the guest bathroom vent. I had a good idea what it was, but wanted to be sure. So I took it to the interview on Sunday, thinking Gustav might be able to identify it. After all, it's his line of work."

"How did you connect with this goon?"

"He picked my résumé off a social media website."

"So you want me to believe it was pure coincidence that you accidently came across a bag of cocaine, and Gustav happens to be in the drug testing business?"

"Sort of. At the time I thought it was . . . *good fortune*?"

"That's about the stupidest thing you've said today. Why didn't you tell me any of this?"

"Tracie, we had serious money problems. What would you have done?"

"That's not the point."

"The truth is—I was curious about what it was worth, if it was the real thing. So I took it along to the interview, and like magic Gustav tells me to take the test kit home and try it on some fake prescription drugs he gave me. Only, I couldn't wait. I went to the parking lot and tested the powder, and sure enough it was cocaine."

"But you still didn't say anything."

"I came home, got up the next morning, and went to the driving range. When I returned, you had taken off with the trailer."

"Did it not occur to you to confide in me?"

"I later searched the Internet and discovered that a bag of this stuff is worth, like, fifty thousand dollars. You want honesty, right?" I looked away. "Well, it was as if I'd won the lottery. I imagined all our problems going . . . *poof*."

"Wait a minute. You said the number was a quarter of a million."

"As you know, the guy unfastened all the connections before he hauled the trailer away. When I returned from the driving range and saw the predicament, I went around back and discovered a bunch of Ziplocs in the ductwork. In fact, there were an additional six. Back inside, I learned you had Gustav's test kit, including the original bag of cocaine."

"And it didn't occur to you to call someone?"

"I called you a zillion times, but you wouldn't answer."

"Then you should have contacted the police."

"I had plans for a second interview and needed to return his stuff. Did I mention Gustav wanted it back *really* bad? That was all I could think about. In an attempt to delay him and get to you, I wasn't thinking straight."

"And then what happened?"

"First and foremost, I wanted you to come home. But you also had the kit, and I figured I could kill two birds with one stone. My backup plan, honestly, still included the drugs as an option. That was, until I found out Gustav knew about the cocaine, *and* the so-called fake prescription turned out to be oxycodone."

"But you returned everything to him."

"I gave him the test kit, oxy, and one bag of cocaine to keep his hit woman off my case."

"That's the one who showed up at Tybee . . . Ariana?"

"In my car, no less."

"Does he know about the rest of the drugs?"

"That's what I'm not sure of. When I came to my senses, I realized I couldn't let him put all of this stuff on the street."

"Trevor, you have to go to the police."

"Gustav and Ariana are watching me. They haven't said anything about the rest of the goods, but it's clear they're not going away. If I slip up, it ain't Santa Claus that's coming to town."

"And you're sure the rest is still under the trailer?"

"Do you want to see it?"

"Maybe later," Tracie said. "What're we going to do?"

"I'm still working on a plan . . . Preferably something that appeases Gustav and doesn't involve jail time."

"Is it safe to stay here?"

"As safe as any other place. They've tracked me from one end of the state to the other."

Tracie set the Bible on the rail. "Were you seriously considering selling those drugs?"

"Not in a million years," I said. "I'm pleading temporary insanity . . . We lost everything, remember?"

"Hold on. Six bags of cocaine at fifty thousand each . . . That's three hundred thousand dollars."

"I may have failed to mention an incident over at our old neighborhood."

"You didn't—"

"There wasn't a felony involved, trust me."

"Then to answer your earlier question, we haven't lost everything," Tracie said, taking my hand.

I looked around and spotted Clayton headed our way. Turning to Tracie, I said, "Can you ever forgive me?"

"Let's just say we have a lot to figure out."

Chapter 49

Suwanee, Georgia
Tuesday, October 15th
10:00 A.M.

When Clayton stepped on the dock, Tracie smiled and gave him a hug. Then she squeezed me, like our lives depended on it, and took off for the Beasleys' place without another word.

"That Tracie's a fine woman," Clayton said. "It's good to see the two of you working things out."

"Clayton," I said, shifting gears. "I want to apologize for the way I've behaved."

"Where in the world did that come from?"

"Starting with last week when you first introduced yourself."

"You mean . . . when you had your bobber stuck up in the tree?"

"You came over to help, but I had . . . well . . . a chip on my shoulder."

"*Trev*, the way I see it a man's bound to be out of sorts when he's experiencing a streak of bad luck. I'd feel differently if it hadn't turned out to be something important, like Tracie leaving you."

"That's all good, Clayton. But it doesn't excuse the way I treated you. If it's not asking too much, I'd like you to forgive me."

"We'll speak of it no more."

"And I wouldn't mind hearing your story . . . the one about how you and Betty Jean landed in Parkway."

"Tracie asked the same thing last night. Maybe we'll cover it with both of you. And I know exactly how to do it."

"If I ever act out again, just run me over with your rig."

Clayton laughed, patting me on the back. "What I really came for was to see what I could do to help you two lovebirds."

"I'm glad you mentioned it." My eyes drifted over to the beach. "Tell me about the sailboat over there."

"That old thing? It's what you call a daysailer."

"I've watched the bigger ones up at Lake Lanier."

"Well, those don't exactly operate on a small lake like this. Believe it or not, I made her with my own hands."

"You built a sailboat?"

"I used to sail on that big, blue sea due east of here."

"The Atlantic . . . You must take it seriously."

"Used to . . . until Betty Jean and I decided to settle down. I built this one just to keep a toe in the water. You interested in sailing?"

"I've been around boats most of my life, only I'm more into power craft. But I just remembered that Tracie said she'd love to sail one day."

"This one will do the trick for a beginner. See up front behind the bow . . . That's what you call a cuddy cabin. It's got just enough room to carry along flotation devices and a picnic basket. As you can see, the rest is an open cockpit outfitted with a tiller, centerboard, and mainsheet."

"What does she draw?"

"Maybe fifteen inches. She's designed to sit high in the water. I've got the sails up at the house."

"She looks to be about twelve feet long, and the mast . . . maybe eighteen feet. That's quite a paint-job. What's with the yellow?"

"Oh, that? It happens to be Pop's favorite color. He gets a hoot out of seeing her on the water with sails a' flying."

"Were you serious about doing something for Tracie and me?"

"I'd be honored."

"How about teaching me to sail?"

"You really think that's going to help?"

"*Me*—I'm built for speed. But I'd like to do it for Tracie." I gazed out across the water, where a gentle breeze was making ripples all the way to the far shore. Then I added, "And that picnic idea sounds interesting, too."

"This isn't some harebrained idea of yours, like fishing?"

"Not even close," I said, giving us both a good laugh.

"'Cause if you were to hook that little woman of yours in the lip, it's game over, sport."

"It's not so much sailing lessons, as it is romance lessons."

"Now you're talking."

"This may be just what the doctor ordered."

"In that case, I have an idea," Clayton said. "A big, beautiful idea."

Chapter 50

Suwanee, Georgia
Tuesday, October 15th
1:00 P.M.

After my first sailing lesson with Clayton, I walked across the beach with a spring in my step, reviewing the key points. "Raise the sail directly into the wind . . . Put the centerboard down once you're underway . . . Tack heading into the wind, and jibe with it behind you . . . Always sit on the windward side of the cockpit . . . Ease off the mainsail if you feel the boat tipping."

I had a new lease on life and considered stopping off to see what Tracie and Betty Jean were up to. But my stomach growled, and I opted to head home for lunch. When I reached the driveway, I spotted Fate sitting on the front steps.

"What brings you over this fine day?" I spouted, flashing a smile.

Fate was nothing but serious as he stood up. "I'm afraid it's official business," he said, meeting me under the palm. "You and Clayton been out for a sail?"

"That right," I said. "What can I do for you?

"First of all, be forewarned. I'm just doing my duty."

"I'll keep that in mind."

"Folks count on me to enforce the rules and regulations, regardless of who's involved. That's the sworn responsibility of the property manager."

"I believe we've covered this ground before."

"You may want to sit down," Fate said, offering me the hood of my car. "I'm afraid I have some bad news."

I leaned against Goldfinger as Fate hung close to the palm. There was something about him I'd never seen. For a moment I wondered if he was about to start up with the zipper, but I sensed he was beyond that phase.

"They got the fourteenth signature on that petition this morning," Fate said. "It happened while you and Clayton were on the lake."

"Seems kind of sudden," I said.

"You want me to give it to you straight?"

"Sure. You've been nothing but fair, Fate."

"Well, sir, while you two were out there on the water, I was at the office scrubbing Clayton's blackwalls. Sometimes he pays me to clean 'em up, seeing how the road grime makes a mess. Now I want to be perfectly clear, it don't interfere with my official duties—"

"Fate."

"Anyway, that was when one of the residents marched right up and slapped the petition in my hand. And I'm telling you, she was madder than a hornet, that one. So I looked at the paper, and there it was—number fourteen."

"Who was it?"

"I ain't supposed to tell, at least not until the board of directors certifies the count."

Without thinking, I reached up and grabbed a handful of hair. "That's all you can tell me?"

"Now I ain't advising you what to do, but in this particular case it just so happens there aren't any rules against asking questions or making guesses."

"You said it was a *she* . . . a woman?"

"No mistaking it, no *sirree*."

"Did she say why she was angry?"

"In a roundabout way. She was mostly talking to herself, but she did fire off something like: 'After all I've done for him, he's down at the dock with that brazen little hussy.'"

"That's no hussy. She's my wife—Tracie."

"Is she the one with the Lexus?"

"One and the same."

"Has she been stirring up trouble since she pulled into town?" Fate said.

Just then I saw something move out of the corner of my eye. I looked next door and noticed a curtain swaying. It was the window with the *Psy-Chic* sign.

"Tammy Faye Fox," I snarled.

"If it was in my power, I'd nail her for that hussy comment."

"Well, it ought to be. Where do we go from here?"

"I took an oath to do things by the book, so I rushed that petition over to the board chairman, thinking the matter was duly out of my hands," Fate said. "And this is where I may have misled you earlier. She told me there was a little-known provision in the bylaws that kicks into motion with that fourteenth signature—that is—until the next board meeting. In fact, she instructed me to give notice as soon as you returned home."

"What does the provision say?"

Fate raised his shoulders, like he was standing at attention. "As an authorized agent of the Parkway Community board of directors, it is hereby my duty to notify you that you have three days to comply with the official covenants, or said trailer at

Parkway 12 must be removed from the premises by the end of the third day."

"That's Friday. Are you kidding?"

"I never kid about business," Fate said. "But I've been meaning to ask you—where exactly is the other half of that trailer?"

"It's in South Georgia."

"Did the aforementioned hussy haul it down there?"

I gave Fate a look, but could tell he intended nothing by the comment. "Call her Tracie . . . And yes, she took the trailer."

"Sounds to me like you need to have another one of those meetings down at the dock."

"That's not a bad idea," I said.

Fate stuffed his hands in his pockets. "I'm sorry about this, *Trev*. I've become quite fond of you. Sometimes I just hate doing my job." He started down the driveway.

"Hey, Fate," I called after him. He stopped and turned. "That board chairman . . . what's his name?"

He glanced across the street and back at me. "It's not a *he*, no *sirree*. It's a *she* . . . Betty Jean Beasley."

Chapter 51

Suwanee, Georgia
Tuesday, October 15th
1:30 P.M.

I tagged along with Fate as he headed up Lakeview Circle for the Parkway office, parting ways when we were within sight of the tennis court. I wasn't about to let anyone or anything knock me off the horse I had been riding all morning. The carnage left in my wake was still fresh in my mind, and I knew for a fact I didn't want to go back there. *Change my way of thinking*, I reminded myself. And then it happened.

BOOM! BOOM! BOOM! . . . KA-BOOM!

I hit the ground, facedown in the middle of Lakeview with my hands over my head. The final KA-BOOM! ricocheted across the lake like a thunderclap, and then washed over me a second time on the rebound. I could feel the hair on my neck standing on end.

I used my elbows to crawl into the grass on the side of the street, lifting my head like a turtle poking out of his shell. Fully expecting to see a mushroom cloud rising above my house, I was instantly thankful Tracie had decided not to move in last night. As I eased to my feet for a peek at whatever disaster had struck, there was no visible sign of damage anywhere. Not even a smoke plume. Dusting myself off, I spotted Clayton down at the dock, straightening chairs as if nothing had happened.

I sprinted past my house and down the bank to the lake to check on him. I knew he would have a good explanation for whatever had just taken place. Halfway across the gangway another round of explosions ripped loose, only this time they were close enough to rattle my teeth.

BOOM! BOOM! BOOM! . . . KA-BOOM!

I hit the deck and almost fell in the water, but managed to roll on my side and tuck into a fetal position. The shockwaves from the blasts recoiled across the water and shook the dock. By the time things settled down, I had a sick feeling in my stomach. With the attack so close, there was a good chance Clayton might have been blown to smithereens. I looked up, and to my surprise he was rummaging about like everything was A-OK.

Climbing to my feet, my knees wobbled as I limped out on the dock.

"Clayton!" I screamed. "Get down . . . we're under attack."

He hadn't seen me coming and did a double-take when he caught sight of me hunched over, wild-eyed, and stunned. "Why is your leg bleeding?" he said. "What did you say?"

"That-that explosion," I said, expecting the next salvo any second. I had no doubt we were about to be vaporized on the spot. "Are you all right?"

"Oh, that," Clayton said, casting his eyes to the shoreline. "Ted's zeroing in a new scope."

Following Clayton's line of sight, I noticed what looked like an archery target fifty yards down the beach. The entire center was missing, with bits and pieces scattered all over the sand. Snapping my head around to Ted's trailer, I spotted the Ford

Bronco and a man in an olive green razorback, camo cutoffs, and hunting boots. There was an orange bandana tied around his head, and below it a ponytail draped over his shoulder. He had on a pair of sleek-looking sunglasses that gave the distinct impression: *Don't tread on me.*

I was taking it all in when a real shocker hit me. In his hands was the biggest weapon I had ever seen in my life. If I didn't know better, I would have sworn it was a missile launcher.

"Ted Nugent," was all I managed to mumble.

"That there's one of the nicest people God ever put on this earth," Clayton said to me. "Of course, if you mess with him . . . may the force be with you."

"Roger, wilco, and out," I said.

"Folks feel the community is a safer place with Ted over in number fourteen."

"That man runs a charity?" I said, recalling my prior discussion with Betty Jean.

"That's right. He has a freezer full of game, just in case you've changed your mind about the food offer."

"Clayton, the board of directors doesn't have a problem with Ted firing that cannon in the neighborhood?"

"Parkway has always supported outdoor activities."

"What if he misses . . . and a stray round takes me out while I'm sailing?"

"No worries," Clayton said. "Ted don't miss."

"Oh, *jeez.* So you're telling me—*he's* a model citizen?"

"He's planning to sponsor a nature hike for orphans in the spring. You might want to think about signing up as a counselor. The neighbors all warm up to that kind of stuff."

"That reminds me. I have a question about our board chairman."

"I'll answer it if I can."

“Why is Betty Jean trying to run me out of here?”

Clayton rubbed his chin, and then cut his eyes at me. “Now that . . . you’re gonna have to take up with her. But it’ll have to wait. The girls have gone out for a spell.”

Betty Jean headed inside Starbucks to place an order as Tracie found a table on the patio. She grabbed a chair, took out her phone, and dialed.

“Neely here,” he answered.

“Where are you?” Tracie said.

“Do you have an update?”

“You might say that.”

“Have you met with him?”

“Just like we agreed,” Tracie said. “And he’s convinced me the bag and all its contents have been returned to Gustav.”

“What makes you so sure?”

“Because I trust my husband.”

“You do realize we’re talking about drug dealers. Big time. These guys are killers.”

“Trevor has issues, but drugs aren’t one of them. You should forget about him and focus on the real villains.”

“We ran the VIN on his car, and do you know what we found?”

“He’s past due on the payments.”

“The lease was purchased by a shell company owned by an offshore entity controlled by one, Dr. Frederick Gustafson.”

“The last time I checked, there’s nothing illegal about leasing a car,” Tracie said.

“But you’ve got to admit it’s interesting.”

"Maybe Gustav's going *legit*, I don't know. But listen to me. Trevor turned over the goods, so his part in all of this is over. *Finished*. Do you hear me?"

Betty Jean came out with their coffee and joined Tracie at the table.

"It's an ongoing investigation. That's all I can say," Neely said.

"You also made a commitment, and I want to collect—*now*."

"You can't be serious. This is far from over."

"Not my problem. We're done, okay?"

"Tracie, it could be dangerous."

"I want the trailer delivered by the end of the week." Tracie hung up and glanced across the table.

Betty Jean handed Tracie a latte, raised an eyebrow, and smiled.

Chapter 52

Suwanee, Georgia
Tuesday, October 15th
4:30 P.M.

Hefting a duffel bag onto my shoulder, I slammed Goldfinger's trunk and limped inside the Nifty-Thrifty. Penny was posted behind the counter with a smile that widened as I entered. A strange beat was thumping out of the eight-track speakers.

"My newest, most favorite client," she beamed.

Plopping the bag next to the cash register, I loosened the drawstring. "Just wait 'til you see what treasures I have for you today."

Penny seemed to be in a festive mood and grabbed a clipboard, bouncing her head to the music. When I dumped the contents out, the enthusiasm evaporated before my eyes. A pair of pants slipped off the counter and hit the floor.

"What's this?"

"Practically everything I own," I said. "The outfit I'm wearing is also available."

"These are all *guy* things."

"My loss is your gain. Figure up the damage, and I'll be out of your hair." I looked around and spotted a rack of men's clothing as Penny picked through the pile. But I could tell her heart wasn't in it.

"This is more than you brought in last time," she said. "Don't you have anything else in the ladies' department?"

"These are top-shelf," I said, taking a jacket by the lapel. "Just feel that fabric."

"Hey, don't insult me. I know fashion, okay?"

I held up my hands. "My apologies, but you do understand there's a gold mine here?"

"It's just . . ."

"What?"

"Menswear doesn't turn as well."

"Yeah, but you and me have an understanding, right?"

"I'm afraid you're only as good as your last sale in this business." Penny finished sorting through the clothes, making notes on the clipboard. "Fifteen pairs of dress slacks, a dozen pinpoint oxfords, eight golf shirts, and two wool suits. We're looking at a market value of five hundred and fifty dollars. Your share is half when they sell. I'll need an address and phone number."

"How about advancing me two hundred, and you keep all the profits?"

"No can do," she said. "You know the policy."

I leaned across the counter, close to her ear. "Come on. You know they don't really appreciate you around here. You've got to look out for—"

Penny planted a drugstore fingernail on the tip of my nose. "The ruse is over, pal. Everything is by the book from now on."

I made a strategic decision to back off, but as I did I noticed a display next to the counter. It was a southwestern skirt in vibrant rust and turquoise tones. Then it struck me. It was one of Tracie's. *Oh, jeez,* I thought. *Look at what I've done.* Taking a second look, I noticed that the skirt had been matched with a woven blouse, coordinating scarf, distressed leather belt, and silver jewelry. Peeking from beneath the skirt was an exotic pair of cowgirl boots.

"That's an amazing display," I said.

The glow returned to Penny's face as she pushed a strand of hair behind her ear. "Thank you."

There's my girl. I crossed my arms. "What's the story with the boots?"

"They're awesome, aren't they? The owner claims they're Australian, but I've never seen anything like them."

"Are, *uh*, all the sizes sort of . . . proportioned to the skirt?"

"Hang on." Penny took down the display and disappeared in the back. Five minutes later she waltzed out, twirling as she came through the doorway. "*Ta-da!*"

I couldn't take my eyes off of her. It was the perfect look. Absolutely perfect. "How much for the entire outfit?" I said.

"You do realize you brought in the skirt, right?"

"Not important," I said. "How much?"

"One-sixty-five."

"Can you gift wrap them?"

"You don't want to haggle?"

"Did I not say you were going to be glad to see me?"

"I have Nifty-Thrifty totes in the back."

As an afterthought, I decided to crunch the numbers in my head. When I was done, I said, "I'm afraid I may have a slight problem."

Penny's smile drooped. "What do you mean?"

"I can offer you one hundred and thirty-six dollars and seventy-five cents . . . one-thirteen-seventy-five in cash, and the rest on credit card."

"Are you seriously that hard up?" Penny glanced out the window. "You're driving a BMW."

"I'm offering you every penny to my name—*Penny*."

"Then let's make it an even one-thirty-five. I'll take the rest out of your share of the consignment sales."

I pulled into the Parkway entrance, watching Goldfinger's fuel gauge bounce just above empty as I spotted Fate. He was coming across the tennis court faster than I had ever seen him move, waving his hands in the air. Not far away, Ol' Lady Wilbanks's kids were giving it their best on the trampoline. I parked in the middle of the street, waiting for Fate to scramble over. It was after five, so I was positive it wasn't good news.

"I was hoping you'd show up," Fate said, stopping in the grass next to the street. "This letter came for you while you were out. They needed a signature." He stepped over to the car, then back on the grass.

"Is there a problem?" I said, taking another look at the fuel indicator. It dipped, so I switched off the engine and opened the letter. A refund for my cable deposit was inside—one hundred and fifty less a twenty-five dollar rush-charge.

"Do you know anyone who drives a black van?"

"What sort of van?" I said, folding the check.

"One of those delivery-type vehicles. They're everywhere. They run up and down the highway all day long."

"I'm not expecting another package, if that's what you're asking."

"I spotted the sucker right up there on the shoulder of Peachtree Parkway." Fate pointed to a spot about thirty yards away.

I looked over my shoulder. "Maybe they had a flat. There's nobody there now."

"That's what they want you to think," Fate said. "But right over there next to the property line is an old logging road."

I followed his finger to a row of pines, but didn't see a road or a van, for that matter. "I'm missing something," I said, shaking my head.

"A service truck, like the one that brought your check, used to pull down that road and sit there for hours at a time. I haven't seen 'em for weeks now, but they showed up again today."

"Why would I know anything about it?"

"Well, sir. They always preferred parking at the end of the road right behind the Dorsey Place."

"You mean, my place?"

"It wasn't yours at the time. But this new van, it's got me all worked up again."

I knew he was right about that, so I leaned across the seat and focused on the gap between Tammy Fox's trailer and mine. The pine trees ran all the way to the lake, only there was no van down there. "Have you notified the police?"

"No *sirree*. Ted used to sneak in there with his gun. But they would hightail it out of there, like a jackrabbit.

I started the engine. "What do you say we both keep an eye on it?"

"That's a fine idea," Fate said. "Don't forget about that eviction notice."

Pulling into my driveway, Tammy Fox's sign was already beginning to glow. I got out of the car and made a beeline over to the Beasleys'. After a couple of knocks, Tracie came to the door.

"Hey, *Trace*," I said. "Did you and Betty Jean have a good day?"

"She's wonderful, just like you said."

"I was wondering . . . Maybe you'd like to do something tonight."

"Like what?" Tracie said.

Suddenly remembering my cash position, I cringed. "How about joining me at the house for beer and pizza?"

Tracie looked across the street, rubbing her arms like she was cold. "*Uh*, I'm a bit tired."

"A drink might warm you up."

"That's sweet. But let's do it some other time."

"Will I see you at the dock in the morning?"

"Bright and early."

"One more thing. Could you ask Betty Jean to step out for a minute?"

"I'm afraid she's unavailable," Tracie said, reaching for the door handle. "But I'll let her know you dropped by."

"*Trace—*"

"Goodnight, Trevor."

Chapter 53

Suwanee, Georgia
Wednesday, October 16th
7:15 A.M.

The sun had just cleared the treetops, when an unidentified object slammed down on the dock's tin roof. Tracie jumped, spilling coffee as a metallic ringing resonated in her ears. Two seconds later there was a splash, and she climbed out of her chair for a look in the water. Shaking the lingering drips off her hand, she spotted ripples spreading out across the lake.

Behind her she heard a mysterious whirring, accompanied by a series of bumps and rattles. When it stopped, a pair of crunchy-sounding footsteps approached, and she turned to find a man in plaid slacks making his way across the gangway. He had on a red shirt and dark cap, wielding a golf club that was long enough to be a fishing pole. Behind him, a golf cart was parked on the beach.

"Morning, ma'am," he said, tipping his hat. "Did you happen to see a number-two Titleist land anywhere in the vicinity?"

Tracie pointed to the lake, where the ripples had all but disappeared.

"*Hellfire!*" the man yelled, snatching off the cap. "That's going to cost me a stroke."

"Sorry," Tracie said, feigning sympathy. *What is this guy's name? . . . Trevor told me.* Then it hit her. "You must be Walt."

He froze, diverting his eyes from the splashdown site. "What's it to you?"

"I'm Tracie—Tracie Wentworth—a houseguest of Betty Jean Beasley." She waited for a response, but instead Walt pumped his eyebrows. He gave her a nervous look and snapped the cap tight over his forehead. "Are you all right?"

"You've just ruined a perfectly good round of golf, young lady. Does that answer your question?"

"Me? . . . What did I do?" Tracie said, her jaw dropping.

"What in the name of Arnold Palmer are you doing out here this early in the morning?"

"You *are* Walt Mobley, right?"

"That depends."

"Well, you see, I was enjoying sunup, reading my Bible, and having a cup of coffee. That is, before your golf ball nearly scared me to death."

"*Pshaw*," he said, waving her off. "But that's mighty peculiar . . . what you said about the Beasleys. Don't you live over in the Dorsey Place?"

"What's it to you?" Tracie said, letting out a giggle. "I'm sorry . . . Yes. Guilty as charged." She walked over and extended a hand.

"Guilty? What's that supposed to mean?"

"It's a figure of speech," Tracie said. "I don't generally meet nice-looking men on the golf course."

Walt smiled. "That's a good one. So you're not a golfer, like your husband?"

"Let's just say he wastes enough time on sports for both of us."

"Hey, that's pretty sassy," Walt said. "You must be a real go-getter."

"Just making conversation." Tracie retreated to her chair and pulled out a thermos. "Would you care to join me? You look like you could use a pick-me-up."

"Don't mind if I do," Walt said, taking the Adirondack next to Tracie. He leaned the club against the rail and removed his golf glove. "I take mine black."

"Looks like you get the thermos top," Tracie said, handing it to him. "This dock is positively the most perfect spot on the property. I can appreciate why you like to play golf out here."

"I teed off from your front lawn . . . Hope that's okay? I was shooting for that hole over there on the beach."

Tracie looked past the sailboat and noticed a flag on the shore. "You must know everyone in the community, playing through the neighborhood like you do?"

"Well, me and Jess—that's my wife—we've been here for quite a while. But I tell you, it was that man of yours that inspired this golf course idea."

"He's a charmer."

"Does that mean you know?" Walt said.

"About what?"

Walt glanced over his shoulder, lowering his voice. "After you took off with that trailer, let me tell you, things got pretty interesting around here."

"And how does that relate to me?"

"It's like this. You returned on Monday. But Saturday night, I spotted that Fox woman slinking out of your husband's front door."

"What was she doing?"

"That's what I'd like to know," Walt said, now whispering. "Have you seen that sign in her window?"

"Back up. You said she was at our place?"

"That's a fact—and it was going on ten o'clock."

"You're not suggesting she was . . . shall we say . . . sleeping over?"

"Not in that negligee. I'd say it was more of a house call."

"Did you see anything else?"

"Perception's nine-tenths of the law, I can tell you that."

"You mean, *possession*," Tracie corrected.

Walt took a gander through the trees at Parkway 12. "That house is nothing but trouble—with a capital *T*."

"Are you suggesting other things have happened?"

"Besides you taking off like you did and someone stealing your husband's sports car?"

"I'm listening . . ."

"Strange goings-on started long before the two of you showed up. They first began when Leland and Sarah lived there."

"I heard the Dorseys were nice people."

Walt gave Tracie a look. "*Huh*, nice and weird."

"Like how?"

"Does the word *Woodstock* mean anything to you?"

"Are you referring to the concert in New York decades ago?"

"Those two were still rocking to the vibe. Only they were doing it in that trailer, if you know what I mean."

"Loud music and parties?" Tracie said.

"Hippies, bell bottoms, bean sprouts . . . and dope."

"Do you think they were dealing drugs?"

"That's not the half of it. They were orbiting mushroom planet nearly every weekend. But I'll give them this, they didn't bother anyone. They pretty much kept to themselves."

"So they were nice people—in a sense. What happened?"

"It all went down a few weeks before you moved in. In fact, it's the reason the place became available." Walt looked around, making sure no one was within earshot. "The entire episode took less than ten minutes, but it woke me and Jess. It was after two in the morning, and we heard tires screeching—like someone robbing a bank and making a getaway. When I looked out the window, all the lights were on and the front door was open. Leland was doubled over the front rail and Sarah was lying in the foyer."

"Were they passed out?"

"Not exactly."

"They were hurt?"

"They were dead . . . *murdered*," Walt said.

"What? Nobody said anything about a murder house. Why didn't someone tell us?"

"Would you have bought it, if you knew?"

"I—I'm not sure," Tracie said.

"And get this, the police report said the killers used silencers, and they didn't turn up much in the way of drugs. The neighborhood scuttle is that the killers robbed the Dorseys and took all their dope."

"Wow. That's really strange," Tracie said, biting her lip.

"Makes you think, doesn't it?" Walt said, getting up. "Guess I better hit the links."

"Yeah . . . Thanks for stopping by."

"Well, you and Trevor seem like decent folks. I hope the two of you work everything out." Walt grabbed his club and started across the gangway. He raised his hat. "And sorry about the profanity when I walked up."

Chapter 54

Suwanee, Georgia
Wednesday, October 16th
7:15 A.M.

By now I half-expected a swift jolt to launch me out of bed in the morning. Today was an exception. The only sound I heard was Walt teeing off, followed by a distant pop that reminded me of a baking pan hitting the floor. It was nothing, really. So I went back to sleep.

When I awoke the second time, I began to reminisce about how well yesterday's visit with Tracie had gone. I checked the time, bolted into the kitchen to start the coffee, and rushed out on the front stoop. Before I could focus on the dock, something caught my eye.

Rounding the end of the trailer, I spotted Ted marching out of my backyard. His hair was loose and hanging around his shoulders, and he was shirtless with a belt of bullets draped across his chest. Below the waist, he wore the usual camo cutoffs and a pair of hiking boots. Bouncing next to his hip was an impressive holster.

I started to call to him and ask what he was up to, but decided to let it go. Down at the lake, I noticed Walt's golf cart parked in front of the dock. Since I knew better than to leave home in my boxers, I headed inside to get dressed.

The morning chill had raised goosebumps on my legs, so I opted for a flannel shirt, jeans, and my Patagonia vest. Grabbing some coffee, I found my shoes and made my way outside, where it suddenly dawned on me to check out back before joining Tracie.

Once in the backyard, I slipped over to the dislocated garage and peeked around the corner, taking a long, hard look in the woods. Since I knew approximately where the old logging road ended, I concentrated on that area. There was no sign of a vehicle. Before leaving, I checked Tammy Fox's place to make sure I wasn't being watched. Then I examined the ductwork to confirm that the Ziplocs were undisturbed.

When I arrived at the dock, Walt had advanced down the beach. He was standing near a flag, lining up a putt.

"Good morning, Little Miss Sunshine," I said to Tracie.

She beamed at me, bouncing out of her seat for a hug.

"This is my newest, most favorite place in the entire world," she said.

This could go better than yesterday, I thought. Then I pointed to her Adirondack. "Is there room in there for two?"

"Actually, it's reserved for my alone time. But pull up a chair. We have a few things to talk about."

"Our future is going to be better—I promise." I patted my heart and smiled. "Did you happen to see Ted earlier?"

"Somebody traipsed by, but I didn't get a good look at him. He went inside that trailer over there. In fact, I'm pretty sure the same guy went by yesterday." Tracie sat down and coddled her coffee cup, perching her feet on the edge of the chair. "Not to change the subject, but is there anything you haven't told me about Tammy Fox?"

I sat next to her, grinning when I noticed her bare feet. Reaching for the pashmina she was wearing, I tucked one end around her toes. "Sorry, I don't want to lose any of those to frostbite," I teased. "Tammy Fox—let's see—I already told you how she's branded herself as the *Psy-Chic*. What I didn't tell you was . . . she came over a few nights ago to sign me up for her services."

"What services? Like palm reading?"

"That, tarot cards, and the crystal ball."

"Nothing else?" Tracie said, lifting a hand.

"First of all, I didn't purchase anything. So regardless of what you may have heard, I wasn't buying. Does that answer your question?"

"More or less," Tracie said. "I saw her sign last night, so naturally it made me think."

"There's nothing to worry about in that department, but since we're making true confessions maybe you could explain about that guy at Tybee the other night."

"Before we go there, Walt just told me something very disturbing. Do you know about the Dorseys?"

"Just that they lived in the house before us. Everyone thinks they were nice people."

"That's what I thought. But it's actually more creepy than that," Tracie said, setting down her coffee. She rested a hand on my arm and looked me in the eyes. "Trevor, they were murdered."

"Murdered!" I shouted, gripping my chair. "What do you mean?"

"Walt said they were shot in our house. Evidently, they were into drugs . . . *big time*."

"Who did it?"

"They don't know. The police never arrested anyone. And as it turns out, they expected to find more drugs."

"Why didn't someone tell us?" I said. "God help us all."

"Trevor, these *are* nice people."

"We both know nice when we see it, but the neighbors must be out of their minds to think these druggies—the Dorseys—were nice people."

"They are accepting and give others the benefit of the doubt," Tracie said, cutting her eyes at me. "Sort of the way they did with you."

"That's not fair . . ." I said, my words losing steam. I couldn't bear to look at her, so I turned to the lake. At least, *it* didn't judge me.

Tracie let me shrink for a spell before snapping me out of it.

"Trevor, about Tybee . . . The guy's name is Neely. He's with the FBI."

That was the instant I thought I might jump in the lake. But the tone in Tracie's voice suggested I should listen to the rest of her story.

"Is he after the bag?" I said.

"The drugs."

"How does he know about those? Did you report me to the FBI?"

"Of course not. They were working a case, and Parkway 12 was part of the investigation."

"Our home?"

"Trevor, you found cocaine under the house. They know about Gustav and your interview. They suspect him of running a drug ring—and our house, the Dorseys, *and you* are mixed up in all this."

"But I was looking for a job."

"It was clearly a setup. Gustav lured you in because of the address. The Dorseys must have worked for him, but they apparently skimmed some of the stuff for themselves. When he found out, Gustav had them murdered."

"And now the FBI thinks I work for Gustav? Is that what they think?"

"They know about the bag. It had drugs inside—"

"And a drug test kit."

"Clearly a front."

"So you're saying TestEZ isn't *legit*," I said, the mental fog beginning to clear. "Maybe . . . Gustav is using major employers to find addicts."

"You think that's how it works?" Tracie said.

A light bulb went on in my head. "Try this. He's got a mobile process set up to not only collect test results, but everyone's personal information as well. What if he bypasses company officials and stiff-arms the employees when they test positive?"

"You mean—he blackmails them into buying drugs from him?"

"And if they don't, he reports them and they lose their job," I said.

"Executives with bad habits would be a gold mine for Gustav."

"*Trace*, I had no idea—I swear."

"How could you have known?"

"One thing I do know. Gustav isn't done with this. I'm pretty sure he has Ariana watching the house."

"So he suspects the cocaine is still nearby."

"And he's right, but he doesn't know for sure."

"It doesn't matter. Neely thinks it's here, and he's going after everyone involved . . . including you."

Chapter 55

Suwanee, Georgia
Wednesday, October 16th
6:10 P.M.

I was pretty worn out from the secret project Clayton and I had been working on all day. The lights around the tin roof were just beginning to cast a flicker across the lake as I headed for the dock. With a bag of chips in one hand, I swung a bottle of pinot in the other, whistling along the way. Betty Jean was busy at the hibachi, Tracie was pairing napkins to silverware, and Clayton chipped away at a chunk of ice in the cooler.

"Smells wonderful," I called out, crossing the gangway.

"We were about to send the bloodhounds after you," Clayton said, raising his head.

"I was just freshening up a bit," I said.

"Hope you like New York strips," Betty Jean said. "Tracie marinated them in a secret sauce."

"Actually, it's Trevor's recipe," Tracie confessed. "He's the master-griller in the family."

"But it's the people around you that make it a meal." I raised my hands and breathed in the evening air. "Even though *you* have been avoiding me," I said, casting a look in Betty Jean's direction.

"I see you've brought chips," Clayton broke in.

"And a bottle of red," I said, setting it on the cooler.

"I've got baked potatoes, so help yourselves to munchies in the meantime," Betty Jean said.

Tracie started chopping up fresh vegetables as I walked up behind her, dropping my chin on her shoulder. She smiled and pressed her cheek to mine.

"We've peppered Clayton with a million questions, trying to figure out what the two of you have been up to all afternoon," Tracie said.

"I could ask you girls the same thing."

"You've been sneaking around this lake like you're hiding something," Betty Jean said to me. "I know for a fact Clayton's up to no good. Otherwise, he would tell me. He tells me everything."

"Now you know better than that. When's the last time you caught me doing something out of the way?" Clayton said.

"How about my birthday?"

"That don't count. Those are special, a time of celebration. A man's got a right to surprise a woman on her birthday."

"That's a smokescreen if I ever heard one. It's not my birthday, and it's not Tracie's. We've already considered every occasion known to mankind."

"Can we discuss it in the morning?" Clayton said to Betty Jean.

"Pinky swear?"

"With a cherry on top."

"Hey, what about me?" Tracie said.

"That's a horse of a different color," I piped in.

"We're getting a horse?" Tracie let out a snicker.

"If you keep asking them dad-burn questions, you're getting a goat," Clayton said.

"The steaks are coming up. Everybody grab a plate."

A few minutes later we were all seated in a circle, with our plates piping hot. There was silence as everyone settled in, like we had known each other for a lifetime. At that instant an unspoken bond was born. I didn't know how or why, but I was certain it was the *when*. It hung in the air until Clayton did something that put an official stamp of approval on our sentiments. He raised his wine glass, and the rest of us followed suit.

"May the Lord grant us peace and gravy," he said.

"Amen," we all responded, clinking our glasses.

Afterwards, I reached over and placed a hand on Tracie's. She seemed to melt at my touch, the look on her face pondering if she really knew me. There was a tear in her eye.

"Everybody dig in," Clayton said.

The evening couldn't have been more perfect. After dinner, we set the hibachi in the center of the dock for warmth. And for a short, uncomplicated time there was serenity. We were on another planet. It was filled with stories, laughter, friendship, and even a little Kenny Chesney.

Around midnight, Clayton got up and stretched. "I don't know about the rest of you buzzards, but I can't remember when I've had a finer time. If you don't mind, I'm moving my celebration up to the boudoir. I've got things to do in the morning."

"You boys run along," Betty Jean said.

We all hugged and parted ways. Clayton and I took a path across the bank toward his house, saying our goodnights when we reached the tip of the street. Moments later, I stepped onto my front lawn and stopped to take in the night. I heard the girls finishing up down at the dock. It kindled a special feeling inside of me. But then something else caught my attention. It was a distant sound. Then I heard it again.

Somewhere behind the trailer, a crunching noise rose out of the darkness. Even though it was faint, I set a course in the general direction. When I reached the corner of the trailer, it seemed to be moving away from me. *Crunch-Crunch-Pop.* I sprinted over to the sagging garage, careful to blend into the shadows. *Crunch-Crunch-Pop.* And then I saw it.

A black van eased up the logging road, heading toward the highway. The lights were off, but for a second the driver tapped the brakes, shrouding the rear panel in red. The van seemed to match the description Fate had reported a day ago. Once it was out of sight, I waded through the brush over to the road. In the darkness tire tracks were barely visible, but real. Nothing else had been left behind.

Returning to the backyard, I was about to head around front when panic struck me. Rushing over to the trailer, I knelt down and poked around for the ductwork. I fumbled in the abyss until I found it, plucking out handfuls of insulation. Reaching in, I extended my arm as far as I could. I felt nothing. Gripping the junction box in both hands, I tore it loose from the house and stood it on end, banging it against the ground. It was empty.

I looked into the woods, running my eyes all the way up the logging road to where it spilled out onto Peachtree Parkway. The van was sitting there on the side of the highway with its lights on. That's when reality punched me in the gut.

I know that van, I thought.

It was part of the shiny new fleet I had seen at the Arts Center . . . a Mercedes . . . Gustav had returned to the scene of the crime.

Chapter 56

Suwanee, Georgia
Thursday, October 17th
9:00 A.M.

After calling Tracie to warn her about the van, I sat up most of the night, peeping through a slit in the tarp. By the time three o'clock rolled around, only an owl had stirred in the tall pines out back. I could think of nothing further to do, other than hit the sack and get a little shut-eye.

When I crawled out of bed, the sun had been up for hours. Yesterday's outfit was conveniently scattered across the floor, so I collected the pieces, put them on, and stumbled into the kitchen to brew a pot of coffee.

Happy to have Mr. Coffee gurgling away, I stepped in the breakfast nook as I heard a familiar car rumbling down the street. Pulling back the curtain, the Grand Prix blasted by and swung into the Beasleys' driveway. Still buttoning my shirt, I hurried out the front door, hoping to get a better look. My jaw dropped as I spotted Tracie climbing into the car with Neely. They backed up and zipped out of the neighborhood.

"Well hello, good looking," someone called out.

I cocked my head, feeling a lump rising in my throat. There stood Tammy Fox on her lawn, wearing a slinky peignoir. Take it by faith, the ensemble wasn't intended for yard work. She bent over to pick up a newspaper, and I bolted inside.

Blazing a trail to the kitchen, I dug into a cabinet and fished out a bottle of Bird Dog. I grabbed my mug, filled it with coffee, and stormed out barefooted. I stuffed the bourbon in my vest and descended the front steps, marching down the drive. When I reached the street, I turned for the lake.

"Hey, is the deal still on?" I heard Tammy Fox yell behind me.

I raised a hand in the air, brushing her off without uttering a word. Moving on, I blew past Walt, who appeared to be "in the zone", teeing up a golf ball in his yard. At the tip of the horseshoe, I almost fell, sliding down the bank to the gangway. When I reached the back rail of the dock I paused, realizing I didn't have a clue why I had bothered to come here. Looking around, I spotted Tracie's Adirondack and sat down.

Pulling out the bottle I toyed with the notion of cracking it open, staring long and hard at the label before putting it aside. I decided to kick back and propped my feet up, wrapping my hands around the warm coffee mug.

With nothing better to do, I knew I had to get my mind off things, so I pulled out my wallet for a much-needed financial review. Tuesday's Nifty-Thrifty shopping spree had not only depleted my cash (except for a dollar seventy-five), but had maxed out my credit card. Fortunately, the cable refund had shown up in time to put me in the black, covering yesterday's trip to Costco. That set me back fifty-two bucks—forty-five for wine and seven for chips. Combined activities for the two days left me with the tidy sum of just under seventy-five dollars. Since Tracie had never complained about money, I was a little irritated she was getting along so well. I put away the thought, along with my wallet. As it turned out, this little diversion wasn't doing a thing to lift my spirits.

Instead, I tried another tactic as I sunk lower in the chair, longing to rekindle the incredible feelings from last night's dinner—starting with the magic in Tracie's eyes. Everything had been spot-on, more than I could have hoped for. It was the best thing that had happened in days. And now, all of a sudden—*Zap!* The sparkle was gone. Taking a sip of coffee, the muse poked me again.

Change my way of thinking.

Then I heard rumbling, returning just as quickly as it had departed. I couldn't bear to look. Somewhere behind me the Grand Prix came to a stop, and I willed myself to remain calm. I heard footsteps coming my way, and then the dock bounced as they drew closer. Ever so slowly, I shifted for a glimpse. Tracie was standing behind me, alone. Up at Lakeview Circle, the Grand Prix snarled off in a fury.

Tracie's eyes locked onto the Bird Dog. "What are you doing?"

I settled down, fully aware there wasn't enough bourbon in the bottle to get a goldfish wasted. "Not a lousy thing," I said.

"What's in that mug?" Tracie didn't wait for an answer. "Trevor, it's nine in the morning."

"It's coffee," I said, offering her a whiff. "Where have you been?"

"I, *uh*, had to call Neely this morning."

"Funny—I could have sworn that was you climbing out of his car a minute ago."

"He wanted details about last night."

"So in lieu of examining the actual evidence, he takes the blonde in for questioning?"

"The FBI is still watching."

"Then why do they need you? I'm the one who knows about the bad guys. What's his problem?"

"I don't know, but I warned you they were anxious to make arrests. I told him how Gustav took the cocaine last night—all of it. And I explained there's no reason to be watching you anymore."

"How did that go?"

"He claims he's only doing his job."

"*Huh*, sounds lame to me."

"I gave him an ultimatum. I told him if he took you in, then he would have to arrest me, too."

That stopped me.

"You're just saying that," I said.

"You think?"

"I think—*not*," I said, resigned. "I've been sitting here going nuts ever since you drove off with the guy. And now the only thing that matters is . . . I don't want to spend another day without you. And if that means getting a jail cell for two, then I'm in. But I don't know why you'd sign up for the gig, because you haven't done anything wrong."

Tracie smiled as she walked over to the rail and sat next to my feet. "What are you doing out here with no shoes?"

"Sometimes you make me stupid."

"Is that the reason for the Bird Dog?"

"They say a dog is a man's best friend."

"Really?" Tracie said, opening her eyes wide.

"I'm pleading the fifth on the bourbon."

"Very clever . . . I get it," Tracie said. She shook her head, taking in the pearly-white beach, like she longed to be out there.

"You're staying, right?" I finally said.

"What do you say we jet off to the Riviera?"

"In case you've forgotten, I'm broke."

"*Nah*, you just need a little cheering up."

I dropped my feet on the dock, sitting up.

"Tell me about this secret project you and Clayton are working on."

"Let's just say, if I'm not locked up, it might be a good idea to keep your calendar open Saturday evening."

"Well, I may have a surprise for you as well."

Standing, I took her in my arms. "Lay it on me."

Tracie raised up on her tip-toes and pecked me on the cheek, then pulled back. "You'll be the first to know when it's time. Right now, I have to go see Betty Jean."

"Works for me," I said, looking across the lake. "I've got to meet up with Clayton anyway. It's going to be a busy day."

Chapter 57

Suwanee, Georgia
Thursday, October 17th
5:00 P.M.

The boat glided up to the dock as Clayton and Trevor grabbed the rail, maneuvering it around to the gangway. They secured the lines and climbed out. Clayton helped Betty Jean ashore, just as she spotted Tracie with pizza boxes.

"How long have you been standing there?" Betty Jean said to Tracie, heading toward her.

"Where did you get *that*?" Tracie replied.

"This is what you call a bass boat," Clayton said.

"It's all sparkly . . . and the engine is gigantic."

"Friend of mine does some serious fishing up at Lanier. He loaned it to us."

"The three of you have been fishing all afternoon? Is that why you abandoned me?"

"Don't be silly, darling," Betty Jean said. "Trevor doesn't know how to fish."

"That's a fact. My fishing pole is in retirement."

"Get him to tell you about the big boy bass that got away," Clayton said, as he pumped an elbow in my side.

"Maybe later," I said, heading over to help Tracie with the pizza. I set the boxes on top of the hibachi.

"Don't forget Clayton's cooler," Tracie said.

It was on a small red wagon, so I wheeled it over to the grill.

Clayton snuck in and popped the lid. "It's time to knock-off, and I'm buying the first round."

Betty Jean turned on the string lights, while Clayton and I arranged the chairs.

"So, what does one do with a flashy boat—that is, if you're not fishing?"

"Sweetheart," Clayton said. "That little puppy can zip you across the lake at sixty miles an hour. What do you say I take you for a ride?"

"No thanks." Tracie cut her eyes my way.

"Don't look at me," I said.

"First, Betty Jean sends me away shopping, and then Trevor calls me to pick up dinner. Now, Clayton seems to be having trouble giving straight answers. Does anyone see a reason to be suspicious, or is it just me?"

"Hey, you've got secrets of your own, so don't go casting stones," I said to Tracie. "If you tell me yours, I'll tell you mine."

"That's a good one," Clayton said, raising his beer.

After happy hour, pizza was served and the conversation waned. It was dark by the time the boxes were empty.

"If you're not fishing, and it takes all of you to go out on the lake . . . let's see . . . three seems to be about the right number for a conspiracy," Tracie said, prodding.

"It takes three to tango," I teased.

"Nonsense . . . three's a crowd," Clayton said.

"Stop it!" Tracie snipped.

"I'll drink to that."

"Me, too," Betty Jean added, clanking her bottle to Clayton's.

“I have this interesting theory,” I said, drawing silence from everyone. “There was a two-day window where Betty Jean decided to avoid me, just like that.” I snapped my fingers. “And I know for a fact it wasn’t my dirty laundry, because Clayton smells worse than me—”

“Don’t you let these women go dividing us men up,” Clayton interrupted.

“It has to be something else,” I said, searching everyone’s eyes. “The way I figure it, Betty Jean is at least knee-deep in Tracie’s secret. While *us* so-called conspirators have been on the lake all afternoon, Betty Jean may have pulled a fast one. That’s right, she’s holding out on the menfolk.”

“Honey Bunch, you wouldn’t go and keep a secret from me, would you?”

“Clayton Beasley, you know more about what’s going on than I do.”

“Now we’re getting somewhere,” I said.

“Everybody—hush,” Tracie said, making a hand puppet. She snapped it shut for effect, her eyes growing big.

“Come on, Clayton. Don’t let a couple of girls bully you.”

“If you say one word, you’re sleeping in that bass boat tonight,” Betty Jean said.

Clayton turned to me. “Sorry, sport. But you’ll thank me later.”

“You’re a girl,” I said to Clayton.

“This will get sorted out soon enough,” Betty Jean said. “In the meantime, let’s just change the subject.”

“I’ve got something,” Tracie said. “When I was shopping today, I found the cutest little boutique. Has anyone been to the Nifty-Thrifty?”

“I stop by all the time,” Betty Jean said.

“She likes the fashions those ladies from *The Springs* drop off,” Clayton said.

"And I've found a few things for Clayton there."

"She's always looking out for me," Clayton said.

"You're a girl," I repeated.

"They have really nice stuff," Tracie said. "I spotted three dresses that are identical to ones I have hanging in my—"

"That's it for me," I cut in, hopping out of my chair.

"What's the rush?" Clayton said. "It's barely nine o'clock."

"If I stay much longer, I'm afraid I'll say something to ruin our little secret."

"But we're talking about clothes," Tracie said.

"Don't I know it," I said, patting Tracie on the head. "A good night to all."

Back at the trailer, I brushed my teeth and pitched camp in the hallway next to the tarp. Bracing myself for another sleepless night, I did my best to get comfortable. Somewhere in the wee hours of the morning, I dozed off . . .

Chapter 58

Suwanee, Georgia
Friday, October 18th
8:15 A.M.

I awoke in a stupor, somewhat disoriented when I felt the floor vibrating beneath me. All of a sudden it stopped, leaving me with a bad feeling. Even though I had grown gun-shy about Parkway wake-up calls, this one was different.

The floor shook again, only this time it buzzed, reminding me I had fallen asleep on top of the hallway vent. Scrambling to my feet, I assumed a sumo stance, doing my best to get a bearing on whoever might be snooping around. I turned full-circle, ever so slowly, noticing how the tarp was bright blue this morning—a sure sign daylight had arrived. I reached in a pocket for my phone, but before I could locate it the vibration went off again.

It took me by surprise, and I nearly slipped as I felt a tingle on my leg. Then I realized it wasn't the floor. It was my pants. Fumbling in the pocket I took out my phone, not bothering to check caller ID.

"Yeah," I said, wiping sweat off my forehead.

"Trevor?"

"Trace . . . whew . . . it's you."

"What's wrong?"

"I'm a little on edge. I spent the night in the hall."

"Did something happen?"

"If it did, I slept through it," I said, tugging at my collar. I looked down and my shirttail was half-out.

"Today's the day."

"For what?" I said, still fighting cobwebs.

"Your surprise. Can you be dressed in five minutes?"

I checked my outfit. "Give me ten."

"But no more . . . Text me when you're ready."

I hung up and started shedding clothes as fast as I could, working my way down the hall in the process. The ensemble I was wearing had been with me for two days. Taking a detour into the kitchen, I set the coffee maker, peeling things off as I went. In the master closet I remembered the warmth coming in through the tarp and picked out a pair of shorts. Pulling on a button-down in front of the bathroom mirror, I took a moment to finger-comb my hair and brush my teeth.

Back in the kitchen, I was tempted to peek out the breakfast nook window, but decided better. After pouring a cup of coffee, I stepped into my shoes next to the fridge. Whipping out my phone, I texted Tracie: *Ready or not, here I come.* I had no idea what was in store for me, but I had a sense it was a brand new day.

When I opened the door, I couldn't have been more surprised. Shocked is actually more like it. Sitting in the driveway was the notorious lime-green Grand Prix. "Oh, *jeez*," I said out loud. "This isn't happening." Then I spotted him leaning on Goldfinger. It was *GQ*, the FBI guy—aka Neely.

I took a strategic sip of coffee, just to let him know he hadn't ruffled my feathers, and then eased off the front steps. When I was within spitting distance, I cocked my hip and clung to the coffee cup for dear life. "Is there something I can do for you?"

"You're Trevor Wentworth?"

"Neely, is it?"

"That's right . . . Federal Bureau of Investigation, narcotics division. Do you know Tracie Wentworth?"

"Let's not play games. What do you want?"

"Ms. Wentworth recently entered into a settlement agreement with the FBI for certain . . . considerations, shall we say?"

GQ was wearing a pair of dark aviators, so I couldn't see his eyes. Things seemed to be headed south, and fast. So I stared into my cup, wondering if I should throw it at him and run. Better yet, maybe I could barricade myself inside with the last of the Bird Dog. I couldn't imagine Tracie selling me out like this. "Do whatever it is you came to do, or get off my property," I said.

"We've had your place under surveillance."

"Do you have a search warrant?" I said, remembering how it always seemed to work in the movies.

"That won't be necessary, Mr. Wentworth. The hounds have already been over the entire property."

"Inside my house?"

"Don't get excited," Neely said. "The place is clean."

"You sound disappointed."

"Just doing my job."

"What are the charges?"

I hadn't noticed until now, but *GQ* gripped something in his hand. "You can thank me later." Raising a walkie-talkie, he said, "Now."

I heard a roar and stiffened up. It was the sound of a tractor trailer coming down Lakeview Circle, growing louder by the second. Just past Tammy Fox's driveway, the full rig came into view. It rumbled past my yard, slowing when it reached the tip of the horseshoe. The airbrakes hissed, and the truck came to a stop. Behind it was Tracie's half of the doublewide. I heard a loud beeping as it started backing up. In the cab, I spotted Tracie leaning out of the passenger window, waving with a smile on her face. My jaw dropped as she hopped out and ran over.

"Are you surprised?" she said, wrapping her arms around me.

I spilled coffee on both of us, but couldn't have cared less. Looking over Tracie's shoulder, *GQ* grinned from ear to ear.

"I love these plea bargains," Neely said, removing the aviators.

Still clinging to Tracie, I reached out and offered him my hand.

"Is it over?" I said.

Instead of responding, *GQ* put on the glasses and walked over to the Grand Prix. He popped the trunk and pulled out a colossal burlap bag, heaving it on the driveway. It landed with a plop and crackle next to my loafer.

"What's this?" I said.

"A little housewarming gift," Neely said, tossing a silver object my way.

I let loose of Tracie and caught it midair.

"Is that what I think it is?" Tracie said.

"It's a nutcracker."

Tracie giggled. "That's sweet."

I looked at the bag, puzzled. "Is it over?" I repeated.

"Not by a longshot," Neely said.

Chapter 59

Suwanee, Georgia
Friday, October 18th
5:00 P.M.

The knock at the door was expected, this time by invitation. It felt strange to be having guests over, but there was reason to celebrate. With the two halves of the doublewide now reunited, I was feeling pretty festive, despite the fact that the garage remained in pretty bad shape out back. "Tracie and Trevor Wentworth welcome you to our humble home," I rehearsed, heading into the foyer. Carefully opening the door, Betty Jean and Tracie greeted me with armloads of drinks and munchies. I helped the girls into the breakfast nook and made sure they had everything they needed before excusing myself.

"Clayton's picking up Chinese, so don't be long," Betty Jean said.

I hurried up the street and cut through the grassy area next to the tennis court. Over behind Ol' Lady Wilbanks's place, a swarm of kids with droopy tongues pounded away on the trampoline. If I didn't know better, I'd wager they hadn't taken a break since the day I first spotted them.

Fate was seated on the pew in front of the Esther Williams memorial cabana, dressed in the flight suit with a paper in his lap. A light breeze ruffled his hair, reminding me of a fluffy wad of cotton candy. By now, I had developed a knack for reading Fate's ticks and was pretty sure he had good news.

"I'd offer you a Dr Pepper, but it's after hours," Fate said as I walked up.

"I came as soon as I could," I said. "What's the emergency?"

"The first part is personal business. It's another piece of registered mail."

I took the envelope and tore it open. There was a fifty dollar refund check (seventy-five dollars less twenty-five in rush charges) from my Internet provider. I thanked him and took a seat. "I don't want to keep you," I said, knowing full-well it was knocking-off time.

"No worries about that, no *sirree*. My brother's picking me up, so I'm just waitin'."

"The one with the Lincoln?"

"Yeah . . . You know him?"

"Not exactly, but I've heard about his car."

Fate gave me a funny look. "I'm the one who told you about that car."

I smiled.

"Have you been talking to him behind my back?"

"Why would I do that?"

"You ain't fixing to make him an offer, are you?"

"You know me better than that."

"Well, sir. You tried to rent it for that road trip. People can surprise you sometimes."

"I have my car back now."

"Sorry, I just don't like it when folks talk about my brother."

"You must be proud—"

"You're darn tootin'. That kitten's a collector's item. He's got people leaving notes on the windshield all the time. He could be a rich man, if he had a mind to."

"Fate, was there something else?"

He peeled the paper out of his lap and shook it at me. "This right here is one of the finer things about being a property manager. Do you understand what I'm talking about?"

"I will as soon as you tell me what it is."

"It's the signatures of the fourteen property owners that wanted you thrown out of this neighborhood." Fate gestured to the *No Singlewides Allowed* sign, now safely swinging from the rusty chains. "Because of that sucker right there."

"Oh, no," I gasped.

"Just a while ago, the chairwoman stopped by and gave me the word to tear up the petition. Yes *sirree*, the covenants specify that upon resolution of an alleged violation, the board shall deem all malfeasances null and void. That means we shall speak of it no more," Fate said, giving his head a nod. "Ashes to ashes, dust to dust."

"That's poetic, Fate."

"Well, sir. I never much cared for conflict, seeing how I'm what you call a peacemaker." Without warning, Fate stuck an ear in the air and turned on a dime. "Say, you want to stick around and meet my brother?"

"I've, *uh*, got people over at the house."

"Then some other time," Fate said, handing over the petition. "I'll let you do the honors."

Plotting my escape, I hurried past the tennis court and waved to the kids on the trampoline as I bounced along with a spring in my step. They just kept on doing their thing.

Back at the house, Clayton and the girls had been busy. The table was pulled away from the wall to make room for four, and a paper lantern flickered in the center. I noticed how all of the place settings had been set with fancy chopsticks.

"A little bird told me you had official business with the property manager," Clayton said.

"Word travels fast in this neighborhood," I said.

"What did he want?" Tracie said.

"He gave me this check."

"A what?" Betty Jean quipped.

"Actually, he told me he got into a rumble with the Parkway chairwoman and stiff-armed her into quashing the petition. He also said she was a mean old biddy."

Betty Jean squinted, snakelike. "He did no such thing."

"Fate is an honest man, unlike *some* people we know."

Clayton slapped me on the back. "You tell her, *Trev.*"

"Trevor Wentworth, you apologize—and do it now," Tracie said.

I walked over to Betty Jean and gave her a hug. "Thank you, Madam Chairwoman."

"For the record, the deadline was intended to light a fire under that posterior of yours. You'd do well to thank your wife. She's the one who put Humpty Dumpty together again," Betty Jean said.

I grabbed Tracie, keeping my eyes glued to Betty Jean. "So explain this three-day clause in the covenants."

"I'll have to look it up and get back to you."

"She pulled it out of thin air," Clayton said, letting out a cackle. "These womenfolk sure know how to work the system. Sometimes Betty Jean even uses a little voodoo."

"She must get it from Tammy Fox," I said, getting a good laugh.

Tracie pulled loose and eased into the hallway. "I've been dying to know why this tarp is still blocking our family room."

"That was Clayton's idea," I said. "He thought it would be memorable to have the two of us tear it down together . . . You know, removing the barrier that separated us for the past few days."

"It's what you call a symbolic gesture," Clayton said.

"Hang on. I want to get a picture," Betty Jean said, pulling out her phone.

I joined Tracie in the hall, each of us grabbing a corner of the tarp. After a couple of photos, we ripped it down and slipped inside to check things out. Betty Jean and Clayton followed us, bringing along beer for a celebratory toast.

"*Trev*, why don't you do the honors?" Clayton said, handing me a matchbook.

I walked over to the fireplace and raised the petition high. "To Parkway Community—home sweet home," I said, before lighting it up.

"And to our new friends, Tracie and Trevor," Clayton said, raising his beer.

"Cheers," Betty Jean said.

After the ceremony, we headed into the breakfast nook for dinner, where Clayton covered the finer points of reconnecting a doublewide. I didn't have a clue about most of what he said, but was happy to poke at him as he went along. I even joked about selling the flatscreen, explaining to Tracie how we no longer had cable service. But the part that felt really good was this—I'd gotten my hands dirty for once. In a good way. And as it turns out, I had been part of something much more important than rejoining two halves of a trailer. For once, I could see the bigger picture. It even inspired me to flirt a little with Tracie during dessert.

After cleaning up, everyone seemed pleased to put a cap on the perfect evening.

"I know you have plans tomorrow," Clayton said, "but we'd like for the two of you to join us at the dock in the afternoon."

I wrapped an arm around Tracie. "We'd love to."

Tracie wiggled free, and to my surprise withdrew to Betty Jean's side, her eyes betraying her.

"*Uh, Trev,*" Betty Jean said. "We've been talking, and Tracie feels it might be best to spend one more night over at our place."

I hadn't seen this one coming, and it almost derailed me. I lowered my eyes. "I thought tonight was a home run. Was it just me?"

"Why don't we let these lovebirds talk?" Clayton said to Betty Jean, sweeping her out the front door.

Tracie led me by the hand into the night air, and then snuggled her arms around herself. She turned to face me. "All of this is wonderful. In fact, it's more than I dreamed possible just a few days ago. You've changed. I've changed . . . Our entire world has changed. But I want to make sure it's real, not just show and tell. I think about us all the time—and the way our lives used to be. I need to be sure we want the same things for the future."

"I think—I understand. But you can be certain of one thing. The *you* that you're referring to—that's the *you* I want most," I said, taking her hand. "The person I married, and the one I'll always treasure."

"You're not mad?"

"That old guy who lived here in half a trailer, he's mad. But he doesn't live here anymore. The man standing in front of you, he's different—a bit jittery, but hopefully more patient."

Tracie gave me a kiss. "I can't wait for our special day tomorrow."

"Today was pretty terrific, if you ask me," I said, walking her to the driveway. When we came alongside Goldfinger, I popped the trunk and pulled out some bags. I handed them to Tracie.

"What are these?" she said, holding them up for a look. "Are they from . . . Nifty-Thrifty?"

"A present for our outing," I said.

"You *are* full of surprises."

"And there's more where that came from," I said, pecking her on the cheek. "Now get out of here before I screw things up."

I waited as she crossed the street. When I turned, Tammy Fox's *Psy-Chic* sign nearly blinded me. I decided to hurry inside, just in case she was watching.

When I got to the steps, a rustling at the far end of the house caught my ear. It was only there for a second, and then disappeared. I decided to sneak over for a look, pausing as I reached the corner. When I didn't spot anything, I eased around back for a closer look.

Ten yards ahead, a man scrambled across the lawn and slipped into the woods. He moved deliberately, clearly on a mission. Even with the bad lighting, the camo cutoffs and rifle gave him away. At that moment it was like a flash went off in my brain.

It was Ted . . . and he was headed for the old logging road.

Chapter 60

Suwanee, Georgia
Saturday, October 19th
2:20 A.M.

Sometime around the witching hour, I convinced myself it was time to turn in. I wasn't crazy about Ted snooping around in the backyard, but that was the least of my worries. Considering his appearance, he was most likely on the trail of a wild boar. The woods were full of creatures I didn't even want to think about. And with the big day coming up, I needed my rest and made up my mind that one last night in the spare bedroom wasn't such a bad idea. It wouldn't be any fun fluffing the pillows in the master suite without Tracie at my side.

A bit after two in the morning nature called, and I stirred from a sound sleep to go to the bathroom. As I rolled out of bed, it occurred to me that the guest bath was back in service. Feeling my way in the darkness, I was only half-conscious and managed to get across the hall without stumbling. After a few more steps the room opened up, but much larger than I remembered. Looking around for the toilet, I suddenly smacked my head on something. Stepping back, I raised my eyes to discover I was standing in front of a window. *We don't have a window in the bathroom.*

I focused on a pair of frilly curtains that were definitely out of place, prompting me to pull them aside for better light. Mystery solved. I had missed the entrance to the bath and wound up in the back bedroom. Yawning, I glanced out the window and froze. There was something afoot in the woods.

"What the . . ." I said out loud. Instead of Ted the lone wolf, I spotted two prowlers in dark outfits combing their way across the backyard. Their zigzag movements could have come straight out of a SWAT team playbook. Looking past them, I spied the one thing I feared most. And there it was beaming in the moonlight . . . a black van.

They're back, I thought.

I took a second look at the silhouettes now zeroing in on the house. It didn't take a brain surgeon to figure out that neither was Ted. One was tall and slender, graceful as a swan. The other had a polished bald pate that bounced up and down in the darkness.

Gustav and Ariana.

In my state of grogginess, I couldn't imagine why they had returned. They had already taken the cocaine, so I had nothing left to my name except a hundred and twenty-five dollars in cash.

When they reached the trailer, I figured they would dip underneath where the drugs had been stowed. Instead, they veered off and disappeared around the corner.

Now fully awake, I didn't have time to think. I tip-toed into the hallway, catching a glimpse of my rod and reel in the corner. *It's not much, but it's all I've got.* I grabbed it and marched on. When I reached the kitchen, another thought surfaced, suddenly transforming me into ninja mode. I raised the fishing pole.

They've come for Goldfinger.

I darted into the breakfast nook, desperate to locate them without being seen or heard. Then I looked out the window at Goldfinger, sensing nothing suspicious. Next door, Tammy Fox's driveway was dusted in the *Psy-Chic* sign's neon colors.

"Freeze!" I heard someone shout outside. The command was followed by a couple of heavy thumps, like dead weight being dropped off the front stoop. I couldn't see anyone, but the sound of footsteps pounded across the front yard to the far corner. And then the world exploded.

BOOM! BOOM! BOOM! . . . KA-BOOM!

I hit the floor and let loose of the rod and reel. It rattled across the laminate as someone outside repeated, "I said . . . freeze!" Covering my head, I said my prayers. But then there was only silence, so I mustered the courage to crawl on hands and knees to the front door. Something slammed into the trailer, and the entire house rocked back and forth. Raising up on my knees, I put my shoulder into the door and barreled headfirst onto the stoop.

Smacking my face against the rail, I opened my eyes to see Clayton, Betty Jean, and Tracie crossing the street. I hoisted myself to my feet—I had to warn them to run for cover. Before I could utter a word, I noticed they were headed toward a skirmish that had broken out on the lawn.

I leaped off the stoop and sprinted over to protect Tracie from the mayhem. Firmly wrapping my arms around her, I did my best to size things up. With his bald head shining, Gustav laid in a bed of pine straw—out cold. A few feet away, Ted was deflecting blows that were coming fast and furiously from the lovely Ariana.

At that very moment Neely's Grand Prix came rumbling out of nowhere and passed Tammy Fox's house, screeching to a stop at the end of my driveway. Tearing around it, two police cars slid up on the lawn with sirens blaring and blue lights flashing. We all braced ourselves as grass and dirt sprayed everywhere.

Still alarmed at Ted's predicament, I turned in the nick of time to catch Ariana leaping into the air, poised for a blow to Ted's face. He snagged her boot, and then leaned in and delivered a swift chop. Ariana collapsed to the ground like a ragdoll.

By now, Neely had jumped out of his vehicle and made his way over to Gustav. The police surrounded Ariana in assault team fashion with guns drawn. Exhibiting no further resistance, both were handcuffed and stuffed into one of the black and whites. And then like ants, neighbors began to crawl out onto Lakeview Circle from every direction. Tammy Fox appeared by my driveway, hiding behind the palm tree.

"Who the hell are these people?" Clayton said to Ted.

With a lopsided ponytail and a bloody lip, Ted reached into his cutoffs and pulled out a badge.

"FBI?" Betty Jean and Clayton said in unison.

"Narcotics division," Ted said as Neely waltzed up.

"Ted is my partner," Neely announced, cutting his eyes over at Tracie.

Tracie tore free from my arms and stormed over to Ted, sizing him up, eyeball-to-eyeball. *What's she doing?* I thought.

"Wait a minute," Tracie said, shaking a finger. "I knew you looked familiar. You're the guy who hauled my trailer out of here last week."

"Half a trailer," Neely corrected, stepping in. "This is special agent, Ted."

"Just plain *Ted*?" I said, unbelieving.

"Actually, it's not his real name," Neely said.

"But what about *Kill It and Grill It*—your charity?" Betty Jean said to Ted. "Was all that just nonsense?"

"I'm afraid it was cover."

"Cover for what?" Clayton said.

"The Dorsey case. We knew they were trafficking cocaine out of Parkway, but needed to trace the goods to the source. We wanted to bust the kingpins—those two in the squad car. But the Dorseys were murdered before we were able to wrap up the investigation."

"The Dorseys were dealing drugs?" Betty Jean said.

"They were the biggest operators in this area."

"But they . . . they were such nice people."

"Hold on," I said, pointing at the patrol car. "Gustav and Ariana took the cocaine a couple of nights ago—all of it. Why did they come back?"

"I can handle that one," Neely replied. "You see, they weren't the ones who removed the drugs from your trailer."

My hand dropped. "Then who did?"

"*Uh*, that would be me," Ted said.

"But how did you know?"

"Who do you think put it there?"

"You put cocaine under my trailer!" Tracie said.

Neely snickered, and then bobbed his head like he thought it was funny. "It was bait. We set a trap for them."

"I don't get it," I said. "Was it just a coincidence I hooked up with Gustav? I may be stupid, but I'm pretty sure I arranged that."

"Every once in a while we get lucky," Ted chimed in. "We never dreamed someone from the pharmaceutical industry would move in at Parkway 12. It was perfect."

"Biotech," I corrected.

"Whatever," Ted said. "Once you showed up, we made sure you discovered the goods. Neely did a little Internet hocus-pocus to put Gustav onto your résumé. Gustav knew the Dorseys had stashed what was left of his inventory, only he didn't know where. The rest of the story played out on its own. And like I said, we got lucky."

Tracie planted a finger in Neely's chest. "You risked Trevor's life—and mine—to catch these thugs?"

"To be honest, we couldn't rule out the possibility that you guys were involved. We thought you might be here to take over the Dorsey operation."

"But they were such nice people," Clayton said.

"So Gustav *is* using the drug testing business as a front to sell drugs," I said to Neely.

"He was blackmailing his way into the Fortune 500."

"Tell them about the reward," Ted added.

"There's a bounty on these guys?"

"If you're agreeable to making a statement, we can work something out," Neely said.

"Oh, *jeez,*" I replied, realizing the gravity of the situation. "You want me to blow the whistle on those two animals?"

"It's the end of the line for them," Ted said. "They're going away for a long time."

I looked over at Tracie. "If that's true, then—"

"Time out," Betty Jean interrupted. "Trevor deserves everything he's got coming to him, but you've wreaked havoc on our neighborhood. Before you close down this little operation, I think Parkway Community deserves some consideration."

Ted scratched his head. "What did you have in mind, Betty Jean?"

"I want you to finish setting up that charity. Instead of supplying drugs to the area, Parkway will be known for something positive—like a big heart."

"Well done," Clayton said.

"The reward and a charity . . . Is that the deal?" Neely said.

"Trevor?" Tracie said, looking at me.

"Who gets my car?"

Chapter 61

Suwanee, Georgia
Saturday, October 19th
2:05 P.M.

The trip to Atlanta ate up the entire morning. After my statement to the FBI, I could only pray I would never run into Gustav and Ariana in a deserted parking lot late one night. By the time I stopped off to cash the refund check and eat lunch (eleven dollars and twenty-five cents) at Five Guys, I was running late for the Beasley get-together. A text message from Tracie confirmed she would meet me down at the dock when I arrived.

With no time to change, I decided to stick with the corduroy blazer, red shorts, and Italian loafers I had worn to the FBI office. I tucked in my t-shirt and descended the bank toward the dock.

"You look relieved," Tracie said, greeting me on the gangway with a kiss. She took a long, pitiful look at my outfit, but managed to smile anyway.

"We have an awesome reward in the works, just so you know."

"When do you take the witness stand?"

"Hopefully, never," I said. "I'll only be called if my testimony is necessary for a conviction."

"And you're comfortable with the reward?"

"We got Goldfinger," I said, pointing up at the driveway, "and five thousand in cash."

"They gave you a car?"

"She's practically family," I said, a little hurt by the tone.

"Who also needs *major* repairs."

"Hey, who doesn't?"

"I guess you're right. We'll work on finances later," Tracie said, giving me another kiss. Then she surprised me. "I tried on the outfit from the Nifty-Thrifty. It's absolutely perfect."

"I can't wait."

She beamed at me and took my hand, glancing ahead at the dock. "This is quite a gathering. Do you know all these people?"

I was tempted to plead the fifth on a couple of them. "More or less."

"Then let's do this," Tracie said.

No sooner had we stepped on the dock than *Murphy's Law* struck, like an anvil falling out of the sky. A woman broke away from the crowd.

"Well, hello . . . And you are?" she said, squaring off with Tracie.

"This can't be happening," I said, attempting to get out of harm's way. It was too late.

"I'm Tracie Wentworth—Trevor's wife."

I did my best to imagine what was going on inside Tracie's head, but the process was eclipsed by a sudden insight: *I'm a dead man.* The home-wrecker had on an outfit best described as vintage gypsy. Her hair was puffy, the earrings large and dangly, and the lip gloss, lustrous. I was afraid to look at her shoes, but knew for a fact she was a good three inches taller than usual.

"Well, *this* is awkward," she said, fidgeting.

"*Trace*, this is Tammy Faye Fox, our next-door neighbor," I said.

"*Ohhh* . . . the *Psy-Chic*. What a lovely outfit," Tracie said with a flair that warned me to run for the hills. "So how exactly do you know my husband?"

"Tammy was close friends with the Dorseys. Being the neighborly type and all, she stopped by to introduce herself when we moved in—after you took off for the beach," I explained.

"Oh, he's just being modest," Tammy Fox said, patting Tracie's arm. "He was my first premium customer."

I looked into the crowd, plotting an escape route. *Maybe I should just jump in the lake*, I thought. Clayton and Betty Jean were in a back corner, too engaged to be of any assistance. Rejoining the conversation, I put on a diplomatic hat and clenched my teeth to restrain my true sentiments. "Tammy, I believe we agreed not to pursue the matter."

"Says who?" Tammy Fox shot back.

"I'm referring to your association with the lynch mob that tried to kick us out of the neighborhood," I said, making eyes at Tracie. "And I may be mistaken, but weren't you the last one to sign the petition—number fourteen?"

"I don't recall a quid pro quo in our agreement," Tammy Fox said.

"Perhaps, you would like to clarify that remark," Tracie said. "The two of you were having a quid pro quo?"

"It's not what you think, *Trace*," I said, pleading. "I swear."

"Tammy, will you excuse us?" Tracie said, taking me by the lapel.

"I'll see you in court," Tammy Fox called out behind us.

We shouldered our way through the mass, making a path to the punch bowl at the back rail. As I started filling our cups, Walt Mobley stepped up.

"Care to hit the links later, *Trev*?" Walt said.

"Hi, Walt," Tracie said, jumping in. "We met the other day in the water hazard."

"That sucker cost me a par," Walt said, turning to me. "How about it?"

"Wish I could, but I've got plans." I leaned close to Tracie's ear. "Watch this," I said, pointing my cup at Betty Jean. "Say, Walt . . . Betty Jean is sure looking fine this afternoon, isn't she?"

Walt's eyebrows did a double-pump.

Tracie slapped a hand over her mouth to hold back a snicker, spilling punch in the process. "I'm sorry."

I handed her a napkin.

"What kind of talk is that at a neighborhood party?" Walt said.

"I was just saying—"

"If you'll excuse me, I need to check on Jess." Walt marched off.

"Wow. You really ruffled his feathers," Tracie said. "What was that eyebrow thing he did?"

"Get Betty Jean to explain it. Come on. Let's circulate before lightning strikes."

We worked our way around the dock, spending time with Fate and a few neighbors before the crowd started to thin. After a few more introductions and handshakes, only Clayton and Betty Jean were left standing in the corner. There was an old man sitting in a chair, but he wasn't a Parkway resident. I kept an eye on him.

Clayton and Betty Jean greeted us like family, wanting to know if Tracie had met everyone. I noticed Clayton was wearing the old camel hair jacket and leather belt from the day we first met. Betty Jean was much more polished as usual. After a bit of chitchat Clayton excused himself to fetch punch for the old man, whom he had somehow neglected to introduce. I couldn't quite put my finger on it, but there was something familiar about him.

Betty Jean and Tracie continued with their conversation as I took another peek at the man. He kept to himself, silent as a stone. He was wearing a cowboy hat—an expensive one—with a distinctive braided band. I couldn't see much of his hair, but it appeared to be well-groomed and a perfect match for his jet-gray mustache. He sported a woven shirt, pressed jeans, and the shiniest western boots I had ever seen.

Clayton returned with a cup, only for some reason the contents were golden brown—not the same color as the punch bowl. He handed it to the man, and then gave me a pat. "How'd it go with the Feds downtown?"

"Not bad," I said. "We reached an agreement, so I'd say it's time to refocus on the job search."

"Well, I still have a few connections to make under your trailer, but after that I'm happy to help where I can," Clayton said. "Of course, let's not go worrying about tomorrow just yet. Tonight is your special event."

"I really appreciate . . ." I stopped mid-sentence, taking a closer look at the old man. He was sitting quietly, taking in the lake and sipping his drink. I had seen him before. *But where?* Puzzled, I pictured him without the hat. That's when it dawned on me.

Clayton watched out of the corner of an eye, but didn't say a word as the wheels churned in my head. It was almost like he was reading my mind. Watching—waiting—expecting something to happen. Clayton tapped Betty Jean on the shoulder, who in turn poked Tracie just in the nick of time.

"*You* . . ." I said, feeling a cloud lift. "You were at the bank on the day of the foreclosure."

The man took a sip of his drink. "This is mighty fine bourbon, Clayton."

Tracie stared at me. "Trevor, no. He's—"

"Sir, do you remember me?" I said, squatting down in front of him.

"Go ahead, Pop," Clayton said, smiling.

The man removed his hat, his face as warm as the afternoon sun. I was right about the hair, only his eyes were different—I could barely look into them.

"I don't understand," I said, standing again.

"*Trev*, I'd like you to say hello to someone special," Clayton said.

Pop eased out of the chair, his smile as soothing as brushstrokes on a canvas. "You can call me Ol' Man River," he said.

Chapter 62

Suwanee, Georgia
Saturday, October 19th
3:00 P.M.

Parkway had revealed its share of mysteries, even a few secrets. But what I felt at the moment was almost like another out-of-body experience, one where I had just been dropped on a different planet. I could tell by the way Tracie was staring at me, something was about to change, and there was no going back. My entire existence had been shattered by an economic meltdown that all the experts labeled a system failure. It was totally beyond my control, but in the blink of an eye, I now figured they were all wrong. It wasn't the job loss or the toxic mortgage that nearly did me in. *It was me* . . . Not my career, the house, golf, the boat, my car . . . I looked deep into Tracie's eyes.

Change my way of thinking.

Then I remembered something I had said to Clayton a few days earlier. *Working my way through a setback.* And he assured me: *Ain't we all.*

I was still dazed, but turned to Ol' Man River. "That banker took my house and what was left of my pride. But you were just sitting there outside his office, reading a newspaper."

"It just so happens I take my morning coffee at the bank sometimes," Ol' Man River said.

"Me and Pop know that banker well."

"But Clayton, you live in a trailer park. You're a truck driver," I said.

Ol' Man River sat down and picked up his drink, like he didn't have anything further to say. Then he winked at Clayton.

"It was a little over forty years ago," Clayton began, "Pop was one of the finest real estate developers in the area. He built more homes in Atlanta than you can shake a stick at, but it took what you might call a roller coaster ride for him to discover true success. Life is full of surprises, and oddly enough it was a poker game that changed his way of thinking. I was only a teenager, but I saw it with my own eyes. He won the deed to three hundred acres of property that most people thought was worthless. And they were right at the time. Well, sir, Pop is the one who turned it into Parkway Community."

"He owns Parkway?" I said.

"Every single acre of the place, only not the doublewides. He developed the property on the heels of one of the worst economic busts in our lifetime. He and my mom had some challenging times in those days . . . lost almost everything they owned. It wasn't long afterwards they moved the family into number thirteen, including yours truly."

"So he lost it all?"

"No, I said *almost*. As it turns out, Pop was mighty proud of what he had accomplished here at Parkway and decided it was the one thing worth fighting for. Of course, I was nothing but a pain in the rear in those days, but he kept us all together—right here on the lake until things turned around."

"I don't' get it . . . Why are you still here?"

"By the time we got back on our feet, I was working for Pop. He and Mom eventually moved further north, and by then I had married Betty Jean. But he wouldn't budge until we agreed to make Parkway 13 our home."

"You told me you were working your way through a setback, like me."

"Like *us*," Tracie corrected.

"Well, we did suffer one a few years ago, when the economy soured again. Pop had turned the business over to me, and the mortgage situation hit us pretty hard. In fact, it just about finished us off. Fortunately, I saw the whole mess coming and had the foresight to diversify into the trucking business."

"So you started driving for CBJ Logistics?" I said.

"How'd you figure that out?"

"I spotted the logo on your truck."

"There's just one teeny-little tweak to your observation. Betty Jean and me *own* CBJ."

"Hold on," I said. "That's not possible."

"Trevor, why would you say such a thing?" Tracie said.

"CBJ Logistics is the second largest transportation company in the country."

"That's a fact," Clayton said.

"We're actually *the* largest that's privately-owned," Betty Jean said.

"But you're living in a trailer, and you're parking your rig on a condemned tennis court."

"It's a doublewide," Betty Jean corrected.

"I commute to work in a rig most mornings, just to test out the new vehicles," Clayton said. "And in case you missed it, Parkway is a friendly place to live. Especially, for folks that have a quirk or two."

I cut my eyes at Betty Jean, then at her boots. "So you guys are worth like—"

"I was wondering how long it would take to get around to that," Ol' Man River said.

"What were you doing at the bank?"

"Besides having coffee, doing the usual and dabbling in real estate. It's a hard habit to kick when you've been doing it all your life. I think of that bank lobby as an office nowadays. Of course, I also sit on the board."

"Believe it or not, he does it like clockwork, every time a Parkway unit hits the market," Clayton said.

"You gave me the classified ad and advised me that Parkway 12 was perfect for my situation. How did you know?" I said to Ol' Man River.

"I sized you up the minute I laid eyes on you. Call it instinct, or whatever you like. The fact is I've known folks like you all my life—although I figured you might have to go through a rough patch to find out for yourself. And as you may have noticed, my children seem to share that view. I'm thinking the glimmer I saw that morning was the love you have for this little lady of yours. She just might be the one thing that's going to pull you through this. That's the kind of magic I like to wager on."

"After all these years, Pop's still playing poker of sorts. Every once in a while he loses a hand, like with the Dorseys. But he typically knows when to lay down a bet."

"So you're saying . . . you bluffed me into coming here for my own good?"

"I made a couple of bucks selling you Parkway 12—fair and square. If that's the price you pay to find yourself, then it's well worth the cost."

"Not a bad deal—considering it all started with a poker game," Clayton said.

"A poker game," I repeated, struggling to wrap my mind around it all.

"All of this was swampland," Ol' Man River said, waving his hand at the lake.

"The same way they built Disney World," I mumbled, mostly to myself.

"It's his way of helping folks these days."

"We've witnessed every kind of problem you can imagine," Betty Jean said.

"And with the proper amount of time, they just kind of melt away, sitting right here on this dock," Clayton added.

"I'm not so sure everything I've just heard is true," I said.

"Is that a fact?"

"Ol' Man River didn't sell me anything."

"Watch it, Pop. He's one of those professional advice-givers."

"He sized me up pretty good. There's no doubt about that," I said. "He somehow knew it was important for us to be here."

"What are you getting at?" Tracie said.

"She dealt you a hand, now play it," Ol' Man River broke in.

"You showed me life through a different set of eyes. I was doing everything I could to claw my way back into a world that both of us once believed was the answer, but you've taught me a thing or two about what's really important."

"It takes a special man to own up to it."

"Trevor thought we were being punished."

"At first, we all do," Ol' Man River said.

"So it's not Parkway Community per se, is it?"

"It's the people," I said, turning to Clayton and Betty Jean. "We've landed in a crazy slice of paradise, where folks tend to take care of one another—quirks and all."

Tracie took me by the hand. "Quirks and all," she repeated.

Chapter 63

Suwanee, Georgia
Saturday, October 19th
5:00 P.M.

Combing a hand through my hair, I climbed the steps to the Beasleys' place, pumped up about what was sure to be an evening like no other. When I reached the stoop, I straightened the collar of my striped oxford, checked my khakis, and examined the laces on a pair of new Topsiders (a last minute gift from Clayton). Satisfied everything was in order, I knocked. The door opened, and Tracie stepped out wearing the amazing Nifty-Thrifty outfit, taking a twirl.

"Sacré bleu," I blurted out, not even knowing what it meant.

She giggled. "A girl never knows what to expect from you nowadays."

"You're one to be talking," I said, not wasting any time. "What do you say we get this show on the road?"

Tracie started down the steps, but then stopped and looked at me. "Where's your car?"

"Goldfinger?" I said, nudging her forward. "She won't be needed for this evening's festivities."

We headed down the driveway and crossed the street. I took her by the arm, easing down the grassy bank toward the lake. Continuing onto the gangway, we slowed to admire Clayton's sailboat. She was floating in the water, her yellow hues shimmering like a Monet painting.

"Someone's been out sailing this afternoon," Tracie said.

"She's pretty awesome, isn't she?" I said, stopping alongside. "What do you think she draws . . . maybe fifteen inches?"

Tracie gave me a funny look, like I had lost my mind.

"And the sheets are in Bristol condition," I added, moving Tracie along to the dock.

The string lights were already lit, casting a warm glow beneath the tin roof. Tracie stopped abruptly. She stared into the corner where Fate stood like a statue, wearing a white jacket with a towel draped over his arm. Using his free hand, he wiggled a pair of horn-rimmed glasses, and then gave a nod as he pulled out a chair for her.

"A bistro table," Tracie said. "What in the world has gotten into Fate?"

"Just remember—quirks and all," I whispered into Tracie's ear.

"Please have a seat, ma'am," Fate said, clicking his heels.

We eased over, and Fate helped Tracie get comfortable. I sat opposite her, both of us taking a front-row seat to the sun working its way toward the horizon. Tracie made eyes at me.

"For starters, we have a nice Sonoma pinot noir . . . 2009," Fate said with flair. "Will that suit Madame?"

"I took the liberty of picking the wine," I said. "I hope you like it."

"Full of surprises," Tracie said. "Fate, it sounds perfect."

Fate poured a taste for my approval, afterwards setting the cork on the table. I hadn't noticed until now, but he had on a pair of white gloves. When he was done serving us, he retreated into the shadows.

I raised my glass. "Here's to new beginnings."

"I must have been gone longer than I thought," Tracie said, as our glasses clinked.

"Let's put it this way. Every day at Parkway has been an adventure."

"Tell me everything." Tracie scooted closer to the table.

"Life happened," I said. "There's a lot to talk about, but first things first. I'm broke, you know?"

"*We're* broke."

"The good news is I spoke to Cal Hunter."

"Not about Zuritech, I hope."

"*Uh*, no. He and Kate are still on hiatus, but he's offered to assist with the job search. He even agreed to provide a reference when the time comes."

"Well, Brenda and I had a similar conversation last week."

"About Cal?" I said.

"Actually, the job situation. She and Jon are getting ready to sail off on their honeymoon, but she believes he may need help with his new firm when he returns."

"I've never worked in venture capital."

"You've got an MBA and all that experience with biotechs, and that's one area Jon intends to focus on."

"Aren't you forgetting something? He witnessed that fiasco with the FBI and Ariana."

"Nonsense. He knows you better than that."

"You really think so?" I said. "Wait—you'd be agreeable to moving to Savannah?"

"What do you think?"

"Well, I'm not going anywhere without you."

Fate returned to the table with the wine, poised for a refill.

"We've got to take off, Fate," I said. "But thanks for everything."

He leaned into my ear and whispered. "Just to be perfectly clear, I'm doing this on my own time."

I gave him a pat on the shoulder.

"It's such a beautiful evening," Tracie said, admiring the lake.

I helped her up from the table and took her arm, heading for the gangway. When we were alongside the sailboat, I slowed. "So tell me, are you serious about Savannah?"

"Well, to be honest, Brenda already dropped your résumé on Jon's desk," Tracie said, fighting back a smile.

I stepped into the sailboat, offering her my hand. "Are you familiar with the punishment for mutiny?"

"What are you doing?" Tracie said, almost in a panic. "Get out of there before someone sees you, or you fall in the lake."

I took her by the hand. "The next step in your adventure awaits."

Tracie studied the boat from bow to stern, like she was afraid. Then she checked to see if anyone was watching. "Trevor, you don't know anything about sailing."

I gently helped her into the boat, arranging two cushions in the cockpit once aboard. When I was certain she was comfortable, I tugged on the halyard to ready the main. Next, I untied the line from the gangway and used a paddle to clear the dock. After we were a safe distance out, I put away the paddle and lowered the centerboard. Then I hoisted the sail and snuggled in next to Tracie.

"Watch this," I said, taking ahold of the tiller. A steady breeze filled the main as I tightened up on the sheet. The sailboat eased into the wind, heeling as we picked up speed.

Tracie looked up at the mass of fluffy-white canvas overhead, amazed at how it stirred such emotion. She clung to my arm, not sure whether to laugh or cry. "We're sailing," she squealed, looking back at the shore. "Oh, my gosh. This isn't happening."

"See that tree on the opposite bank? That's our mark."

"How far is it?"

"According to Betty Jean, about three hundred yards."

"And what do we do when we get there?"

"We'll turn around and crisscross the lake until sunset."

Tracie tightened her grasp and scooted closer, closing her eyes. She raised her face into the wind, basking in the fading sun. "I love that sound . . . wind and water."

"And the popping of sails," I added.

"Like the joining of two souls."

I glanced over, taking her in from head to toe. I tried to imagine the moment lasting forever. When I finally broke the silence, I said, "I didn't get a chance to tell you how nice you look."

"I had a little help with the outfit. These boots are awesome. How did you know I would like them?"

We were approaching the shore, so I had to delay my response to ready us for a tack. "Follow my lead . . . Duck when the boom swings this way, and then stick close to me. After it passed overhead, we slid to the opposite side of the cockpit. The wind filled the sail, sending us on a new bearing.

"You're really into this," Tracie said.

"And you aren't? You give it a try," I said, handing her the tiller. "Hold her on a steady course."

"You make it sound easy."

"About the outfit," I said, picking up where we left off. "I see and hear things—*sometimes*."

"What do you mean?"

"The boots, for example. I know your likes and dislikes . . . what's important to you . . . things like that."

"Did you know I always wanted to sail?"

"Truthfully, yes. But I ignored the obvious and bought you the fastest cabin cruiser on Lake Lanier anyway."

"Well, I didn't mind."

"Here, let me do this," I said, taking the tiller. We turned and started a second pass across the lake in silence. When we reached the halfway point, I set a course for the north shore, pointing to the trees.

"Something's back there," Tracie said. She leaned for a better look as a cove opened up. "Look, it's a dock."

The sun was setting behind us, and the palm trees in our wake were now turning into silhouettes above Parkway's pearly-white beach. I swapped places with Tracie, handing her the tiller. "I'm going to drop the sail while you steer us over to the dock. "Wait for me to tie her off, and then I'll help you out."

Tracie brought us in perfectly, waiting patiently to climb ashore until I finished up and gave her the sign. Taking her by the hand, she stepped out on the dock and straightened her skirt. With a smile, she looped an arm through mine and took a lingering look at the sunset before exploring the bank rising before us.

"So what's up there?" she said.

"That," I said, "is your next surprise."

Chapter 64

Suwanee, Georgia
Saturday, October 19th
6:15 P.M.

A stone path marked the way up the hill, winding gracefully through a stand of pines. When we reached the top, the terrain opened to a breathtaking view. In the fading light, the sharp roofline of the lodge with its massive stone chimney appeared first. It was apparent that patches of wooden shingles had been blown away over the years. The portion of the building facing the lake was constructed of fieldstone, timber, and glass. From the looks of things, it had seen better days, like the roof, yet still storybook charming. Facing us was the faint honey-like glow of an unbelievable window rising four stories into a gable. Hundreds of glass panes sparkled as we followed the path closer. Neither of us said a word, taking it all in.

The path stopped at a corner of the building, where a beefy old door fit for a castle was nestled beneath a portico. I gave the door a push, allowing it to part ever so slowly. Light spilled out into the night, and I stepped aside for Tracie to enter. Hearing her next breath was the closest thing to living in a fairytale I had ever experienced.

Our first steps inside were jaw-dropping, opening up into an exposed wood-beam ceiling that rose four stories into the gables above. The rear wall was a stacked-stone fireplace, casting a spell as big as the embers blazing beneath the hearth. The opposite wall was constructed of the glass panes we had seen from outside, and beyond them a panoramic view of the lake. In the center of the room was an ancient chandelier hanging from the beams, its tarnish bearing the character of a bygone era. Beneath it a woven rug covered the stone floor, with a cozy chestnut table for two perched in the center.

I heard Tracie gasp, as if her heart had just skipped a beat. She remained speechless as Clayton appeared and crossed the room in a black tux. In what had now become a familiar theme, he raised an arm waist-high with a towel draped across it.

"A very good evening, Mr. and Mrs. Wentworth. Welcome to Parkway Lodge," he said, bowing his head. "If you will follow me, I believe we have the perfect table for you."

Tracie stared at me for what felt like an eternity, long enough for her eyes to become a window into her soul. We fell in behind Clayton, only Tracie paused to take in the ambiance, doing a slow turn in place. There was room enough for dozens of tables, but we were standing next to the only seats in the house.

"If I may," Clayton said, pulling out a chair.

Once Tracie was seated, I took my place and reached across the table, offering her my hand. Looking out the window, I could just make out the string of lights across the lake. The dock, the trailers . . . our everyday lives . . . seemed a million miles away.

"Now, if you will excuse me," Clayton said, setting menus in front of us. "I will allow you to get comfortable."

"Trevor, what is this place?"

"It was the crown jewel of Parkway, back in the day when Ol' Man River built the neighborhood—sort of a community gathering place. As you can see, it hasn't been used for quite some time."

"And we're here . . . for dinner?" Tracie said, picking up her menu:

2012 Tigerlily Cabernet Sauvignon
Spinach Salad with Walnuts and Clementines
She-Crab Soup with Sherry
Grilled Alaskan Salmon in a Blackberry Glaze
Fresh Sautéed Asparagus
Banana Bread and Coffee

Tracie set the menu on a piece of bone china, taking a moment to run a finger down the gleaming silverware next to it. In the center of the table was a single rose stem.

"The china and all was Betty Jean's idea," I said. "She's got an eye for what she calls the vintage farmhouse look."

"With a French twist," Tracie said. "I love it, just like this outfit you picked out for me."

"Well . . ." I said, my eyes lowering.

Clayton returned to set out bread, wine glasses, and the Tigerlily. "The cook sends her best wishes to you both," he said, glancing over a shoulder.

Just past the fireplace, Betty Jean stood in a doorway wearing a chef's bib. She curtsied, and then disappeared.

Pouring wine into our glasses, Clayton took leave once again.

"You're not going to believe this, but just a few days ago I was telling Brenda how I dreamed of dining in a quaint French restaurant with a bottle of wine and soft music—"

"Hold on," I said, snapping my fingers. As Clayton turned, I gestured in a twirling motion. He worked some magic in the corner, and music began to float down from the ceiling. It was a gentle island beat selected by Betty Jean, so I was pretty sure it was Kenny Chesney. When Tracie smiled and started swaying her head back and forth, I knew for a fact it was solid gold. "Sorry, you were saying . . ."

"We've never discussed French cuisine, have we?"

"Not lately," I said.

"Try, never," she teased. "So how did we come to be sitting here in our own private restaurant?"

"First, about that dream you shared with Brenda. I was there, right?"

"In real life you were at a football game or off drinking beer," Tracie said. "But in my dream . . . *yes* . . . it was a cozy little table for two."

"Sacré bleu," I whispered.

"How did you do this? . . . What happened?"

"*After* you finish the story," I said, not knowing what to expect.

"Brenda was telling me how Jon was taking her sailing on their honeymoon. It all sounded like a fairytale, something that was never going to happen for us." Tracie's eyes filled with tears. "I told her . . . one day I wanted to sail off into a sunset."

"So this is—sort of like magic," I said through tears of my own.

"Trevor, I admit this place is crazy, but we both know it's special. These people are real, and they get under your skin. But they love you, and for some reason they want us to be happy. They are exactly what friends are meant to be."

"Yeah, I'm still amazed. I don't deserve this."

Tracie let out a sigh, and then reached for my hand. "It is magic . . . our magic . . . and that's all that matters right now."

"Let's have a toast," I said, waving to Clayton and Betty Jean. I poured wine as we waited for them to join us, then continued. "I believe I have just the right words for an occasion such as this. It's more or less a prayer someone once taught me—and I will treasure it for the rest of my days." I lifted my wine glass. "May the Lord grant us peace and gravy."

"Amen," everyone said.

"Clayton and Betty Jean, you guys are incredible," I said. "After dinner we'd be honored if you would join us for dessert."

They retreated to the kitchen, leaving us to ourselves. It wasn't long before a savory mesquite aroma filled the room. As we sipped our wine, Tracie was the first to break the silence.

"I have the perfect ending to this evening," she said.

"Oh?"

"Tonight, I'm coming home . . . if that's all right with you?"

"Don't ever leave me again."

"Never," she said. "We've got magic."

I looked into Tracie's eyes, falling deeper than I ever thought possible. Her eyes were blue . . . my favorite color.

Epilogue

I landed facedown with my nose pinned to the floor, feeling a sharp pain working its way into my head. There was a momentary lapse as my brain struggled to catch up. I heard the ranting of a sportscaster's voice, and then realized it was play-by-play action coming at me, ninety-to-nothing. Drawn to the excitement, I craned my neck and spotted a television over the fireplace. The camera zoomed in, and the crowd went nuts as a scoreboard flashed on the screen. It was a tied ballgame, fourteen-to-fourteen.

I twisted for a peek at the cozy couch behind me, where I had been napping only moments ago. A look around the room confirmed I was alone, except for a beer and bowl of chips on the coffee table. I spotted my loafers in the middle of the floor, crawled over, and slipped them on.

A bit wobbly, I made my way into the hall and called out, "Tracie?"

When there was no response, I wandered aimlessly through the house, eventually winding up in the breakfast nook. Outside the window Goldfinger sat under the palm tree, but Tracie's Lexus was nowhere in sight. I spun around to the refrigerator, hoping to find a note. *Nothing*. Then I reached for my phone pocket, but instead felt only the tail of a football jersey and silky boxers at my hips.

Scrambling to the master bedroom closet, I dug through a pile of clothes and found my pants. Before I could get to the phone, the front door opened down the hallway.

"Tracie?"

I backed out of the closet and hurried into the foyer. When I turned the corner, there she stood with two sacks of groceries, wearing her favorite cowgirl boots. She also had on a plaid shirt and jeans, but the boots always got me.

Rushing over, I helped her with the bags, getting a taste of lip gloss for my thoughtfulness.

"*Hiya,* football fan," she said, frowning at my outfit. "I'm glad we decided to reconnect the cable. I'd hate to find you at Macho Taco wearing *that.*"

"What's in the bags?"

"We're doing hibachi with the Beasleys at the dock this evening . . . Ahi tuna and baked potatoes."

"Don't forget the ginger-plum sauce," I said. "Are we celebrating something?"

"Now that we've accepted the job in Savannah, I want to make the most of our time here at Parkway."

"Ol' Man River already signed the contract and sent over a deposit."

"We lost our shirts on that last place. Who would have dreamed we would turn a profit on Parkway 12?"

"Go figure."

"Don't let me keep you from your game. The radio announcer said it was a clincher—tied with only minutes to go."

I just stood there, amazed. *Change my way of thinking*, I thought.

"Get out of here," Tracie said. "I'll bring you a refill."

"If it's all the same to you, I'd like to go sailing."

"That's your team driving for the goal line in there." She shook a finger.

"Like you said, we're moving. It won't hurt to sit this one out."

Tracie came closer, giving me a nosy that felt better than any football game ever had, especially coming from that someone who really believed in me.

"So Ol' Man River's going to sell the Dorsey Place one more time," Tracie said.

"Not exactly."

"But I thought we agreed?"

"He's selling it all right, but get this. They're now calling it the *Wentworth Place*. That should be good for a story or two."

"Why not?" Tracie said with a glow. "I hear they're nice people."

Dennis Carr lives in Atlanta where he and his wife, Cheryl, enjoy sailing in their spare time. His writing delves into the private lives of corporate executives, where egos and bottom lines make for great mystery. *Parkway 12* is his third novel.

Follow Dennis on Facebook

www.ingramcontent.com/pod-product-compliance
Lightning Source LLC
Chambersburg PA
CBHW031543240626
47153CB00002B/358
9780988186439